REDEMPTION

The Legacy Series
Book Four

Jessica Ruddick

CHAPTER 1

NEXT TO ME, CLAIRE SNORED softly in a way that was kind of cute. When I snored I probably sounded like a lumber mill. But there was no worry of that tonight. My eyes were wide open with no signs of shutting.

I rose carefully so as not to disturb Claire and padded out to the living room. In a daze, I sat on the couch, thinking about everything and nothing. How could things have gone so horribly wrong? Just once, I'd love to not have to ask that question.

Resting my forehead in my hands, I closed my eyes. The memory of Cole standing in the doorway with the envelope in his hands flooded my mind. He'd glared at me—an accusation, but I didn't know what for. Though, it could have been any number of things.

I'd never forget the hurt on his face. I'd seen it before, when we'd gone to visit his mother, and it was a heart-wrenching, gut-clenching pain, the kind that scarred your soul.

But this time, I was responsible for it.

I'd gaped at him, not trusting my eyes that he was really there. It was like time stood still. Finally, Clare had taken the envelope from him and he'd bolted without another word. I hadn't said anything. Even if my mind had been able to figure out what to say, I physically wouldn't have been able to get the words out—I'd been paralyzed. Would it have mattered? Would he have stayed? By the time I'd gotten my wits about me and went after him, he was long gone.

The sound of Chase stirring in his room brought me back to the present. I slipped out the front door, not bothering with shoes. I wasn't going far.

I sat on the curb in the parking lot and wrapped my arms around my knees. It was actually quite pleasant out here—there was a full moon and a nice breeze, almost like it was going to rain soon.

I'd been so stupid, which seemed to be the theme of my life. It had been a double whammy of an afternoon. First Xavier dropping the bombshell that he wanted me to kill him and then Cole showing up. My brain had been overloaded. Still was.

And my emotions? Wrecked beyond belief.

Movement in the parking lot caught my eye, setting me on edge and making me wish I had a weapon. Xavier was no longer a threat, but there was still Linda to worry about.

A lone figure appeared between two cars and recognizing Xena's small frame, I relaxed. Even though I should be angry at her because she'd obviously given my location to Cole, I couldn't help but feel comforted by her presence.

She walked over and sat next to me, not saying anything for a moment. I was hit by her citrusy scent, which reminded me how much Xavier's cinnamon scent had faded.

But that was the least of my concerns in his changed demeanor.

"How are you?" she asked, breaking the silence.

I considered for a moment before shrugging. I wasn't ready to talk about it yet, especially with Xena. Although, who else was there who understood the complexities of the situation?

"I'm sorry," she said quietly. "I didn't tell him. He found the address in my phone and left before I could stop him."

I let that tidbit of information roll around in my mind. I didn't know if it made me feel better or worse because if he'd been so eager to find me, then why did he leave without talking to me? Did he have some other reason for coming all this way? It felt self-important thinking it was because of me, but I couldn't come up with any other logical reason for him to make the trip.

"How's Bill?"

Now it was her turn to consider the question. "About how you'd expect."

In other words, not good. *Damn.*

"Is he pissed?"

"Not pissed. More like...*disappointed.*"

Ouch. I'd rather he be pissed at me. The last thing I wanted was to hurt him.

"How much does he know?" I asked.

"Enough to understand why you had to leave," she replied. "The less he knows the better."

We agreed on that front. I didn't want to drag Bill into this mess any further than he already was.

"Linda was here," I said. "She found me at my hotel. Niles, another handler, tipped her off."

Xena scrunched her nose. "Niles is vile."

So she knew him. Despite everything, I chuckled. "Did you just rhyme on purpose?"

She shrugged, a pink sheen gracing her cheeks. "He doesn't have much of a backbone."

"I picked up on that, too." I paused. "He's in love with Claire."

"I assume that's who Niles is assigned to."

I filled her in on Chase and Claire's general situation, but I tried not to get into specifics about their family dynamics. That was their business.

"Do you know if Linda learned anything else about Cole?" I asked.

"I don't think so," Xena said and I let out a breath of relief. "From what I can tell, she's been focused on finding you. She's absolutely pissed you slipped away." Xena smirked, happy my shenanigans had gotten under Linda's skin.

I was beyond caring. I just wanted that toxic woman out of my life. And away from Cole. I didn't know how I'd manage to accomplish both, though.

"She's not going to give up, is she?" I asked.

Xena's expression sombered. "No." She didn't ask whether I was referring to Linda trying to find me or find Cole. I figured the answer was the same in both scenarios.

I was a fool to think I could outwit Linda. When had I ever been able to stay one step ahead of a handler?

By now, the sun was starting to peek on the horizon and I yawned. *Figures.* Now that it was daytime my body finally decided it was ready to sleep.

"Have you talked to Shenice?" I asked.

"She came home a few days ago." Xena didn't say anything else, but she didn't have to. I could read the implied disappointment in her tone.

I stood. This conversation had run its course—I didn't want to hear any more about how I'd disappointed and hurt the people I loved and had been trying to protect. And anyway, my brain was fuzzy.

Just as I turned to go inside, Chase came up from our basement apartment steps dressed in running shorts and a t-shirt. He slowed when he saw Xena, eyeing her suspiciously. I was sure he'd have a sharp comment waiting when he learned my former handler was here. I didn't have the patience to deal with it right now.

"Chase, this is Xena," I said, pointing. Then I pointed in reverse. "Xena, Chase."

Xena nodded coolly, giving Chase a run for his money with her own suspicious look, more than holding her own.

"I'll see you later, Xena." I brushed past Chase, leaving the two to sort things out themselves.

I WENT BACK TO BED where Claire was still snoozing away.

And dreamed of my mother.

I got the sensation of being in the ocean with the waves lapping against my skin. The water was cool and warm at the same time. I couldn't describe the temperature other than to say it was just right—it felt like the water was embracing me.

My mother stood in front of me, looking exactly like I remembered her. Her auburn hair that was the same shade as mine fell in waves around her shoulders, and there were tiny wrinkles around her eyes when she smiled. She was beautiful. When she opened her arms, I walked into them and the sensation of being in water shifted.

It felt like I was surrounded by pure love. I choked on emotion as tears streamed down my face.

"What's wrong, baby girl?"

"I messed up," I told her. I wished I could tell her all my problems and that would be the end of them. She'd take care of me like she had when I was a little girl.

But I was no little girl anymore. And she wasn't here. Not that I'd expect her to solve my problems, but she couldn't if she tried.

She stroked my hair. "You can fix it."

"I don't know. I don't think I can." There was no way things could go back to the way they were. Anyway, things had never been *right* in the first place. My birthright was always looming over me, ensuring I could never live a normal life. And because of me, neither could Cole.

Damn it, I was trying to save him from the burden of being a seeker. But now it seemed my sacrifice was for nothing. He'd tracked me down, which brought him that much closer to Linda, that much closer to his role as a seeker being exposed.

My mother pushed me away from her and held me at arm's length, so she could stare into my eyes. "You can, Ava. You can fix *everything*."

She stressed that last word like it was supposed to mean something important, something big, something I was not understanding.

"But how?" I hung my head.

I'd alienated everyone I loved. My intentions were good, but that didn't change the end result. Truth be told, I didn't know if I should try to fix it. I was toxic. Nothing good could come for anyone who was close to me.

I knew before I looked up that my mother was gone. With a sob, I held my hand out to where she'd been, but all I felt was cool air. The rhythmic wave sensation turned cold and choppy, beating against my skin, its former comfort gone.

I was alone.

IT WAS NEARLY NOON BY the time I stumbled into the kitchen still in my PJs. Chase and Claire sat at the kitchen table not talking, but I'd heard muffled voices before I'd come out, making me suspect they had been talking about me. I flashed them a tight smile and Claire's expression turned guilty. Yup, they'd definitely been talking about me.

"So your boyfriend brought your handler here," Chase said. Leave it to him not to beat around the bush. I actually appreciated it. I didn't have the time or patience for bullshit.

But he had it wrong. If anything, Xena had led Cole here. Cole was never supposed to come.

"*Chase*," Claire hissed. "Leave her alone."

I squared my shoulders. While I appreciated Claire's concern, I could fight my own battles.

"Xena isn't like Linda or Xavier. Or Niles for that matter."

"She's a handler," Chase retorted.

"I know, but she's not like them. I can't begin to tell you how much she's risked to help me."

"Why would she do that?" His voice was laced with suspicion. "What's her motive?"

"I don't know." I crossed my arms. I wasn't any happier about my answer than Chase was, but there was no point pressuring Xena. She'd tell me what she wanted to tell me and so far, her motives weren't on that short list.

"I can't believe you shared our location." Chase's voice was laced with anger, but I'd take that over disappointment any day.

"Xena helped me get away from Linda. She's not going to turn us in," I insisted. "But I can tell there's nothing I can say to convince you, so you can talk to Xena yourself and make up your own mind."

I could tell by the look on his face that wasn't happening.

He pushed back from the table. "I have an interview." When he stood, I noticed he was dressed in khaki pants and a shirt and tie. The fact I'd missed that before showed just how out of it I was. The sleep had done me well physically, but mentally, I was still a wreck.

Moments later the door slammed and Claire jumped.

I sighed, sinking into the seat Chase just vacated. "I'm sorry," I said. "If it really bothers him that much, I can leave. I don't want to cause trouble for you two."

Claire reached out and squeezed my hand. "Don't be silly. He'll get over it. He always does."

I wasn't so sure. He was pretty mad, and he had reason to be. I understood his position completely. Maybe it would be better for everyone if I left.

Except I couldn't. I still had the Xavier situation to deal with, but I couldn't tell Claire that. She would be horrified. I was fairly horrified myself.

You wouldn't think I would be. After all, I'd been thinking about killing Xavier for almost a year. But wanting to do it and actually being given the opportunity were two entirely different things. It turned out I wasn't as fierce as I led myself to believe.

I couldn't wrap my head around it. Xavier had done everything in his power to make me miserable and basically ruin my life. And now he was giving me what I wanted.

Except not really. If I went through with it, it would be a mercy killing. An assisted suicide. Where was the justice in that? I'd be giving *him* what *he* wanted. He'd effectively put me in a no-win situation.

And stolen my vengeance.

"Can I make you some breakfast?" Claire asked.

I shook my head. "I'll just have some cereal."

"Are you sure?" She peered at me, concern in her eyes. "I don't mind."

"No, I'm good. Thanks."

Her concern actually made me feel worse. I felt like a jerk just thinking it, especially because I knew that wasn't Claire's intention. In the past, my mom had been the one to try to cheer me with food. So Claire's behavior was an in-my-face reminder of what I had lost, especially in the wake of my vivid dream.

Seeming to sense I wasn't up for company, Claire retreated to the bedroom, closing the door behind her with a soft click. I dragged myself out of my chair and foraged in the pantry for cereal. But holding the box in my hand, I knew I wouldn't be able to eat. I sighed and shoved the box back on the shelf.

While I showered, tears filled my eyes and for a moment, I gave in, letting them stream down my face. Then my hands clenched into fists.

"*No.*"

Taking a shaky breath, I wiped at my eyes. Crying and self-pity wouldn't fix anything.

It may have been a jerk move for me to leave like I did, but that didn't make it okay for Cole to pull the jerk behavior, too. My intentions were good. And right now, I couldn't say the same for Cole.

I got it. He was hurt. *I'd* hurt him. But what the hell had he expected? Why drive all this way just to run out?

I turned off the water and yanked the shower curtain to the side, nearly pulling it down. I wrapped a towel around myself and stalked to my and Claire's room, my hair dripping all over the place.

Claire looked at me with wide eyes but smartly didn't comment.

I picked up my phone that had been gathering dust these past few weeks and pulled up Xena's number.

"Where's Cole?" I asked as soon as she answered, not bothering with a greeting. I didn't worry about offending her, though. She appreciated directness.

I could almost hear her grin through the phone. "It's about damn time."

CHAPTER 2

MY HAIR WAS STILL DAMP by the time I parked in front of the hotel. It was a nice one, or at least much nicer than the one I had been staying in. This one had interior hallways and exterior doors that required a key card to open.

I stormed through the lobby, going straight for the stairs. If I waited for the elevator, I might lose my nerve. I had to keep moving.

Housekeeping carts loaded down with towels and cleaning supplies blocked the hallway. *Crap.* They only cleaned rooms when the guests were out. I suddenly became fearful Cole wouldn't be here. For all I knew, he could have left already.

But Xena hadn't said so and anyway, I didn't think that was the case.

I went in search of room 304, but I didn't have to go far. It was the second one. I stared at the numbers on the door, my hand poised to knock. After a few seconds, I rapped my knuckles on the wood.

Right away I could hear movement inside the room, and I was temped to bolt. *Hypocrite.* I swallowed.

The door opened a crack and Cole leaned against the doorframe. We stared at each other for a moment. I had no clue what was going on in his head, but I drank him in. His presence had always affected me, no matter what mood he was in, whether it be playful or brooding. There was never an in-between with him and today was no exception.

I wanted nothing more than to wrap myself around him and press my face to his chest to listen to his heartbeat. My own heart thudded in my chest, my hands shook, and my mouth suddenly became dry.

He towered above me, guarded dark eyes peering at me suspiciously.

That hurt, but I supposed I'd earned it.

He didn't make a move to let me in, so I pushed past him into the room, catching a strong whiff of the peppermint gum he always chewed. I closed my eyes, the scent bringing memories powerful enough to make me sway on my feet. I dug my fingernails into my palms to bring me back to the *now*.

I opened my eyes and turned to face him. "We need to talk."

"I don't have a lot to say to you right now." His voice was flat, emotionless.

I shook my head. "You don't drive six hours just to *not* talk to me."

"I brought your birth certificate."

"Really?" I said dryly. "That's the best you have? Xena could have overnighted it."

He shrugged, then moved toward me. As he did, a small burst of hope he'd take me in his arms rose in my chest. When he passed by without so much as touching me, I squeezed my eyes shut as the hope sank deep within me where it belonged. *Stupid. You know better than that.*

When I opened my eyes, Cole was stretched out on the bed with his hands behind his head, his gaze focused on the ceiling.

He wouldn't even look at me.

How did we get here again? It was eerily similar to when Cole had learned I'd made the decision for Areli to save him, thus making him a seeker.

But this wasn't exactly the same. In that situation, I'd made a decision for him. In this case, I'd made a decision for myself.

"Cole, look at me." I half-expected him to refuse, but he wasn't that obstinate. As his gaze shifted to me, he let his guard down. A rawness consumed his features.

It was a dagger to my gut. I'd done that to him. His life had been filled with shitty people, and I knew how hard it was for him to trust. Yet, for some reason, he trusted me. And I'd let him down.

Again.

"I did what I thought was best." I paused, but he didn't speak, only continued to look at me.

I didn't know what I expected. An olive branch maybe? Because, damn it, didn't he realize this was hard for me, too? If he didn't get that, then he didn't know me at all.

I pressed on. "Do you know who Linda is?"

He focused on the ceiling again. "Your overzealous new handler."

I was surprised he knew that much. "She's more than just that." I waited for a moment but got nothing. "Do you want to know why I left?"

He sat up in one swift motion, resting his elbows on his knees. "I don't even know anymore."

I reeled back like he'd slapped me. "Why did you bother to come?" I asked. "What do you want from me?"

"I don't know." Scrubbing his hands over his face and hair, he let out a shaky laugh. "I don't know why I still care."

All the breath left my body in one fell swoop. I was getting a dose of my own medicine, and it was sour, making me want to throw up. I'd hurt him and now he was hurting me back.

There was so much I'd planned to tell him, so much I *wanted* to tell him.

But now wasn't the time.

"You should ask Xena about Linda," I said, trying not to choke on the words. "There's some stuff you should know."

Maybe my actions had been shortsighted, but it all had happened so fast. Linda showed up, and then five minutes later Xena was pushing me out the door. When I thought about it that way, she was as much to blame as I was.

But Xena wasn't the one Cole had placed his trust in.

"You know where to find me when you're ready to talk." I used *when*, not *if*, because I refused to believe the time wouldn't come.

He regarded me coolly for a few seconds, giving no sign of encouragement before turning away.

I let myself out.

And he let me go.

I DIDN'T GO BACK TO the apartment. I wasn't in the mood to deal with Chase and Claire. Chase because, well, he was *Chase*, and Claire because I couldn't take her pitying looks.

Instead, I went to campus and found a bench in the shade. Pulling my knees up to my chest and wrapping my arms around them, I watched people come and go and wondered what it must be like to have a normal life. Considering it was summer, there was still a fair amount of people. Then again, I had no point of comparison. I wondered how busy campus got during the normal school year. It would be starting soon, and the campus would probably overflow with students.

It would be so easy to get lost in the crowd, to be surrounded by people but still be alone.

I thought about Xavier. I wasn't sitting in the same place we'd chatted, but I wouldn't be able to come onto campus without thinking about it. It wasn't every day someone asked me to kill him.

Assisted suicide.

That was essentially it. He wanted to die, and it wasn't something he could accomplish by himself. I hadn't even considered what would be involved. I imagined it would be...gruesome.

My stomach lurched just thinking about it.

I turned my head and rested my cheek on my knees. I was a coward. For all my talk, I didn't know if I could actually do it and I didn't know how to feel about that fact, either. I had no doubt I would have no trouble inflicting mortal harm in the middle of a fight or to save a loved one, but this was so much more cold-blooded, calculated, *premeditated.*

Pre-meditated murder.

I gulped, squeezing my eyes shut. *Don't think about it like that.* Assisted suicide—that was what it was. By definition, no one could ask to be murdered. Right?

God, I hated Xavier. I hated him for killing my mom, for his part in making Cole a seeker, and now for demanding this of me.

I feared that even if I went through with it, I would still never be free of him.

I TRUDGED DOWN THE STAIRS to the apartment, wishing we'd gotten a place on a higher floor. There were windows and everything, but it still felt like descending into the ground, like a grave.

When I opened the door, Cole was sitting on the couch next to Claire and it appeared they were in deep conversation. Claire looked up at me with wide eyes and removed her hand from his knee, then rubbed her palms on her thighs.

Why was her hand on his knee? I narrowed my eyes at her. *And sweaty palms?* Exactly what were they talking about?

Cole didn't meet my gaze, making me even more suspicious.

More jealous.

For the first time, I wondered what it might have looked like when he saw me and Chase sitting on the couch. Surely he would know I wasn't *with* Chase.

Yeah, just like I know Cole isn't with Claire.

She might be better for him. She probably wouldn't hurt him like I keep doing.

Jealousy sucked. Even though I knew it was irrational, I couldn't shake it. I never thought I was the jealous type, but I guessed where Cole was concerned, all bets were off.

"What are you doing here?" I asked, coming across way harsher than I meant to. But a few hours ago it had seemed like he wanted nothing to do with me. And now here he was practically cuddling with Claire.

How the hell had I missed his car in the parking lot? The Rustinator didn't exactly blend in. Either I was really not paying attention—*not good*—or he'd driven another car—*not likely.*

"Can we talk?" He still didn't get up from the cozy spot on the couch next to Claire.

"Sure," I said cautiously, wondering what had changed in the last three hours. I knew Cole, and he wasn't one to do a one-eighty this quickly.

Claire stood. "I'll go into the bedroom to give you privacy."

"Thanks," I murmured, not able to take my eyes off Cole. Only when I heard the quiet click of the bedroom door closing did I join him on the couch, but I sat on the other end, leaving space between us.

It was so hard to be near him and not be *with* him.

"I think you should come home," he said.

I blinked. That wasn't what I expected him to say. Though I didn't know what I expected.

"Did you ask Xena about Linda?"

"Yeah." He rubbed his brow, obviously uncomfortable. "She said I'm unique, a special snowflake or some shit."

I couldn't help but grin at his description. "Xena called you a special snowflake?"

"Her words, not mine." The edges of his lips tugged, like a smile was threatening to burst through, but his expression turned somber again. "If any of that is true, I can't hide from it. Someone will always be looking for me."

When he said it like that—so logically and sure—I felt like an idiot for trying to protect him, to draw Linda away from him.

I shook off the unpleasant feeling. It had worked so far. While I might not be able to keep him safe forever, I could at least buy him a few years, long enough to get Kyle through high school. Speaking of which—

"What's going on with Kyle?" Though Cole's brother was a big reason I'd wanted to keep Cole from having to live the life of a seeker, I hadn't actually given him much thought.

"He's staying with Bill right now. We're working on making that arrangement permanent."

"Really? Like Bill would foster him?"

"Something like that. The child welfare office is slammed with kids younger and more vulnerable than Kyle, so they wouldn't mind not having to worry about him."

That made me sad. Kyle might be a teenager and a pain in the butt, if truth be told, but he was still a kid. He deserved consideration.

But honestly, this was better. Kyle would get the tough love he needed from Bill and Cole instead of falling through the cracks of the foster care system. Since he'd already spent time in juvie, there wouldn't be a lot of families willing to take a chance on him.

"Are Kyle and Bill getting along?" I asked, seriously curious. By the time Bill became Cole's mentor of sorts, Cole had already decided he wanted to stay on the straight and narrow. Kyle still had some growing up to do before he reached that conclusion. Although Bill appeared gruff and rough around the edges, he was a big softie. But I also had no doubt he could be a hard ass if the situation warranted it.

With Kyle, it most likely did.

"Bill put him to work in the shop."

"Wow. Really?"

Cole nodded. "He's good with his hands."

That must run in the family.

My gaze dropped to Cole's hands and memories of other ways Cole was good with them overwhelmed me.

I dragged my eyes away. "Good," I whispered.

Cole cleared his throat. "Anyway, you need to come home."

No, I don't. Learning about Kyle hardened my resolve to keep handlers away from Cole. As long as I'd known him, he'd wanted to help his brother and I'd do everything in my power to make sure he was able to.

I shook my head.

"Look," Cole said, getting angry. "I don't hide from my problems. If Linda or another handler finds me, I'll deal with it."

"It's not that simple."

"It is."

I shook my head again, fuming this time. He didn't get it. Sure, he witnessed some of what Xavier did, but he wasn't there when my mom was tortured. If Cole was as important as the handlers were making him out to be, then they'd stop at nothing to force him to cooperate, including hurting Kyle and Bill. Cole might be willing to sacrifice himself, but was he willing to put Bill and Kyle on the line?

"You don't get it." I stood, too angry to stay seated.

Cole rose and towered over me. "Why are you underestimating me? I get it. I know what you went through. Xavier tortured and killed your mom. He hurt me. But that doesn't mean the same thing will happen to Kyle."

Okay, so maybe he did get it, just a little. But he was missing the main point. "You can't protect them."

The only way to keep them safe was to keep them out of the line of fire, which couldn't happen unless Cole stayed under the radar.

He crossed his arms and looked at me, his eyes cold and hard.

Realizing what was going through his mind, I took a step back as if he'd pushed me. "You think you can deal with the handlers where I couldn't. Where I *failed*."

His expression remained unflinching.

"You're an asshole," I whispered, my voice dripping with rancor. "I can't believe you think that."

He had no idea how hard it was for me to walk away from not only him, but also Bill, Shenice, and Kaley, the one friend I'd managed to make in the last two years. My sacrifice meant nothing to him.

I knew he'd be pissed when he found out why I left, but I realized now I also partially expected him to understand.

"Why do you want me to come home?" I asked the question I should have posed at the beginning of this conversation.

He hesitated. "For Bill. Losing you like that was like losing another daughter. You should come home for Bill."

I closed my eyes. *But not for him.*

How could I possibly go home knowing Cole didn't want me there? His brother was living with Bill, so it wasn't like I could avoid him.

But even if I wanted to, I couldn't leave here. Not yet. Not until I'd dealt with the Xavier situation.

I stepped back as I opened my eyes, wanting space. "I'll think about it."

Cole gave me a look that told me he knew what that meant—I wouldn't be going home.

"At least call him."

"Yeah, okay," I said, my gaze fixed on the carpet. "You should go."

The front door opened and Chase walked in. It took all of two seconds for him to size up the situation and move beside me in a protective gesture. He scowled at Cole, and Cole scowled right back.

Just what I needed—an overloaded display of alpha maleness.

I didn't bother to introduce them. Chase knew who Cole was and quite frankly, I didn't really care if Cole knew who Chase was.

"Is everything okay?" Chase asked. Though he might be pissed at me, he wasn't going to let anyone hurt me, either. I knew if I gave the slightest indication that it wasn't, he would forcibly escort Cole out of the apartment.

Cole cracked his knuckles. He obviously got that memo, too.

Chase was a former athlete who still kept obsessively in shape, but Cole was no slouch himself. Physically, they'd be evenly matched. Cole, however, most likely had more practical experience. He'd lived a rough life before coming to work for Bill, and I'd witnessed him kick some ass before.

"I was just walking Cole out," I said. I wasn't. I'd been perfectly fine with Cole letting himself out, but the testosterone in the small apartment was suffocating. I could use some air.

"Okay." Chase strode purposefully over to the window that overlooked the parking lot. *Yup, got the message loud and clear. He'll be watching.*

I opened the front door and gestured for Cole to walk out. When he passed me, I thought I heard him mutter "asshole," but I couldn't be sure. Whatever. I couldn't care less if Chase and Cole got along.

At the top of the stairs, Cole stopped and his entire body tensed.

"What the fuck?" he growled.

Damn it. What now?

I tried to push past him, but he put an arm out, holding me back.

There, casually leaning against the Rustinator, was Xavier.

CHAPTER 3

COLE KEPT HIS ARM IN place, effectively shielding me from Xavier. I pressed against his back and in doing so felt the outside of a gun tucked into the back of his pants.

Shit. This could escalate really quickly. Rage emanated off Cole. I bet if I peeked at his aura, it would be bright red.

I tried to shoulder my way in front of him, but that wasn't happening. Even though he wanted nothing to do with me, Cole's protective streak was alive and well. I'd have to dissect that later.

"Stupid boy," Xavier drawled, taking a final puff on his cigar before dropping it to the ground. "I won't hurt her."

Cole's expression clearly said he was calling *bullshit* on that, and I couldn't blame him. He didn't know about Xavier's recent request and his overall change.

I took a moment to examine him. The last time I'd seen him, he was peaceful, contemplative, but standing in front of me now was the old Xavier—the calculating and brutal one.

It made me wish I had my own gun.

"What do you want?" I said. I knew what I wanted— for him to go away. I didn't want him anywhere near Chase and Claire. Hopefully they would stay in the apartment.

Except *damn*, Chase had been watching out the window. As soon as I remembered that, I glanced over my shoulder at the window, but I was too late. Chase was bounding up the stairs. He took a place next to Cole, blocking me from Xavier.

I rolled my eyes. While I appreciated they were both willing to protect me, I wouldn't hide behind them. I put my arms between them and pushed. They each shot me a glare in unison but shifted so I was able to see.

"You know what I want," Xavier said darkly. "I've given you more than enough time to get used to the idea. If you don't comply with my wishes, there will be consequences."

Twenty-four hours was more than enough time to get used to the idea of committing murder? For him, maybe. Though to be fair, I had definitely thought about killing him at least a million times.

His gaze flicked to Chase, then to the stairway leading down to the apartment as if he knew Claire was down there. He probably did.

I didn't get it. When Xavier had asked me to end his life, he'd been a sad and broken being. Absorbing the souls had given him just enough humanity to see what he'd become, for him not to want to live like that. But in front of me was the ruthless Xavier I'd always known. I couldn't believe he still felt remorseful enough to want to end his life.

"What consequences?" I peered at him. The whole reason he supposedly wanted to die was because he couldn't live with what he'd done. So were the consequences more of those same actions?

He took a step toward us, and Chase and Cole closed in their ranks again.

"You have a choice." He took another step, allowing me to clearly see his eyes. The void look from before was not as prominent and in its place was something deadly.

Before, something had taken hold of Xavier, giving him a come-to-Jesus moment. Was that something fading? Losing its influence?

Shit. That wasn't good. As horrible as killing him might be, unleashing him on humanity would be much, much worse.

"What's the choice?" I whispered.

"I think you know." His gaze held mine, and it was all I could do not to squirm and look away. He looked through me, *in* me. It was like he could see right into my soul.

And I had to wonder—was it as black as his?

AS SOON AS XAVIER LEFT, Chase whirled around, glaring at me.

"What the hell?" he growled.

"Hey man," Cole said. "Leave her alone."

"Screw that," Chase shot back. "How the hell did he find us?"

"I don't know," I said, but I realized I also wasn't surprised. I'd learned never to underestimate Xavier.

Chase cursed under his breath and put his hands on his hips, looking in the direction Xavier had gone.

"What's wrong with his face?" Cole asked. I'd forgotten he hadn't seen Xavier since my mom shot him. Though I'd gotten used to his Freddy Krueger-like appearance, it was jarring.

"My mom shot him there, remember?"

"Yeah, but..." Cole put a hand on his forehead, seeming disturbed. "I thought he had healing powers."

"Not anymore," I said. "He's changed."

"Is everything okay?" Claire had come up the stairs.

This was turning into a regular powwow out in the parking lot. I could almost hear Chase grinding his teeth.

"Fine," I said. "Let's go inside."

As we went down the stairs, Cole took his phone out and made a call. I frowned. Who could he possibly be calling right now?

"Xena," he said. "You should come."

Right. Good call. If I'd been thinking straight, I would have called her myself. I needed information. Hopefully Xena would be in a sharing mood.

Once we were all inside the apartment, the tension ratcheted up to an all-time high. Claire seemed to perceive it too because she put on a bright smile and asked, "Is everyone hungry?"

It didn't faze her when no one responded.

"I'll make dinner," she said.

I considered asking her if she needed help, but I didn't think it was wise to leave Cole and Chase unattended. They might have put up a united front against Xavier, but all bets were off now.

I sank into the couch cushions, clasping my hands between my knees. Cole and Chase stayed on their feet.

"Why was he here?" Cole asked.

"I saw him on campus...yesterday." God, was it only yesterday?

Wow, Xavier had changed a lot in a short amount of time. If I waited much longer, would he change his mind about wanting to die? Would I lose my chance?

Assuming I'd even go through with it, that was.

"Why didn't you say anything?" Chase asked. "I *knew* something was up after you'd come home yesterday."

"I was a little preoccupied by everything else." I gestured in Cole's general direction. What I'd said was true—I *had* been preoccupied—but I'd also made a conscious decision to not tell Chase because I didn't want him involved.

You'd think I would have learned by now that things like that were out of my control. The universe seemed to want everyone I cared about all up in my business and in the line of fire.

Chase shot Cole a dirty look and Cole stepped forward. "Do you have something to say to me?"

"Stop it," I said, getting to my feet. "Both of you are being stupid."

I stepped between them and Cole backed up immediately. I might as well have been Cole-repellent. He couldn't stand to be near me.

"I'm going outside to wait for Xena," Cole said. I jumped as he slammed the door behind him.

"What the hell, Ava?" Chase asked, but his tone was softer this time, more sympathetic.

"I left without telling anyone. I didn't say goodbye or give any kind of explanation," I said quietly. "So he has a right to be pissed. Cut him some slack."

Chase exhaled slowly. "You should have told us Xavier followed us here. If he's as bad as you say he is, then we need to be on guard."

"What was your impression of him?" I was curious because Chase hadn't met him before—he'd only seen him briefly while we retrieved my stuff from the hotel. I thought Xavier seemed menacing as hell just now, but my judgment was clouded by my past interactions with him.

"He seemed sadistic. Dark. I can't explain it."

"Yeah," I said quietly. "Nothing like Niles."

"No, nothing like Niles," Chase admitted. "I'd take that shifty chap over this guy any day." He looked at me with pity in his eyes.

The front door opened and Cole came in, followed by Xena.

"That was quick," I said.

She shrugged. "I was in the neighborhood."

Of course she was. Or had she done her freaky teleporting thing? I still didn't know how that worked.

Claire came out of the kitchen, wiping wet hands on her shorts. "Hey," she said. "I'm Claire. You must be Xena."

Xena nodded, coolly looking her over. Claire must have passed the test because Xena stuck her hand out.

Smiling, Claire took it. "I just put dinner in the oven. I hope you'll stay. Ham and mac 'n cheese casserole."

Chase's gaze slid to his sister, but to his credit, he didn't say anything. I was sure he wasn't wild about having a handler over for dinner.

I totally understood why he'd be wary. It was good he was being forced to spend time with Xena. Maybe then he'd realize she wasn't like the others.

Well, not completely anyway.

"Tell me what's going on," Xena said.

"Let's sit down first," Claire said, ever the thoughtful hostess. We were all hovering just inside the front door. If left to our own devices, we probably would have stayed there while we hashed things out.

Xena and I sat on the couch, Claire sat in the side chair, and the guys remained on their feet. Cole leaned against the wall and crossed his arms and Chase widened his stance, also crossing his arms.

I shook my head. Those two idiots didn't even realize how alike they were.

"So, what's going on?" Xena prompted again.

"Xavier."

I told them all about how Xavier had been hanging around Hershey Park, with Claire chiming in. Then in a rush I recounted everything I remembered from our talk yesterday—about how he'd absorbed the souls that were unaccounted for, how it had failed, and how he wanted to die. Considering how tight-lipped I'd been about the whole thing, the words poured from my mouth like water over a ledge. Surprisingly, no one interrupted me.

It felt good to get it out in the open. Though I'd only kept this secret for a little over twenty-hour hours, I'd been drowning in secrets for weeks. I suddenly felt lighter.

"So let me get this straight." Cole laughed bitterly, shaking his head. "The psycho wants you to kill him? Because he's finally developed a conscience?"

That was oversimplifying it a bit, but it more or less summed it up. I nodded.

"I'm not buying it," Cole said, earning a nod from Chase.

"I don't know," Claire said thoughtfully. "If he's a fallen angel, then at one point he had to be good. Is it that hard to believe some of that goodness has returned?"

"Yes," Cole and Chase said in unison.

"You didn't see the guy just now," Chase said. "There's no way he has noble intentions."

"Oh, his intentions aren't noble," I corrected. "They're still self-serving. He wants to die because *he* doesn't want to live. It has nothing to do with the good of mankind."

Cole started pacing. "Part of that I agree with. Nothing he does is ever for the greater good. He is always self-serving. But I still can't believe he wants to die."

"What does he have to live for?" I played devil's advocate, even though I'd had the same thoughts. But no one had seen him yesterday when he'd been stripped of all his *Xavier-ness*. Seeing him like that, I could start to believe he'd been an angel like my ancestor, Areli. It scared me to think how far he'd fallen.

Cole's mouth tightened into a thin line. He didn't have an answer to my question, but he still didn't believe Xavier was ready to throw in the towel on life.

I wouldn't have believed it either if I hadn't seen it with my own eyes.

"Yesterday, he was different," I said. "He was harmless, weak, pathetic."

"He definitely was not any of those things just now," Chase said.

"I know." I chewed on my lip. "I don't get it."

"The question we need to ask is what he really wants," Cole said. "This could be some kind of trap."

"That was my first thought," Chase said.

Those two were like two peas in a freaking pod all of a sudden. I couldn't decide which was more annoying—when they were at each other's throats or when they agreed on everything.

I turned to Xena, who'd remained silent throughout the whole discussion. "What do you think?"

"I don't know," she said slowly. "I have to admit I didn't expect this."

No one did. But what had me worried was that Xena was thrown for a loop. That never happened.

"Do you think he's for real?" I asked.

"I don't think it's a trap, if that's what you're asking. If he wanted to kill you or hurt you, he would've done it by now."

That didn't really make me feel any better.

When my mom had shot him, he'd been badly hurt. A normal person would have died. But other than some scarring on his face, he seemed fine. The scarring was a result of his absorbing the souls gone wrong, so how much would it take to kill him? I was scared to know, but there was no way around it. I couldn't make any kind of decision until I had all the facts.

"How can he die?" I asked. What I really meant was *how do I kill him?* But I couldn't say those words aloud.

Xena shifted uncomfortably. I imagined she didn't want to talk about it, considering she'd also be sharing the method to killing her. For a minute I didn't think she was going to tell us, but if it wasn't just some sick trick, I'd find out eventually anyway. When she began to speak, I guessed she came to the same conclusion.

"It won't be pretty," she said, "and it won't be easy."

I waited for her to say more but she clamped her mouth shut, true to form. She'd basically told us nothing. I could've guessed it was going to be difficult. Everything with Xavier was difficult.

"He said you need to make a decision," Cole said. "Did he give you any other information, like where and when to meet him?"

"Sort of," I said. "He said everything was ready and I should call him when I was. I was surprised to see him. I didn't get the impression it was urgent."

I realized now that was foolish thinking. Xavier was accustomed to calling the shots and everyone bowing to his commands. So even though he'd changed in some ways, in others he was still the same old Xavier.

"When were you planning to call him?" Chase asked.

Claire looked horrified. "Why are you assuming she's going to do it?"

"I would," Chase said without hesitation. "And considering everything this asshole has done to her, I'm surprised she hasn't done it already."

"How can you think that?" Claire stared at her brother with pain in her eyes. "You're talking about killing someone in cold blood."

"He's not exactly innocent," Cole said.

"It's still taking a life."

Chase's face tightened. "What do you think happened to the people we turned into Niles?"

Claire looked away, a stricken expression on her face.

"He's right," I said. "If someone doesn't end him he's just going to absorb more souls, or try to anyway."

"Do you want this on your conscience?" Xena asked softly. "You'd be giving him exactly what he wants. Are you okay with that?"

I intertwined my fingers in my lap and stared at them. It was like Xena read my mind. I didn't want to be responsible for more death, but killing Xavier would most likely save innocent lives. I couldn't be sure though because it seemed there was no shortage of handlers. At the very least I could prevent Xavier from doing something unnatural with the souls.

Not that the practice of seeking was natural, either.

I had two questions—could I actually do it? And could I live with myself for giving him exactly what he wanted? My mother's death would never be avenged. Justice would never be served.

God, I hated him. He'd taken everything from me, even this.

"What are you going to do?" Cole asked. His eyes bore into mine, and for a moment I got lost in their darkness. Like Xena, he understood why this was hard for me. But though he understood, I wondered if he cared.

"What would you do?"

Cole didn't hesitate. "I would kill him." He looked away. "But I know it's not that simple for you."

It was a shot to the gut that he delivered this sympathy without looking at me.

Chase and Claire had already stated their opinions on what I should do, but I didn't really factor that into account. Even though they were seekers, they hadn't dealt with Xavier like the rest of us had. They didn't really understand.

"What about you?" I asked Xena. "What would you do?"

"I can't say."

"Can't or won't?"

She shrugged. "It's the same thing."

It wasn't. One meant she didn't have an opinion and the other meant she didn't want to state her opinion. It was too bad because there was no way I could get it out of her, and I really wanted to know what she thought. She seemed to understand my dilemma more than anyone. In a way I respected that she didn't try to influence me. But that didn't make it any easier.

"Before you make a decision," she said, "you should know what's involved."

My palms grew slick, and I felt sweat gathering down my spine. I knew I needed to know, but I wasn't sure I was ready.

"Tell me," I whispered. All eyes were glued on Xena.

"Fallen angels are impervious to disease and they heal quickly from injuries, but they can't recover from excessive blood loss."

"But any wounds he gets will heal before he loses an excessive amount of blood..." I trailed off as I realized what that meant. Not only would it not be pretty or easy, it also wouldn't be quick. I would have to injure him again and again so he continued to lose blood. He couldn't be allowed time to heal. But how long would that take?

Cole's eyes met mine again, and I could tell by his expression he'd put the pieces together too. I could also tell he was still willing to go through with it.

Unfortunately, it wasn't up to him.

CHAPTER 4

AFTER EVERYONE LEFT, I RETREATED to an empty bench in the parking lot. I had a lot of thinking to do, the least of which was about Cole. He'd been the first to leave. Once the group had finished talking he barely looked at me. I'd have been lying if I said it didn't sting.

Not long ago, he couldn't keep his hands off me.

Dinner had been awful. Not the food—that was fantastic—but the way Chase glared at Xena suspiciously as he shoveled mac & cheese into his mouth, the way she evenly met his stare, the way Cole continued to coldly assess Chase. Claire was the only well-behaved one. Was it too much to ask for everyone to just get along?

Stupid question.

Chase and Claire cleaned up the dishes even though I offered. They both plied me with pitying stares, acting as if I would break any minute. Their sympathy made me squirm. But each of their gazes also carried undertones. Chase wanted me to go through with killing Xavier while Claire didn't. Every look they gave me was a plea to choose their side.

Or perhaps it was all in my head. I was completely mental these days. It didn't help I had no one to talk to.

I pushed off the bench and turned toward the apartment but a flash of light on the other side of the parking lot caught my eye.

Xavier.

He leaned casually against a tree with a newly lit cigar hanging from his lips. Though he seemed to realize I saw him he didn't approach or signal me in any way. He merely puffed on his cigar like he hadn't a care in the world, like he hadn't just threatened me hours earlier.

What was he up to? I thought he'd left. Had he been here the whole time or did he come back?

Either way, I didn't like that he lingered so close to Chase and Claire. If it came down to it, would he use them against me?

Another stupid question. Of course he would.

He turned to stare at me, his gaze boring into me. Another expectation. It was like he already knew what I would decide and that pissed me off, especially because he was right. But that didn't mean I was ready to give in so soon. I needed to come to terms with things before I blackened my soul beyond redemption.

I met Xavier's gaze defiantly. After a moment, he grinned and slithered away. The breath expelled from my lungs in a whoosh. I'd like to think my waiting to take action was a power play, but we both knew who held the power.

And it wasn't me.

With a final look across the parking lot at the spot Xavier had vacated, I sent a group text to Cole and Xena, letting them know what was going in. Then I schlepped down the steps to the apartment. Chase and Claire were still in the kitchen and as soon as the door opened, their chatter ceased.

"Xavier was just out there." I flopped onto the couch, not even perturbed they'd obviously been talking about me. If I were them, I'd be talking about me, too.

Chase's eyes filled with fury. "What the hell?"

I shrugged. "It's not all that surprising."

Claire twisted a dish towel in her hands. "What did he want?"

"Nothing," I said blandly. "Actually, that's not true. He wants to screw with us. Or with me, anyway."

I sighed as I realized I knew Xavier much better than I claimed, much better than I wanted to. At least, I knew his sinister side. His newfound side with a conscious was still a mystery.

But soon it wouldn't matter. He would be dead.

Chase cursed under his breath. "We're sleeping in shifts tonight."

"I don't think he'll try to come in," I said. But it wasn't a bad idea. While I could understand a lot of Xavier's actions in hindsight, he was still unpredictable.

"What are you going to do?" Chase asked. I guessed he had taken off the kid gloves. That was fine. He had a right to ask. Now that Xavier was stalking the apartment, the situation affected him and Claire.

"She can't..." Claire's gaze shifted to me and her eyes widened, shock registering on her face. "You're going to go through with it."

It wasn't a question. It was a fact.

"I don't have much of a choice."

"There's always a choice."

"What's the alternative?" I said quietly. "If I don't do it, he'll take more souls and who knows what else? I have to end him."

The expression on Claire's face told me she understood my sole concern—after it was done, I wouldn't be able to look in the mirror without seeing a murderer stare back at me. The way she was looking at me now, you'd think she was already looking at one.

Yet, Claire offered no alternate choice because even if she wouldn't admit it aloud, she knew I was making the best choice.

I wouldn't go so far as to say I was doing the right thing because was murder ever right?

A soft knock sounded on the door and all three of us tensed.

I forced myself to relax. Xavier wouldn't knock. And if he did, it wouldn't be softly. I stood to go to the door, but Chase beat me to it.

He looked through the peephole. "It's Xena." He didn't bother hiding his disgust.

"Let her in," I said, annoyed. But I wasn't going to bother explaining yet again that Xena was one of the good guys. Chase was too hardheaded and I didn't have the patience.

He let her in. As he was closing the door, Cole appeared, putting his hand on the door to stop it from closing.

"What the hell?" Chase growled. "It's like deja vu from earlier."

I shot Chase a nasty look. He didn't have to be such an ass. His attitude didn't help anyone.

Chase checked the foyer before closing and locking the door a final time. He looked at me expectantly, but I shook my head. Although I'd let Xena and Cole know about Xavier's lurking, I hadn't expected them to show up.

Neither one of them said anything, though. I guessed it was up to me to start the conversation.

"You didn't have to come," I said. "We had it under control. Actually, there's nothing to control. I think he's gone."

"He's more likely to stay away if I'm here." Xena sat on the couch, slipped her shoes off, and tucked her legs under her, making herself comfortable. *Guess she's staying.*

My gaze shifted to Cole. He crossed his arms, the look in his eyes daring me to tell him to leave. It wasn't a friendly look, but at least he was actually meeting my eyes.

"I'm coming with you," he said.

It took me a minute to realize what he meant.

I shook my head. "No, I'm not putting you through that."

"Damn it, Ava, stop trying to make decisions for me."

"This one isn't yours to make."

"That's a first."

My chest heaved as I stared him down.

"You'll probably need help," Xena chimed in, like this was just a normal conversation and Cole and I weren't allowing our festering issues to leach to the surface. I tore my eyes away from him to look at her.

Dread trickled down my insides. She was right. I might not be able to manage it on my own. And I'd rather not take the chance.

Claire took a step forward, her chin held high. "If you need help, I can—"

"No way," I said at the exact same time Chase said, "Hell, no."

At least we were in agreement there.

"This isn't your fight," I told Claire, then I nodded at Chase. "Yours, either, for that matter."

"But it is mine," Cole said.

"But he didn't..."

I was going to say, *"But he didn't ask you."* I let it go. Cole definitely had a stake in the fight against Xavier.

"Isn't this a fight for seekers?" Claire asked. "Doesn't it involve all of us?"

Sort of, but not really. This was definitely personal.

"You and Chase left home so you wouldn't have to deal with seeker stuff anymore," I said. "I'm not dragging you into this."

"I'm learning we might not be able to escape being seekers," Claire said quietly. "Are we supposed to stay in hiding forever?"

"If that's what it takes," Chase said.

Claire shook her head. "I don't want to live like that. Never being able to settle down. We're young now, but I always dreamed I'd have a family of my own someday."

Her words brought to mind the time I proclaimed to my mother I was never having kids because I didn't want to pass on my seeker genes. My mother had said the same thing, even going as far as attempting suicide when she found out she was pregnant.

Of course, Claire's children wouldn't be seekers. No, that joyous privilege was mine and mine alone because I was a descendant of Areli.

Or was it?

My eyes slid over to Cole. Though he wasn't Areli's descendant, Areli's blood flowed through his veins, which made him part of Areli's line. Would he pass on the seeker gene to his children? I hadn't considered it, but there was no way to know until the time came.

I looked at Claire, who had tears glistening in her eyes.

"Your children won't be seekers," I told her.

"But yours will," Chase said.

I couldn't help it—my gaze swung around to Cole. His expression was tight. I couldn't read it.

"Not if I don't have any." I was so done. All my energy was spent. "I'm going to bed. We'll come up with a plan tomorrow."

THE EVENING SOMEHOW TURNED INTO a warped slumber party. Xena slept on the floor in our room—despite Claire's repeated offers for her to take the bed—and Cole slept on the couch in the living room. Knowing he was just on the other side of the wall, I tossed and turned all night. Despite that, Claire was out of bed before me, whipping up pancakes in the kitchen.

I hoped she'd get to have a family one day. She was a natural nurturer.

I stayed in my room long after Xena had gone out. I wasn't avoiding everyone, not exactly. I just needed time to think before facing them.

I had hoped I'd dream of my mother, but I'd have had to sleep for that to be possible.

Even though I had no appetite, my stomach growled as the scent of pancakes and sugary syrup wafted into my room. I dragged myself out of bed and pulled on shorts and a t-shirt. After a quick trip to the bathroom to brush my teeth, I joined everyone for breakfast. There was no idle chatter, but no one was giving anyone death glares, so I considered that a win.

"Here's the plan," I said as soon as I sat down. "I'm going to contact Xavier and set things up for tomorrow."

Chase nodded and Claire sighed, resigned. Cole said nothing.

Xena crossed her arms. "Are you sure you want to do this?"

I hadn't expected that from her. She had no love for Xavier, who actually happened to be her distant relative. I'd never learned exactly how closely they were related. It was probably better I didn't know.

"No," I answered honestly. "But I don't think it's about what I want anymore."

I still couldn't wrap my head around everything, and my feelings were all over the place. I wanted Xavier dead, but not like this.

Like what? a tiny voice in my mind asked. When all was said and done, would I feel any better about killing someone if it was self-defense? Or in the heat of battle? Basically, in a way that wasn't so calculated. *Premeditated mur—*

No. Assisted suicide. The sooner I could convince my brain to start thinking of it that way, the better.

"Excuse me." I left the table and grabbed my phone from the bedroom before stepping outside. I needed to do this before I changed my mind.

I half-expected Xavier to be lurking in the parking lot, but if he was, I didn't see him. That was one small saving grace.

It would be easier to text him, but I wanted to hear his voice. I wanted to know if I would be dealing with the changed Xavier or the vicious one.

The phone rang four times before he answered.

"I've been expecting your call," he said and I was immediately annoyed. I hated that he knew me so well. And if he was expecting my call, then why had it taken so long for him to answer?

Prick.

"Tomorrow," I said.

"I'll send you the address."

I waited for him to elaborate, but I was met with silence.

"Do I need to bring anything?" I asked.

"No. Everything is ready. See you soon." Then he hung up.

A few seconds later, a text came through with an address in Lancaster, Pennsylvania.

He'd given nothing away in that conversation, and I shouldn't have expected otherwise. I couldn't ascertain his state of mind. He'd sounded almost bored.

Footsteps sounded behind me, but I didn't need to turn to know it was Cole. He stopped several feet behind me.

"What's the deal?"

I turned to face him. He had his hands stuffed in his pockets, his expression neutral.

"He gave me an address in Lancaster."

He waited a beat. "That's it?"

"That's it."

Cole rocked back on his heels. "Huh."

"What are you thinking?" I asked cautiously.

"I don't trust him. He could be setting us up."

Setting me *up*, I mentally corrected. Cole had inserted himself in the situation. If Xavier was out to get someone, it was me. He didn't even know Cole was coming.

"How so?" I had also considered that Xavier might not be playing straight with us, but I couldn't figure out what his goal could be. If he wanted me dead, he'd had many different chances to kill me and he wouldn't get anything out of me getting arrested.

"I don't know." Cole shook his head. "Something doesn't seem right."

"Xavier isn't right," I said. "You didn't see him the other day."

"He's never been right."

Point for Cole.

"You know what I mean. He was different. He actually reminded me of Areli." After I said that, I realized the comparison would mean nothing to Cole. He'd been dead and then unconscious the only time I'd seen my angel ancestor. "I think he truly wants to die."

Cole shrugged, like he still wasn't buying it. "I don't care what he wants."

"You don't have to go."

"I want to be there when that asshole dies. Besides, who else is going to help you? Like Xena said, you probably can't do it alone."

"Maybe Xena could help."

"She didn't volunteer," Cole pointed out. "And would you really want her to take part in killing a fellow handler? One she's related to, no less?"

"She doesn't like to claim that relation," I muttered.

"Also, I promised Bill I'd look out for you."

"Oh."

Cole was being pragmatic and unemotional in his decision to help, which caused a frost to form around my heart. He wasn't doing it for me. He was doing it because it made sense, and he'd made a promise to Bill.

"Lancaster," he said thoughtfully. "Amish country."

I hadn't put that together, probably because my mind was on other things, like the six-foot testosterone-laden conflict standing in front of me.

"Look, Cole, can we declare a truce?"

He crossed his arms, his expression darkening. "Why do we need one?"

I narrowed my eyes at him. "Cut the shit, okay? You can't act like we meant nothing. I know that's not true. Just like I know there are unresolved things between us."

"Okay." His tone was irritatingly neutral.

"I'm not saying I don't want to deal with those things, because I do, but if we're going to work together on this, we need to be able to trust each other."

"I've never not trusted you." The words seemed to come out of his mouth before he realized he was saying them.

"Good," I whispered.

His eyes met mine, and for a moment all the barriers were gone. Then he turned on his heel and walked away.

CHAPTER 5

CLAIRE INSISTED WE ALL GO out to dinner that night. I would have rather stayed in, but I couldn't say no when I saw the hopeful look on her face. She wanted to take my mind off what awaited me in the morning, as if that were possible. So I figured what the heck. We had to eat and no one felt like cooking.

We went to a local mom & pop place that reminded me of the diner Chase, Claire, and I used to go to. It had the same cheap vinyl seats, waitresses who seemed stretched too thin, and the sweet smell of fried goodness. *Thank God.* I could use some of that in my life. My appetite had been nonexistent. I told myself it was too soon for me to have lost weight as a result, but my clothes seemed baggy on me.

As soon as we were seated, Xena announced, "Order whatever you want. It's my treat."

My eyebrows shot up and I met Cole's gaze. The edges of his mouth quirked into a mischievous grin. I couldn't help but grin back at him and shake my head when he gleefully rubbed his hands together in jest as he surveyed the menu.

"Xena, you have seen Cole eat before, right? You might regret that."

Cole could pack away enough food in one sitting to get someone else through a week in a zombie apocalypse.

Xena waved her hand, dismissing my concern. "I'll be staying with Chase and Claire for the next few days, so we're spending what I'm saving on a hotel room."

When had that happened? I looked at Claire and she nodded, smiling. Chase shrugged. I was glad to see he'd made progress in accepting Xena. Not that it mattered much. She'd probably be on her way and out of their lives as soon as this business with Xavier was finished.

Would I be on my way as well? I couldn't imagine not having Chase and Claire nearby even though I'd only known them a few weeks. *Time flies when you're dealing with a sadistic fallen angel.*

That label could apply to Xavier and Linda. She'd definitely dropped on my priority list, but she was still a problem I'd have to deal with sooner or later, especially if I was going to go back to Bill's.

Guilt tugged at my insides. I needed to call him, but I'd been putting it off. Not because I didn't want to talk to him, but because I knew how much I'd hurt him and I didn't want to face it. He deserved better. I vowed to call him after dinner.

I scanned the menu and decided on comfort food—mozzarella sticks, chicken tenders, and french fries. True to form, Chase ordered bland baked chicken and veggies. Grinning, I watched Xena's eyes widen as Cole ordered a triple bacon cheeseburger with onion rings for his meal and wings and loaded cheese fries for appetizers.

Knowing him, he'd probably still have room for dessert.

"So, are you ready—"

"No," Claire cut her brother off with a stern look. "We're not talking about that. We're *done* talking about that. This is going to be a pleasant dinner."

She was right. Chase had had to go to work and Claire went out job hunting for a while, but Cole, Xena, and I had spent all afternoon discussing and hashing things out. Even still, we knew little more than we did before. Though Xena knew how a fallen angel could be killed in theory, she'd never heard of it ever actually happening. So while I wanted as much information as possible, that little nugget only served to set me on edge even more.

"Sorry," Chase said, but he didn't look sorry. He looked like he wanted to call in sick to work and come with us tomorrow. I didn't like it. Chase said he wanted to forget about all the seeker stuff and live a normal life, but he seemed more than willing to throw that aside and commit this bloody seeker deed.

I worried he had some vengeance issues and my presence only made it worse.

"Any luck with job hunting today?" I asked Claire, trying to get the conversation flowing in a neutral direction.

"Not really." She looked glum. "I was trying to get an office job, but I might have to widen my search to retail."

"Is there a local temp agency you could try?" Cole asked. "That's a good way to get your foot in the door."

"I called one, but they didn't seem too interested. They already have a lot of people on their list. And I don't have any experience."

"You'll find something," I said more confidently than I felt. I knew firsthand how hard it was to find a job. Though, when I had looked, I was seventeen and still in high school. I would have thought it'd be easier for an eighteen-year-old high school graduate. I had been under the impression people like her had been taking all the jobs I'd been applying for. But what did I know?

"Where did you find a job?" I asked Chase. I was really out of the loop.

"At a shipping company. In the warehouse," he replied. "It kind of sucks, but the pay is decent. The benefits are good, but I'm hoping my dad won't bother taking us off his health insurance. If he even manages to keep his job."

Claire pursed her lips. This was a sore subject for her. The one objection she had to taking off was her concern for their father. He was an alcoholic and only able to function with Claire taking care of him.

Our appetizers arrived, and I was grateful for the distraction, which proved temporary since Cole received a text as soon as the server walked away.

"Goddamn it," he muttered.

"What is it?"

He sighed and rubbed his forehead. "Kyle broke into Bill's liquor cabinet. It's barely seven and he's already wasted."

"Other than that, is he okay?" I asked. "Did he stay at Bill's?"

"Thankfully, yes. That kid just can't stop himself from being a screw-up."

"Is this your little brother?" Claire asked.

Cole nodded. "He's a dipshit."

"Is Bill mad?" I asked, once again feeling guilty for not calling.

"Not really. You know him."

"Yeah." Bill was about as even-keeled as they came.

"But he's no push-over either. At six a.m. sharp tomorrow, Bill's putting Kyle to work. Manual labor." Cole grinned. "I kind of wish I could be there to see that."

"That's going to hurt," Chase said. "He'll be hungover as hell. What kind of manual labor?"

"Not sure. He'll probably make him clean the shop with a toothbrush or some shit like that."

"Shop?" Chase asked. "Like an automotive shop?"

Cole nodded and the two of them engaged in a conversation about cars and engines and I didn't know what else. They lost my attention at the first mention of a V8. At least I knew that was a type of engine, but beyond that, I had no clue what they were talking about.

Beside me Xena tensed and sucked in a breath. I might have missed it if I hadn't been tuning out the boys. Aside from announcing she was picking up the tab for dinner, Xena hadn't participated in the conversation. In fact, she hadn't paid much attention to us, instead choosing to people watch.

Now I looked at her, a question written on my face.

When she moved her gaze to the table, I elbowed her. "What?" I said under my breath.

"Nothing," she said quickly, but I looked where she'd been staring a moment ago.

A group of three men, probably in their twenties, had just been seated three tables over from us. And two of them were staring straight at Xena.

"Who are they?" I grabbed her arm and squeezed before she could tell me they were no one. "Come on, Xena. Tell me."

For a moment, I thought she was going to do her normal thing and withhold information.

"Please," I pleaded, begging with both my voice and my eyes. "The secrets are no good."

"Two handlers and a seeker," she said, still not looking over there.

Damn. They had walked right by us, and I hadn't even realized what they were. I needed to work on my seeker-identifying abilities, though I didn't know if that was even possible for me.

"Do they know you?"

Noticing Xena and I whispering, Cole stopped talking and turned to us. "What's going on?"

I inclined my head toward the three men, two of them still looking this way. Cole's expression darkened.

"The Hispanic man is Hector," Xena said. "I don't know much about him other than his name. The light-haired one is Benny. He's the one I'm worried about."

"Why?" I asked.

"He's an ass-kisser and power hungry. Always willing to do whatever it takes to rack up favors."

"Like outing us to Linda." Feeling sick to my stomach, I threw my napkin on the table.

"Maybe. I don't know," Xena said. "Not all handlers keep up with who is assigned to who, so they might not be aware she's looking for you."

"What about Cole?" I asked, noticing she'd only mentioned me.

She shifted. "Everyone is looking for him. They took me off the case, but they haven't formally assigned anyone else yet. I think they're hoping it will turn into a manhunt."

"Were you planning to tell us this?" Cole asked tightly.

"I just found out about an hour ago," Xena said. "I was going to tell you after dinner."

Cole and I looked at each other across the table. Xena had a history of not telling us things, so even though I'd like to believe her, there was always that lingering doubt.

"Should we leave?" Claire asked.

"I don't think it matters," Xena said. "They've already seen us, so the damage—if any—is done."

I noticed she hadn't said anything about the seeker. That wasn't surprising, but it did show me how inconsequential seekers were compared to handlers.

Other than Cole, of course. Everyone was interested in him.

And perhaps me. When Claire had realized who I was, she'd stared at me in awe. Apparently as a seeker who had been born instead of made, I was somewhat of an urban legend to other seekers. So even among the outcasts, I was an outcast.

I peered at the other seeker, trying my hardest to find some sort of signifier that would mark him as such. I came away with nothing. Most seekers recognized other seekers by the translucent shimmer that surrounded them. It was essentially the absence of an aura. But I didn't see that at all. Instead, I saw their auras like I would for any other person.

Focusing on him, I lowered my guards, but he was too old—out of my age range.

I nudged Cole. "Can you check him out?"

He worked his jaw, not happy about my request.

"Please," I said quietly.

Cole sighed but looked in the man's direction, his eyes getting glassy for a moment. "It's dark. Not black, but almost. It will be soon."

Damn. That was the second seeker I'd encountered with a black aura. I wished I could have checked out Reggie's, a surly and unpleasant seeker I'd met. I would have expected his aura to be black, but I hadn't expected it of the other seeker, who was Chase's friend.

This man I didn't know anything about, but I was developing a theory that seeking darkened seekers' souls. Granted, I didn't have enough of a test sample to prove my theory, but the more I thought about it, the more plausible it seemed. We sentenced good, innocent people to death.

We played God when we had no right to.

A somber tone cloaked the rest of dinner, and our poor server flurried around, trying to repair the broken mood. She probably thought we were displeased with the food or the service. Nope. Just worried about our souls blackening.

Since I'd learned about being a seeker, I'd worried about my soul in an abstract sense. But now, I worried about it even more. Best I could tell, Cole and I were the only two seekers in the world who could see other seekers' auras. Why was that?

Maybe the absence of an aura was a way for seekers to identify one another, but somehow I didn't think so. My gut screamed it was to keep the state of their souls a secret.

And if so, why? What did that mean?

Nothing good.

WHEN WE GOT HOME, EVERYONE went into the apartment, but I stayed out in the parking lot, which had become my pseudo living room. It seemed I spent more time out here than inside. I copped a squat on a curb and stared at my phone for a moment before dialing.

Bill picked up on the second ring.

"Ava," he said. "How have you been?"

That was it. No chastising, no yelling, no guilt tripping. Just a straightforward question he honestly wanted to hear the answer to. If not for the thickness in his voice and the fact that I knew him so well, I'd never know he'd been worried out of his mind.

Good old understated Bill. I didn't deserve him.

I opened my mouth to answer with a cheerful "fine" but changed my mind at the last second. There was no need to pretend with Bill. And I owed him the truth at the very least.

"I've been better."

"Hmm."

The events of the past few weeks spilled out of me as Bill made murmuring sounds that let me know he was listening. By the end, I was wiping tears from my eyes.

"It sounds like you've had a hard go of it," Bill said.

"You have no idea." Except he did because I just told him. But I didn't want to talk about it anymore. "Cole said Kyle is staying with you."

"Yeah." Bill sounded uncomfortable. "I put him in your mother's room. I hope you don't mind."

I suddenly remembered I hadn't cleaned out the room the way I'd planned to. I'd put it off to *tomorrow* too many times to count and then I'd left so suddenly I'd never actually gotten around to it.

"No, of course I don't mind. It's your house."

"It's your house, too."

Still? I wanted to ask. *Even after I ran out on you?*

"Thanks," I said quietly. "Sorry I didn't clear it out. I meant to, but..."

"It's no problem. I boxed everything up, so it's waiting for you when you're ready."

"Thanks," I said again and there was an awkward silence. "Cole told me Kyle got into some trouble."

Bill sighed. "That boy needs straightening out."

"Yeah. Any plans for making that happen?"

"I volunteered him to clean out the public restrooms at the downtown park first thing tomorrow morning."

I'd been in that restroom only once and the stench had been so bad I'd gagged. I'd hightailed it out of there, deciding I'd rather take my chances peeing in the bushes. I hadn't even opened any of the stall doors. I could only imagine how filthy and disgusting they were based on the smell.

"I didn't know volunteers did that."

"Oh, they don't." Amusement danced in his tone, and I'd bet there was a twinkle in his eye. "The city is supposed to maintain the facility, but Kyle could stand to do some community service."

I laughed and Bill chuckled.

"I love you, Bill."

I'd never said the words aloud and they were an awkward segue after talking about nasty toilets, but this conversation represented everything I loved and respected about Bill. He was steady, hardworking, and just plain good. Not many men would take in and mentor a bedraggled group of misfits like me, Cole, and Kyle.

"I love you, too, Ava," he said gruffly then he cleared his throat. "I hope you'll consider coming home soon."

"I'll think about it."

"Okay. That's all I ask. I want you to know this home is always open to you, even if it takes a while for you to come around again."

"Thanks," I said. My heart was so full it threatened to burst. I wished I could express to Bill how much that sentiment meant to me, but I didn't want to embarrass him. "I should probably go."

"All right. Take care of yourself. Bye now."

"You too, Bill," I whispered after he abruptly hung up. "You, too."

CHAPTER 6

HOW LONG DID A PERSON have to go without sleep to be considered an insomniac? That was one of the many questions I pondered while I tossed and turned. As usual, next to me, Claire was dead to the world. Xena slept on our floor again, despite everyone's attempts to let her sleep in a bed or on the couch. Considering I barely closed my eyes all night, I felt especially bad taking up valuable bed space.

An anxious buzz zapped through my body like an electric current. I dreaded what awaited me in Lancaster, but I was ready to get it over with. This was the culmination of years of struggle. Soon, I—and the world—would be free of Xavier.

In the morning I took a long hot shower, hoping it would revive me. Though my mind was abuzz, my body was exhausted. Then I packed up the last of my things and put my bag by the front door next to Cole's. He, Claire, and Xena sat at the kitchen table, each cradling a mug. Chase's door was open, but he was nowhere in sight, so I assumed he was out for a run.

I reached into the pantry and pulled out a box of cereal at random. It didn't matter which one it was. I doubted I'd be able to eat much anyway.

"Any last words of wisdom?" I asked Xena as I poured milk over the cereal.

She shook her head. "Be safe. Be careful. Stay alert."

"Check, check, and check." I took the seat next to her.

The scent of coffee assaulted my senses, making me scrunch up my nose. Coffee wasn't my thing, but it normally didn't turn my stomach, either. I pushed the cereal away. What a waste. I shouldn't have even pretended to be able to eat.

Claire noticed my actions right away. "I can cook you something if you want."

I shook my head. "No need for any more food to wind up in the trash."

"You need to eat," she insisted.

I sighed, pulling the bowl back toward me. "I know."

Cole stood, taking his cup to the sink where he rinsed it out before putting it in the dishwasher. "We should leave in ten minutes."

"Okay," I said.

He picked up our bags and went out the front door.

I shoved two bites of cereal in my mouth then stood to follow him. Claire came up behind me while I was taking care of my dishes.

"Good luck," she said.

I smiled tightly, not knowing how to respond to that. It was an odd sentiment considering what I was about to do, but it wasn't like she was going to say, *"May God have mercy on your soul."*

But dear Lord, I hoped someone was looking out for my soul because I sure as hell wasn't.

I nodded to Xena and she nodded back. We'd discussed whether or not I should text her to keep her in the loop, but in the end we decided she was better off not knowing. No news was good news.

Out in the parking lot, Cole stood next to the Rustinator with Chase, who wore running clothes. As I approached, Chase stuck out his hand. Cole took it.

"Call me if you need help," Chase said.

"I will," Cole said.

No, he wouldn't. Cole had never been good about asking for help. No matter how bad things got, Cole would still deal with them alone. It was a result of him more or less raising himself.

Chase looked at me. "I would hug you, but I'm all sweaty."

"No problem," I said. "We'll be in touch."

He nodded and headed toward the apartment.

"Are you ready?" Cole asked.

"No." I shrugged. "But it's time to go."

As I circled around the back of the car where the trunk was still open, I noticed my gun case tucked between our bags and a red plastic gasoline container.

"Hey!" I exclaimed, reaching for it. "You brought my gun."

Cole walked over and put his hands on the trunk hatch. "I thought you might want it."

I removed my hands from the case, even though I was dying to open it. "I didn't mean to leave it behind, but I had to pack in a hurry."

Cole looked at me, saying nothing. He closed the trunk and got into the driver's seat.

The gun had been a belated birthday present and one that had thrilled me to the core. I wondered at what point Cole had realized I'd left it and what he'd thought about that.

I didn't tell him I wore his other gift—a necklace with an angel pendant—hidden under my shirt every day.

I got in and buckled my seatbelt. "Do you need me to pull up GPS?" I asked.

"No, I got it."

Neither of us spoke for the first half of the drive, which was just over an hour. As we neared Harrisburg, Cole turned off and I took out the list we'd made.

Before going to bed last night, we'd pulled up the address Xavier had given me on Google maps and learned it was an isolated old farmhouse. We didn't know much else, like if it even had power. So we were assuming the worst, that there would be no power or water or anything else for that matter.

Cole easily found the Bass Pro Shop and parked. As we walked toward the entrance, I couldn't help but think of the last time we'd gone to a store like this—to get my gun. We'd held hands and had later gotten reprimanded by a store employee for making out in the ski section.

Good times. But note to self—avoid winter sporting goods department.

I couldn't help but wonder if Cole was thinking of that time as well. I sneaked a glance at him, but he was busy reading the signs posted in the store.

"This way." He pointed toward the camping section.

"Hang on." I doubled back to grab a cart. We were going to need it.

We quickly loaded it with sleeping bags, flashlights, a cooler, and other necessities. As we headed toward the register, Cole looked longingly at the weapons section.

"Stay the course," I said. We'd discussed loading up on weapons, ropes, and tarps, like we were in an episode of *Dexter*, but in the end I'd decided against it. Xavier had said he'd provide everything for that part. I was content to let him and save my money.

After the cashier rang up our purchases, my eyes bulged at the total. As we'd grabbed things off the shelves, I hadn't bothered to look at the prices. But holy crap, camping was an expensive hobby.

Cole held out a stack of bills.

"Hold on." I dug in my pockets for the cash I'd brought.

"I got it," he said.

"But—"

"Here's your receipt," the cashier said, handing Cole his change. Damn, she was fast.

Our next stop was a grocery store to load up on provisions. At the register, Cole asked me to grab two bags of ice from the cooler. By the time I returned, he'd already paid.

I threw the ice in the cart and stalked out to the car ahead of him. What was his deal? Why wasn't he letting me pay for anything? Granted, I didn't have as much money as him, but that didn't mean he had to pick up the tab for everything, especially since this was *my* thing. I'd made this deal with Xavier.

As Cole approached, I whirled to face him. "What's your problem?" I asked.

He gave me the side-eye as he lifted the cooler out of the trunk. "What do you mean?"

I angrily ripped open the ice, which made a loud and satisfying crashing sound as I poured it into the cooler. "You know what I mean. Why wouldn't you let me pay for anything?"

"It's no big deal and I can afford it. Anyway, I thought we'd agreed on a truce."

"We did, but...it's just..." I couldn't articulate why this was bothering me. His actions could be interpreted as nothing but polite practicality, but they meant more than that to me. It seemed like he was trying to take care of me, like he always used to. It was almost like it was a reflex for him.

His words echoed in my mind—*I don't know why I still care.*

The question I really needed answered was if he still wanted to care.

THE CLOSER WE GOT TO the address, the more deserted our surroundings became. I supposed that was good. We didn't want anyone sneaking up on us or accidentally wandering onto the property.

Signs on the side of the road advertised real Amish furniture and horse and buggy tours of Amish country. If we didn't already have an agenda, I would have liked to do that. Would it be like going through a time warp? The Amish lived a much simpler life with no electricity and modern conveniences. Did simpler mean easier? I could certainly live with easier, but I wouldn't want to live without technology.

Cole's phone lay on the seat between us with the GPS app open. *Seven minutes.* A trickle of sweat slid down my spine and it wasn't because of the Rustinator's lackluster air conditioning. *Six minutes.* My heart pounded and my tongue turned to sandpaper. *Five minutes.* I was suddenly suffocating and I rolled down the window, taking a gulp of the hot air that blew in.

Cole glanced at me. "Are you okay?"

"Yes," I croaked, wishing I'd thought to bring one of our newly purchased bottles of water to the front seat instead of leaving them all in the trunk.

"Do you want to take a minute? I can pull over."

I shook my head. "Let's get this over with."

Still, he slowed to give me a few extra seconds to collect myself. I managed to regulate my breathing, but that was it. I was still a sweaty, heart-pounding mess.

After a few minutes, he turned down a gravel driveway overrun with bushes and trees. I was glad he was driving because I would have missed it. Branches and leaves scratched against the side and roof of the car. Cole ground his teeth so hard it was almost audible. I held back my eye roll, but just barely. Was he worried the rust would get scraped off?

I'd never understand his allegiance to this stupid car.

It seemed like this driveway to hell would never end, but we took a turn and suddenly there was a clearing in front of us. The old farmhouse we'd scouted on Google maps sat in the middle, and it had seen better days when Google captured its image. In person it was downright decrepit. Paint peeled off the siding and half the rails were missing from the porch. We wouldn't have to worry about opening the windows for airflow because there was no glass left in them.

Cole parked the Rustinator next to an equally rusted out truck. Okay, to be fair, the truck was in much worse shape than his car. The tires had dry rotted and the rust was so encompassing there were holes in spots, some of them big enough I could put my fist through and touch the engine.

Xavier was nowhere in sight, but it wasn't like I expected him to roll out the red carpet for us. Even still, this place oozed of his presence. Though the sun was shining brightly and birds were chirping, there was a darkness.

It was a fitting place for him to die.

"Should we check things out?" I asked.

Cole's response was to get out of the car and circle back around to the trunk. I met him there and he pulled out my gun case.

"Do you still remember how to use this thing?"

I gave him the stink eye. "That's a little insulting."

He grinned. "Just don't shoot me by accident."

He took out his own gun, a Glock, and checked to make sure it was full of rounds. When he looked at me again, there was no trace of a grin on his face. He was all business.

The grass beneath our feet was long and dry and yellow and crunched as we walked toward the porch. It itched my feet and ankles and made me wish I'd worn pants. Or at least proper shoes instead of flip-flops.

The wooden steps creaked as we climbed them. It was no louder than the birds chirping, but to me it was deafening. I inhaled deeply, trying to determine if there was a scent of cinnamon in the air. Months ago that would have given away Xavier's presence, but the last few times I'd seen him the scent had been barely noticeable.

Cole pushed open the old wooden door, which groaned in the effort of its moving. That sucker was only hanging on by the middle hinge. I'd be surprised if we'd be able to open and close it many more times without it falling off completely.

He stepped inside and I followed. Right away we were greeted by the stench of rot. I put my left hand, the one that wasn't holding my gun, over my nose and mouth but it did little to mask the smell.

"What died in here?" I made a heroic effort to stop myself from gagging.

"That."

I looked to the corner where Cole pointed. There was the remains of an animal, but I couldn't tell what it had been in life. All that was left was matted fur and red chunks of—

I turned on my heel and bolted out the door, barely making it off the porch before I lost what little breakfast I had eaten in the bushes. After I was done heaving, I caught my breath and went to the car for a bottle of water. I rinsed out my mouth and spat the water on the ground.

I leaned against the car and pressed the icy bottle to my forehead. After a few minutes, Cole emerged from the house and walked over.

"Are you okay?" he asked.

"Yeah. The smell was a bit much." I felt fine for the most part, other than the hollow emptiness of my stomach. I was more embarrassed than anything.

How was I ever going to make it through this?

"I'll take care of it before you go back in." And there he went, taking care of me again, but I wasn't going to dwell on that now, especially since I was grateful. Lucky for me, Cole had a strong stomach.

"Did you find anything else?" Other than the animal remains, the front room had been empty.

"No," he said. "Just some broken furniture in the bedrooms."

"I guess electricity and running water is too much to ask."

Thank goodness we'd come prepared.

Cole started pulling everything out of the trunk, so I went to help him. We ended up with a fairly sizable pile of stuff.

He stared at it, putting his hands on his hips. "I wish we had a shovel," he muttered.

We hadn't gotten any tools, only focusing on our own survival type items, so we didn't have anything he could use to pick up the dead animal. I wished I could've offered to help, but that would only result in me dry heaving.

"Maybe there's an old one lying around somewhere," I suggested. "Is there a shed around the back or something?"

"Yeah, there's a barn."

I wondered if that was where Xavier was keeping himself. He still hadn't shown, but I couldn't shake the creepy feeling he was around somewhere. I'd feel better if I knew where he was.

"Should we look back there?"

"Probably." The way he said it made me think he also thought Xavier was there. It really was strange he hadn't come out to meet us if he indeed was on the premises.

Cole took hold of his gun again, and we trooped around to the back of the house. The large barn was in slightly better shape than the house. Two huge doors that slid sideways adorned the front, along with a few windows that actually had glass in them.

The doors had been left open just a crack. We approached cautiously, once again with Cole in the lead. He held his gun at the ready and peeked inside. His expression went through several changes—first puzzlement, then dismay, ending in disgust. He motioned for me to look.

I half expected the room to be filled with medieval like torture devices or something along those lines. Instead Xavier sat in the middle, cross legged, with his hands on his knees, meditating.

WTF? Cole mouthed.

I shrugged. I was less surprised than Cole because at least I had seen this side of him. Still, I wasn't used to it.

The barn was mostly empty except for a cot pushed into the corner and a big pile of stuff covered with a tarp. Not much light filtered through the grimy windows, making it dark and shadowy. A slight mildew smell was present as well.

We continued to watch for a few minutes before Cole shook his head and walked away.

I had an *I told you so* comment ready to go, but I held it in. It wouldn't have given me any satisfaction anyway.

Back at the car, Cole emptied all of our groceries onto the back seat, taking the plastic bags and going back into the house. A few minutes later he emerged carrying the bags, now full. I averted my eyes. He walked up the driveway a short distance, and when he returned I had the hand sanitizer waiting for him.

"Thanks," I said.

He rubbed the sanitizer into his skin. "No problem."

"No," I said firmly. "I really want you to know how much I appreciate this and that I don't take you for granted."

I didn't know where that came from because I hadn't consciously been thinking it, but it was true. For the first time in days, Cole gave me an intentional look of something other than indifference, making me glad I'd said it.

"I'm glad I could help." And I knew he meant it.

COLE AND I CARRIED OUR things into one of the back bedrooms, and Cole hauled out the broken furniture. It might have been easier to stay in the already empty front room, but the odor of dead animal lingered. Also I wanted to be farther away from the front door, which was about to fall off and had no lock. At least in the back room we could wedge a chair under the door.

Neither one of us knew what to do with the zen Xavier out in the barn, so we sat on the porch, waiting him out. Cole hadn't said anything, but I think this new Xavier freaked him out more than the old Xavier ever had. I could understand. It was more than a little freaky. In some ways, the old Xavier was easier to deal with. I understood him better.

Cole stood and pulled out his phone. "It's almost lunchtime. Let's give him ten more minutes."

"Maybe we should have lunch first and then approach him," I suggested. "We might want to eat before we get started on...you know..."

"Just because we talk to him doesn't mean we have to get started. We're not at his command," Cole said vehemently. "We can do this on our time."

I'd never had the power when it came to Xavier and I wasn't assuming to now, even though he was the one who wanted something from us. The fact that we were here at all showed he was in control. Our purpose might be to kill him, but that was only possible because he was allowing it. Cole may have conveniently forgotten that but I hadn't.

"Don't you want to get this over with as soon as possible?" I asked.

Cole looked like he was about to reluctantly agree with me when Xavier walked around the side of the house. I jumped up from the porch steps where I was sitting, peering at him to try to determine what mood he was in.

"I'm glad you came," he said in a soft and reverent voice. Okay, so we were dealing with the thoughtful angel side of Xavier. Good to know.

"You didn't give us much choice," Cole said stiffly. I could tell he wanted to unload his Glock into him, here and now. That would get the party started nicely.

Xavier clasped his hands in front of him almost as if he were praying. "There is always choice. Choice is what makes us human. Follow me."

I had a newsflash for Xavier—he wasn't human.

He turned and walked back toward the barn without waiting to see if we would follow.

I looked at Cole with a *see?* expression on my face. I was glad Xavier was showing this side of himself in front of Cole. It was vindicating. However it was also typical. It would've been easier to reconcile killing him if he were acting like the sinister psychopath he'd been my entire life. But of course he was being nice. It made things that much harder.

Cole took a few steps before stopping and gesturing for me to join him. Taking a deep breath, I went to his side.

My heart raced and I wanted to throw up again. Everything about the situation was wrong, wrong, wrong. Cole and I were going to hell.

Oh, wait. We're already there.

As we walked, Cole's fingers brushed against mine and I wanted more than anything to grab his hand and squeeze. Even though we were in this together, we weren't really together. Would it be easier if we were?

Maybe not easier, but definitely better.

The barn doors were closed, and Xavier waited for us to catch up before sliding one of them open. As soon as light poured into the space, I knew what Xavier had been doing for the last hour while we waited.

Gone was the tarp covering the pile of stuff from earlier. In its place was a table laid out with every kind of blade you could think of—hunting knives, butcher knives, scalpels. Was that a machete? They lined several metal trays like you would see in an operating room. There was a line of industrial sized buckets under the table. Next to the cot, chains had been staked into the ground and at the end of the chains were handcuffs.

No, this definitely wasn't your standard operating room. It was more like one Dexter would use, except his environments were usually more sterile than this musty old barn. Though I couldn't say for sure since I'd only ever seen the previews. We could never afford premium channels.

For some reason, I fixated on the buckets. Everything else was somewhat expected, but those seemed out of place. They were shiny and new, though, so I knew they weren't relics from when this barn was in use.

"What are the buckets for?" I asked.

"My blood."

I clutched at Cole's arm, no longer caring I was supposed to keep my distance. He glanced over at me and removed my hand from his bicep. My heart slammed into the concrete, shattering like fragile glass.

Then he put his hand up to mine, lacing our fingers together. And squeezed.

My heart started fusing itself back together.

"What's the plan?" Cole asked, getting right to the point.

"It's quite simple," Xavier said in a tone that showed he thought we should already know. "When I am injured, I heal and reproduce blood at a rapid rate. All you must do is inflict injuries upon me at such a rate that I can't heal from them quickly enough."

He made it sound so clinical and civilized. But what we really had to do was slice and dice him. A lot.

"How long will it take?" I hated that my voice shook.

His shoulders moved up slightly and he tilted his head. "It's never been done before."

"Then how do you know it's going to work?" Cole asked.

It hadn't occurred to me this wasn't foolproof. I hated to think we might go through all of this for nothing.

"I have faith."

Cole snorted, the only suitable response for Xavier's sentiment and word choice.

"Why are there handcuffs?" I asked.

"To secure my arms and legs."

I gritted my teeth. His comment reminded me of Xena who always stated the obvious. Or maybe the problem was my question wasn't specific enough. Either way, they should be able to figure out my intent and answer appropriately instead of making me feel like an idiot.

"You still want to go through with this, right?"

Please God, no, half of me pleaded. The other half was thinking what Cole was when he first saw Xavier—about using Xavier for target practice.

"Yes." Xavier gestured to the setup around him. "Why do you ask?"

"If you want to do this, why do we need to strap you down?"

"It's just a precaution."

"For what?"

"Enough talking," Cole snapped before Xavier could reply. "Let's get on with it." He always was one who preferred action.

With a nod, Xavier walked over to the cot and lay down.

CHAPTER 7

I FELT DIRTY, LIKE I'D never be clean again.

I'd been right that we should have eaten before we got down to business because by the time we'd finished with the first round, all I wanted was a hot shower, a soft bed, and a fire to torch my clothes.

Unfortunately, I had none of those things. A fire could be arranged, but that might draw attention to us, so it was a no go.

I made do by scrubbing myself with baby wipes and then I collapsed on top of my sleeping bag. The window was open, but no breeze graced us, making the air stagnant and stifling.

Cole leaned up against the wall, chowing down on a granola bar. I didn't know how he could eat. Every time I closed my eyes, I saw Xavier's slit wrist, dripping blood into a five-gallon bucket like he was an animal being slaughtered. He hadn't even flinched as I'd sliced through his flesh. If anything, I'd describe his expression as peaceful.

I'd dry heaved in the corner the moment blood started flowing. When I was done, I'd slid down the wall and sat on my butt, as far away from the blood as I could get. With crossed arms and a widened stance, Cole had stood several feet away from Xavier, a scrutinizing stare on his face as he watched.

It had taken less than half an hour for Cole to mutter a curse.

I'd ventured over just as Cole poured water over the wounds to wash away the blood so we could see clearly.

The skin had been smooth, like it had never been cut.

Xavier's eyes had remained closed, and he gave us no further direction. Cole had stalked over to the table to select a large knife.

It all went downhill from there. And we'd made no progress at all.

"You should eat before you fall asleep," Cole said, bringing me back to the present.

"I can't. I'll just throw up again."

"At least drink some water, then."

I'd probably puke that up too, but he was right. Dehydration would make an already sucky situation worse. I hefted myself into a sitting position and snagged a bottle of water from the nearby cooler. Taking a small sip, I willed it to stay down.

"That was so much worse than I expected," I said.

"What did you expect?"

My neck snapped up sharply and I peered at him, trying to figure out what he meant by that smartass comment. The look on his face was genuine, though. It was an honest question.

"I don't know."

Cole waited a beat. "It's only going to get worse."

I closed my eyes and hung my head. "I know."

The last few years had been rough and I'd gone through some hard stuff—attending the funeral of the first kid I'd sentenced to death, clutching Cole's dead body, watching my mom die. I thought I'd be hardened enough—tough enough—to kill the person responsible.

Maybe the fact I wasn't proved my soul wasn't as far gone as I'd feared.

So then what did it say about Cole that he could calmly munch on a snack after the horror we'd just witnessed? No, not *witnessed*. Inflicted. There was a huge difference.

But I was in no position to judge. I'd signed us up for this bloody sideshow.

"I'm setting an alarm," Cole said.

"Why?"

"We'll need to...attend to him overnight or this isn't going to work," he explained. "We can't leave him to heal that long."

"Right." I felt dead inside. "You're right."

"Hey." Cole sat next to me and wrapped his arm around my shoulders. At one time, it might have been comforting, but now it only served to remind me how far apart we'd grown. "We're doing the right thing."

"It doesn't feel that way."

"Would you rather Xavier try to absorb more souls?"

"No." I sighed. "But maybe we could have, I don't know, turned him in to his superiors or something."

"They've turned a blind eye to him all this time. Do you really think they'd do anything?"

"Probably not."

"Exactly. And Xena would have said something if that was a viable option." Cole patted me awkwardly on the shoulder before removing his arm and scooting toward his own sleeping bag. "Let's get some sleep."

MY MOTHER VISITED ME THAT night. I didn't say *I dreamed of her* because her presence was too real, too visceral for that. I could *feel* her next to me. The cool rhythm of waves surrounded me like an embrace, just like last time. If the world could feel the peace, calmness, and love brought by the sensation, there would be a lot less hatred and violence.

"You need to take care of yourself, Ava." She ran her fingers through my hair, which was no doubt greasy. I was a mess.

"I'm doing my best," I said.

"It wasn't a criticism."

I guessed I was a little oversensitive, even with my mom. She looked better than I'd ever seen her. Her luminescent skin glowed, her eyes were bright and sharp, and her hair was a vibrant auburn with no streaks of the gray that had begun to appear right before she died.

But most importantly, she seemed content. I hadn't realized how worried and stressed she'd been in life until now, when she was finally allowed peace.

God, I hope she's found peace.

"Do you watch over me?" My voice sounded small and needy. Part of me desperately wanted to have my mother still in my corner, cheering me on even if I couldn't see her. The other part of me wanted her to be able to wash her hands of seeker business, once and for all.

"No." She frowned. "I've tried, but I'm not able to."

Even though nothing had changed, I felt a sudden loss.

"Are you in heaven?" Although Xena had assured me there wasn't a hell, not all souls made it into heaven the first time around. If they hadn't achieved enough good in life then their soul would be recycled, for lack of a better term. That meant if a person didn't make it into heaven, their soul went on, but the person they were in life ceased to exist. So the fact I was seeing her meant she had to have made it into heaven, but I still wanted confirmation.

She smiled softly. "Yes. I didn't think I'd make it here, all things considered."

I'd never tell her this, but I'd had my doubts as well, especially considering my recent theory about seekers' souls.

"Did anyone ever visit you like you're visiting me?"

"No." She paused. "I don't think this is common."

I took a moment to think about that but came up blank. In a way, it made sense because nothing about my life was common. Why would this be any different?

"What did you mean before when you said I could fix everything?"

"Just that I believe in you." She put her hands on my shoulders and stared into my eyes. "You can do anything you set your mind to. Have confidence."

"Oh." I cast my eyes downward, trying to hide my disappointment. I'd hoped her words had meant something concrete. Instead, they were just the normal blind encouragement of a mother.

The air shifted and when I looked up, she was gone.

"Damn it," I muttered, wrapping my arms around myself. As wonderful as it was to see her, I always felt so alone afterward.

"Ava." Cole's voice snapped me out of my dream, and I groggily peeled my eyes open. *Figures.* When I finally didn't have trouble sleeping, I had things to do.

"Give me a minute." I tried to blink the dryness out of my eyes. "What time is it?"

"Two."

I dragged myself to a standing position and mustered up my game face. "Let's do this," I said with more enthusiasm than I felt. Because seriously? I didn't feel any.

We trudged outside to the barn. Xavier was just as we left him, strapped to the cot, his eyes closed. His hands were folded neatly across his abdomen, yet despite the partially full bucket of blood, there was very little blood anywhere else. He must have healed before moving his arms. This was turning out to be a surprisingly neat operation.

Cole and I gave each other grim looks before crossing the room. As I neared Xavier my gag reflex kicked in and I swallowed as hard as I could, determined not to wimp out on Cole. There was no time like the present to get over my aversion to blood.

Though Xavier's eyes remained closed, I could tell he was awake.

"How do you feel?" I asked, feeling like the creepy prince from *The Princess Bride*. Let's just hope Xavier ended up more dead than Westley.

"Fine." Not the answer I was hoping for. It wasn't that I *wanted* to cause him pain at this point—I'd moved beyond that—but he was supposed to be *dying*. That was an inherently painful process, especially when it involved a buttload of knives, right?

"Do you have any suggestions as to how to make this work a little better?" Cole sounded annoyed.

"You must do as your conscience guides." Also not the answer I was hoping for. What the hell did that even mean anyway? Now *I* was annoyed, especially considering I'd been fighting to silence my conscience ever since we got here. Now Xavier wanted me to listen to it?

Something like a growl emanated from Cole's chest and he stomped over to the table.

"You know, this was your idea," I told Xavier. "You could be a little more helpful."

His eyes snapped open and in them I saw the fire of the sinister Xavier. "I did all this." He lifted his hand to gesture to the room, but his movement was stilted by the handcuffs. "All you have to do is hurt me, something I would've thought you'd enjoy."

I flinched at his accusation. I was glad Xavier would no longer be in my life, but that was the extent of it. *This* did not make me happy.

Even as recently as a week ago, I would've thought otherwise. Ironically, I would've *killed* to be in the position I was in now—Xavier subjected to my wrath. But this was no longer about wrath or vengeance. It was about doing the right thing.

Which just so happened to include murder.

Cole returned, holding a knife with a serrated edge. I shuddered just looking at it. I preferred the scalpel since a cut was a cut and it seemed more humane to use the tool doctors used. But perhaps Cole had the right idea with the serrated edge. There was a reason tools like that weren't used in operating rooms. The damage to Xavier's skin would be greater, taking longer to heal. In theory, anyway.

"Let's do this," Cole said, echoing my words from earlier. Before I could hold my hand out for the weapon, he quickly slashed at Xavier's wrists. I squeezed my eyes shut and turned my head when he moved toward his throat. There was a gurgling sound that made me sick to my stomach.

Cole abruptly dropped the knife on the ground with a clatter and went outside. I followed, still not looking at Xavier. If I did, I would be sick.

Outside, I found Cole leaning against the side of the garage with his head in his hands. When he looked up at me, his eyes were bloodshot. The sight nearly made me take a step back. It was so rare for Cole to look vulnerable. He was always the tough one. Seeing him like that bothered me even more than the scene in the barn. At the end of the day I didn't care about Xavier, but I would always care about Cole. And I hated that he was being affected this way.

He steeled his gaze as he looked at me, but it was too late. I'd already seen.

He stood up straight. "He'll be fine for a few hours."

"Okay," I whispered.

Cole nodded and strode toward the house, leaving me to stare after him.

By the time I got to the bedroom Cole was already lying down on his sleeping bag, facing the wall. I lay down on my own and watched the rise and fall of his shoulders, trying to determine if he was asleep. When I was satisfied Cole was passed out, I rolled over and tried to make myself comfortable. It was a miserable failure.

I didn't think I'd be able to sleep, but I must have because the next thing I knew light was streaming in the window. Cole was gone.

I quickly brushed my teeth, using bottled water and spitting out the window. Then I set out to find him. I didn't have to look very far.

He sat on the porch steps, leaning back on his arms. His eyes were closed and sunlight danced on his hair.

"Good morning," he said without turning around.

I sat beside him. "Did you sleep okay?" What I really meant was, *are you okay?* But I knew he would say he was fine even if he wasn't.

"Good enough."

"Have you eaten?"

"Yeah. I've been up for a few hours."

I reflexively looked to my wrist even though I wasn't wearing a watch. "What time is it?"

"After nine."

"Shit," I said. "We need to get in there."

"I've already been. He's fine."

Funny how warped our definition of *fine* had become.

I was quiet for a moment. "I'm sorry I haven't been pulling my weight."

"It's okay." He shot me a half grin that didn't meet his eyes, but I appreciated the effort. "Kind of hard to help out when you're puking your guts out."

His attempt at a joke fell flat and only made me feel worse than I already did, even though I knew that wasn't his intention.

"I need to get over that. I'll take the next few shifts."

He faced forward again, staring out into the distance. "We can do it together."

"Why are you being so nice to me?" I rushed on before he could respond. "And don't give me the line about making a promise to Bill."

"I thought we'd called a truce."

"We did. It's just…"

Maybe I was wrong. Maybe I was reading into things. Maybe he really just did have a thirst for vengeance against Xavier.

One thing I knew I wasn't wrong about was how this was affecting him. He'd already been through so much crap because of me, and I didn't want to add to it if I didn't have to.

But I needed his help. There was no way I could do this alone and if I was honest with myself, I wouldn't want to. Totally selfish, but there it was.

I realized Cole was looking at me expectantly, waiting for me to finish my thought. But I couldn't. For starters, because when I started that sentence, I didn't know how it was going to end. But mostly because I couldn't take it if I was completely and utterly wrong—if Cole really did care more about hurting Xavier than he cared about me.

CHAPTER 8

EARLY MORNING LIGHT CAST ITS rays on the angry red scars crisscrossing Xavier's skin. Looking at them only made me angry because soon they'd be nothing but a memory. He healed too fast and all this torture we'd been putting him and ourselves through was doing nothing.

It had been three days and I swore I looked worse than he did.

"You seem troubled, my dear." The sound of his voice surprised me. He hadn't said a word since this ordeal started. With every "treatment" Xavier became more and more serene in his silence. It was maddening.

"Ya think?" I snapped.

The barn was hot, sweaty, and musty. I hadn't showered or eaten a proper meal in days, not that I could've kept it down even if I had. My entire body was stiff from sleeping on the floor.

And my mind...that was another story all together. Cole and I might be hurting Xavier physically, but this ordeal was psychological torture for us. One day, a shrink was going to make a crap ton of money off me.

Except, oh wait. Nope. I could never talk about this because what we were doing was illegal.

"I am here to listen." Xavier's voice had a soft and comforting tone to it. I narrowed my eyes at him. Did he think he was a priest in a confession booth or some such nonsense? Probably. He was delusional.

"No, thank you," I said. "You're the last person I want to talk to."

He shrugged slightly. "I thought I would offer since it seems you and Cole are at odds."

I wanted to slap him across his face. How dare he comment about my and Cole's relationship? It made me even madder to know he was right. I never should have let Cole join me. The longer this took, the more my regret festered.

Last night we'd thought we'd heard people on the driveway. Talk about making an already stressful situation even worse. *If we got caught...*

I didn't even want to think about it. Our lives would be ruined.

Neither of us slept the rest of the night. At first light, Cole had gone to inspect the property to determine if people had actually been there or we'd imagined the whole thing. I'd gone to the barn to deal with Xavier.

Who now apparently wanted to talk.

The time for talking had passed around the time he'd killed my mother.

I surveyed the table of tools, which had become messy and disorganized. Blood coated almost every blade.

"This is pointless," I muttered. He'd survived multiple gunshot wounds, even one to the face. Had the bullet come out the other side? I hadn't gotten close enough to see if his brain matter had been blown out. But one way or another, he took a bullet to the brain and lived. So why did he believe we could end him by simply draining his blood? And why did we fall for his trick?

Because that was what this felt like—one big trick. Just another manipulation in Xavier's twisted scheme.

"You can do it," Xavier said.

So what, now he was my cheerleader? I gritted my teeth and grabbed a weapon at random.

Gagging, I sliced his wrist. *Pointless.* I'd lost count of how many times we'd done that.

I can't believe I'm damning my soul for this.

"You're not."

Doing a double take, I realized I must have spoken that thought out loud. The past few days had taken their toll on me, and I was weak and woozy. I couldn't keep this up much longer. But if we failed, what were we supposed to do? Just let him go? Unleash him on society again and hope he behaved?

"What do you mean?" I asked with a sinking feeling I'd regret engaging him in conversation. It was almost always a mistake.

"Areli has made sure his descendants end up in heaven. Granted, none of them have directly killed before, but these are definitely extenuating circumstances."

Despite his fallen status and exile from heaven, Xavier was one of *them.* Would that be enough for the angels to declare his death a tragedy? Or would they finally recognize how evil he'd become? So far they'd turned a blind eye.

"What about Cole?" I hadn't looked at his aura because while I worried for both our souls, I also didn't want to know. I was a coward, but I didn't know how I could live with myself if Cole ended up with a black soul. He definitely wasn't perfect, but damn it, he was a good person.

"He's not a direct descendant."

Damn. I took that to mean he didn't get a "get into heaven free card."

"And all the other seekers? What about their souls?"

Xavier turned his eyes to the ceiling and closed them. "They made their decision."

"But did they know the consequences?"

"Do you think it would make a difference?"

"Yes!" I cried automatically. "Of course—" I stopped, suddenly not sure.

He didn't speak for a moment and when he did, it was like he'd read my mind. "The type of person who'd agree to save their life by sacrificing others isn't going to get into heaven anyway."

"Maybe. But they still deserve to know the facts before they make a decision. And what about Chase and Claire? They aren't the ones who decided."

"They are reaping the benefits of the decision, though."

"I wouldn't call being a seeker a benefit."

"They're not dead. Wouldn't you say that was a benefit?"

"Some things are worse than death."

"How would you know? You've never died."

It was all I could do to stop myself from shoving a scalpel in his eye. It actually might have been a good idea given the circumstances, but I was barely holding my stomach as it was.

"Is everything okay in here?" Cole stood in the doorway.

"Fine," I said curtly. I gouged Xavier's other wrist and then joined Cole outside.

I kicked at some dead grass. "This isn't working."

"I know." Cole's tone showed he was as perturbed as I was. "I don't think he was completely honest with us."

"I don't know. He seemed pretty confident about this working."

"In theory, remember?"

If we succeeded, we'd make history as the first to kill a fallen angel.

"Yeah." I kicked at the grass again, wishing there was something more substantial I could take out my frustrations on. I could always kick Xavier a few times, but I doubted it would make me feel any better.

"I talked to Bill," Cole said, an edge in his voice that made me want to cry.

"What happened?"

"The shop was broken into. Most of his tools were broken or stolen. It's a big mess."

"Damn it," I whispered. The shop wasn't in the best part of town, but I'd always felt safe inside those walls. And Cole *lived* there, for goodness sake. "Did they get into your apartment?"

He shook his head. "No. They probably didn't know it was up there."

"They?" I asked. "Does he know who did it?"

"No. The cops have no clue, either."

I knew Cole felt guilty—if he'd been home, then perhaps this wouldn't have happened. But I was glad he hadn't been there. He could've gotten hurt or even killed if he'd walked in on a robbery.

"That sucks," I said. "Does he have insurance to cover the damage?"

"I assume so, but he didn't want to talk about it. He wasn't even going to tell me, but I pried it out of him."

Of course. Bill knew Cole would feel bad about being away while that happened.

"That sucks," I said.

"Yeah." Cole blew out a breath. "We need more ice."

"You go. I'll stay here with him." The last time we'd needed ice, I'd gone because Cole hadn't wanted to leave me alone with Xavier.

Cole's mouth pressed in a thin line. "Are you sure? I don't mind—"

"You go," I repeated. "I'm not exactly fit to be seen in public." Baby wipes and dry shampoo only did so much.

He hesitated and I could tell he didn't like leaving me, despite the fact Xavier wasn't a threat—he hadn't so much as raised his voice to either of us.

"I'll be back as soon as I can. Do you have your gun?"

"It's in the house."

"Get it. Just in case."

I didn't think it was necessary, but I would keep it on me if it made Cole feel better. After he left, I went into the house to retrieve my gun and decided to give myself a minute. I wasn't ready to face Xavier again quite yet.

Physically and emotionally exhausted, I slid down the wall and laid my head back against it. Talking to Xavier did this to me.

A breeze flowed across my skin. *Impossible.* I was inside.

My body tensed as I climbed to my feet. White light bathed the room and I blinked. The last time this had happened, I hadn't been prepared for what came next.

This time I expected it when Areli materialized in front of me.

He looked just as I remembered—dressed in white with fair skin and light hair. The air smelled of fresh sugar cookies. Again, he brought with him the sensation of being wrapped in warmth and love.

Except this time, it was unwelcome. I could have used him when my mom was dying, but I had this covered. I could damn my soul on my own, *thank you very much.* I didn't care what Xavier said—this wasn't good for the state of my psyche. There was no way I was coming away from this unscathed.

For a moment, Areli observed me like I was the world's largest ball of twine or some such oddity.

"What are you doing here?" I asked.

He tilted his head, eyeing me reverently. "I came to say goodbye to an old friend."

I often forgot Xavier and Areli used to be close and in fact, their stories were quite similar. The main difference was Areli was forgiven for consorting with a mortal woman and allowed back into heaven. Xavier wasn't.

I wanted to feel sorry for him because it really did seem like he'd gotten the raw end of the deal, but I couldn't see past my own bitterness. Lots of people dealt with injustice every day, and they didn't turn into sadistic psychopaths. Xavier was supposed to be inherently good, making his reaction to his apparent misfortune that much worse. Wasn't he supposed to turn the other cheek or something like that?

"He doesn't deserve it."

"Perhaps."

Would Xavier even want to see his former friend? The old Xavier would probably try to rip his throat out on sight. But I wasn't so sure about how this new Xavier would react.

"When you brought Cole back, did you know he was going to be some kind of super seeker?"

"I suspected."

No hesitation. My jaw dropped a little.

"But you didn't say anything." It came out as an accusation, but I supposed it was.

"Would it have mattered?"

He had me there. I would have agreed to anything to save Cole. It still would have been nice to know, though. Maybe this whole thing with Linda could have been avoided.

"Handlers are looking for him," I said.

"I'm not surprised."

"Can you do anything about it?"

He shook his head. "Angels such as myself don't interact with handlers."

Oh, the irony. I barely contained my snort/eye roll combo.

And what a total crock. It was *his* fault Cole was in this situation. My irritation turned to anger. If Areli hadn't messed with Cole's aura, making it white in the hopes he could become my guardian angel, Cole wouldn't be in this predicament.

I pushed down my rage and cocked my head. "Tell me why you're here again."

"To pay my respects."

That made it sound like Xavier was already dead. He might as well be.

It was on the tip of my tongue to ask him about my visits from my mother, but I wasn't sure if they were sanctioned and I didn't want to risk being cut off. Even though they were short and infrequent, they meant everything.

"Have you seen my mother?" I asked instead.

"No. Even in heaven, I'm forbidden from seeing my descendants."

I paused, squinting up at him. "So again, why are you here?"

A small smile played at the edges of his mouth. "I never was good with respecting authority."

I didn't return the smile. His lack of respect for authority was what cursed his line to be seekers, so forgive me if I didn't find it amusing.

His answer also didn't fully answer my question. He'd never shown himself to any of his other descendants that I was aware of—only me. Why was I the lucky one?

"Xavier said you made a deal for your descendants to get into heaven. Is that true?"

"Partially." He seemed reluctant to talk about it. "The stipulation was that they—*you*—wouldn't be judged by your seeker responsibilities. You're judged the same as everyone else."

"What about the seekers who chose this life?"

"They're judged by all of their decisions."

"Are they aware of it?" This was turning into a repeat of the conversation I'd had with Xavier. Hopefully this time I'd get concrete answers.

"No more or less than any other human."

I pondered that for a moment. I supposed that was where religion came into play, and that was one can of worms I wasn't about to delve into.

"Xavier is in the barn," I said, sinking down to a sitting position. I didn't want any part of that happy little reunion.

Areli nodded. "Goodbye, Ava. It's doubtful I'll see you again."

I stared up at him, but his announcement meant nothing to me. I had no emotions to spare.

I GAVE ARELI FIVE MINUTES before I traipsed out to the barn, hoping he was already gone. Though I didn't care much about my angel ancestor one way or another, I still didn't want to see his—or anyone else's—reaction to what we'd been doing to Xavier.

It was sick and sadistic. We were torturing him. But damn it, he'd asked for it. No, that wasn't right. He'd given us no choice. Saying he "asked" implied we'd had another option.

Areli was gone, but the air in the barn was different, tense. One look at Xavier told me he was agitated.

I gritted my teeth. *Great.* What exactly had Areli hoped to accomplish? His visit had done no favors for me or Xavier. Had he been trying to assuage his own guilt for how things went down all those years ago? He should have just stayed away. Now I was left to deal with the mess he left behind.

Typical.

"Is it time for more of your incompetence?" Xavier sneered in a voice I knew all too well, a voice that haunted my nightmares.

I took a step back, inhaling deeply. As I did, I caught a faint whiff of cinnamon, something that had been missing since Xavier's transformation.

Oh, no. Not good.

But I wouldn't let him see I was shaken.

"If you can do better, have at it," I snapped.

A string of obscenities and other filth poured from his mouth. *What a jerk.* Did he think I wanted to go without showering? Did he think I liked picking his dried blood from under my fingernails? Did he think I enjoyed puking my guts out several times a day?

He could go to hell.

Seething, I tried to calm myself as I surveyed the weapons table.

"You know, it's funny," Xavier said in a tone that told me I wasn't going to like what came next. "You couldn't save your mother and now you can't seem to kill me. Rather backward, isn't it?"

My knees threatened to give out and my vision went black for a moment, probably partially a result of not being able to keep down proper food for the last few days. I clenched my shaking hands into fists. My vision returned, but it was cloaked in a red haze.

I was going to kill him.

Grabbing the weapon I'd mentally dubbed the Crocodile Dundee knife, I stalked over to Xavier. Enough was enough. I raised the knife high above my head, pausing before bringing it in a downward descent.

Was I really doing this?

I shook off the unwelcome doubt, locking it somewhere deep in the recesses of my mind. The time for doubt was done. I was already in this so deep there was no turning back.

Gritting my teeth, I pulled the knife down, applying more force when it met resistance.

When it met Xavier's stomach.

I pushed downward, my gag reflex kicking in when it hit something hard. *His spine.*

Taking my now-slick hands off the hilt, I staggered away, clamping a hand over my mouth before I realized what I was doing. Any hope of holding in the bile vanished when I tasted the copper of Xavier's blood in my mouth.

I retched, but there was nothing left to come up.

At one point in the recent past, his blood had been invaluable to me. It had been the only thing keeping my mother alive. Now I just wanted to wash my hands of it.

I wiped my hands on my shorts and took hold of the second knife I'd selected—a narrow one that might have been used to fillet a fish. In one swift move, I slammed it into Xavier's throat. His body jerked.

Backing away, I looked in horror at what I had done.

But I wasn't finished yet.

Before I could overthink it, I ran to the front of the house, hoping to God the red container of gasoline from Cole's trunk was still sitting there.

It was.

Holding my breath, I lifted it to test its weight. Maybe half full. It would have to be enough.

I carried it to the barn, not hesitating this time as I poured some over Xavier's body. Then I flung the remaining fluid on the walls of the barn. It didn't cover as much as I would have liked, but it would have to do. The wood was so old and dry it probably wouldn't take much to set it aflame.

Tossing the empty container aside, I stood over Xavier, staring down at the man who'd caused so much misery. His eyes met mine. They were full of shock, like he didn't actually believe I was strong enough to complete the task he'd given me. But with the knife jammed through his throat, he couldn't talk. With the knife lodged in his stomach, he was pinned to the cot. With his hands still shackled in the handcuffs, he couldn't help himself if he wanted to.

For his sake and mine, I hoped he still wanted this.

I lit a match and when I dropped it onto his chest, I felt no remorse.

CHAPTER 9

THE FLAMES WERE MESMERIZING AS they grew, swallowing the brittle and dry old wood. I stood and stared, listening for Xavier. No screams, nothing as the fire melted his flesh from his bones.

Xavier had once boiled my blood—a freaky ability of his. Would the fire boil his? Or would it simply burn?

I was so distracted I didn't notice Cole behind me until he grabbed my shoulders and spun me around. He held me at arm's length and stared into my eyes, a frantic expression on his face.

"What...did...you...do?"

I turned toward the barn and wordlessly pointed.

Cole let me go and put his hands on his head as he stared at the growing inferno. "Holy shit."

His expletive snapped me out of my stupor.

"We need to leave."

He looked at me and blinked, his eyes clearing as my words sank in. "Let's go."

He took my hand and we ran to the house, tearing toward the back room to retrieve our belongings. Luckily, we'd kept it all neat, so it was only a matter of stuffing a few random things in our bags and hightailing it out of there.

We tossed our stuff in the trunk and before getting in, I took a few steps to the right so I could see the barn around the side of the house. The cackling of the fire was louder and black smoke billowed into the blue sky. It would only be a matter of time before someone noticed and called the fire department. We needed to move, but I couldn't stop staring.

"Ava," Cole called, urgency in his voice. "Let's go."

I walked backward until I could no longer see the barn, could no longer see the source of my misery literally going up in flames.

Good riddance.

Cole peeled away before I even completely shut the car door.

I WAS NUMB. THE FARTHER away we got from the barn, the number I became. I felt like I was in a bubble, and everything around me was happening in slow motion. When I closed my eyes, I saw Xavier pierced through his stomach and his throat. The whites of his eyes were huge as the match fell on him, catching him on fire. Flames licked at his clothing before moving to his exposed skin. Through it all, he remained silent.

But the smell...

Singed hair and burned flesh. It was the most awful smell ever, the kind that stuck with you, never letting go of your senses.

I'd done what I'd had to do. Hadn't I?

Would his wounds alone have been enough to kill him? Could his body heal with metal staked through his organs? Was burning him alive overkill?

Better not think too deeply on that. I might not like the answer.

What's done is done and cannot be undone.

The interstate we were on was in need of repair which resulted in a rhythmic *thud-thud, thud-thud* every three seconds. Not that I was counting or anything. Because that would be crazy, right?

No crazier than killing a fallen angel.

But was he really dead?

Could he be dead? Was it really possible?

How would I ever know for sure? Would I spend the rest of my life looking for him? Wondering when he was going to reappear to make my life hell?

That was a problem for tomorrow.

Thud-thud, thud-thud. One, two, three. *Thud-thud, thud-thud.* One, two, three. *Thud-thud...*

So soothing, like a heartbeat. This was why babies fell asleep during car rides.

Maybe I could sleep. Some shut-eye would be good. I hadn't been doing much of that lately.

I leaned my forehead against the window. *Thud-thud, thud-thud.* One, two, three...

I closed my eyes.

"Ava. *Ava.*"

Why was someone shaking me when all I wanted to do was sleep?

"Ava, you need to stay awake."

I opened my eyes. *Ouch.* It felt like they had sand in them. Why were they so dry? I rubbed at them with my fingers. Why did my hands smell of smoke?

Holy shit. *Xavier.*

It all came rushing back.

"Pull over," I croaked.

The car pulled to a stop on the side of the interstate and I flung the door open, tumbling out onto the pavement on my knees. My stomach clenched, forcing bile up my throat. I spat onto the ground as wave after wave of nausea slammed into me.

Oh...my...God. What had I done?

I seemed to remember Cole asking me the same question. Now, he knelt next to me, offering a bottle of water. I took it and rinsed my mouth but didn't swallow. I wasn't convinced I could keep even water down.

Cars whizzed past us, creating a *whooshing* and *zooming* noise, but it didn't have the calming consistency of the *thud-thud*. I couldn't count out the beats. It wasn't like a heartbeat at all—the heartbeat was no more.

Had Xavier's heart finally stopped beating?

"Ava."

I shook my head, trying to bring Cole into focus.

"Stay with me," he said. "Drink some water."

I shook my head.

"Just a small sip. Please."

He sounded so nice when he said *please*. How could I resist him? That *please* was worth the risk of puking.

I swished a tiny bit of water around in my mouth before swallowing. I clutched at my stomach as the liquid settled in the hollow emptiness.

Mercifully, it stayed down. I cautiously took another sip. That one didn't sit as well as the first. I was too optimistic.

"Are you okay now?" As Cole studied me, he took hold of my hand.

Aww, how sweet.

He turned it over to feel for my pulse.

Nope, not sweet. Medical.

I yanked my hand away. "I'm fine."

He looked like he wanted to call bullshit on that statement. "Just do me a favor and stay awake, okay?"

"Sure."

The bubble surrounding me began to deflate, and the world came back into focus. I wasn't so sure that was a good thing.

Cole stood and held his hand out. I took it and he guided me back into the car. It was then I noticed the blood covering my clothing and dried on my skin. There was also a distinct gasoline odor clinging to me.

"I'd like to take a shower," I said calmly.

We got back on the interstate, and it was only then I realized we'd been traveling south instead of back toward College Park. We'd been going in the direction of home.

Home. For a moment, my heart fluttered. How nice would it be to sleep in my bed in Bill's house and stroll down to the kitchen for breakfast in my pajamas? Then maybe curl up with a book in the living room while Bill watched sports? I'd definitely taken normalcy for granted.

But normal wasn't in my future. At least not yet. I had no intention of going home. The Xavier problem might be more or less solved—*don't think about that now*—but we still had to worry about Linda. As the seeker with no limits, Cole had a target on his back. He had a better chance of staying hidden if I stayed away from him.

So I'd have to discuss our destination with Cole, but later. After I'd taken a long, hot shower.

It didn't take long to find a hotel. We got the cheapest room they had which only had one bed, but that wouldn't be a problem because we weren't actually going to sleep here. We would just clean ourselves up and be on our way.

Cole carried both of our bags into the room and dropped them on the bed.

"You can shower first," he said, not meeting my eyes. I stared at his face for a few moments, trying to determine if I was imagining things. Nope—he definitely wouldn't look at me.

What was that about?

I'd have to think about it later, after I rid my body of the grime of the last several days. For now, I wasn't going to argue with him. I was grateful for the gift of the first shower. Grabbing my bag, I took it into the bathroom. As I undressed and got the water ready, I avoided the mirror. Things sucked bad enough without having to look at my bedraggled state.

Hot water never felt so heavenly. Closing my eyes, I let it pour over me for several minutes while I breathed in the steam. The water that pooled in the bottom of the tub was gray and brown and flat out nasty. I'd probably never been dirtier in my whole life. I washed my hair twice and scrubbed my skin until it was pink, probably taking off the top layer.

When I turned off the water and got out of the tub, I stood in front of the mirror and wiped away the fog with my hand. My eyes looked huge, but that was probably a result of the dark circles under them and my sunken-in cheeks. And had my hip bones always stuck out so much? I'd always been thin, but now I was scary skinny.

I turned my back to the mirror and covered myself with a towel.

Cole wasted no time getting in the shower once I vacated the bathroom.

I lay down on the bed, focusing on a water stain on the ceiling. The cheap polyester comforter was scratchy against my bare legs, but I wasn't complaining. I'd take a sagging mattress and rough bedding over a hard floor any day.

Putting two fingers on my wrist, I checked my pulse, like Cole had tried to do on the side of the road. My heartbeat was slow and steady. While I'd probably been in shock then, I was eerily calm now. I'd even go as far as to say I was relieved.

But at the same time, I felt a heaviness in my soul. This weight was new and different, and I intuitively knew it was one I'd never escape.

When Cole emerged from the bathroom, I was waiting for him. "I'm going back to Penn State."

He eyed me wearily. "Why?"

"For starters, I don't want to abandon Chase and Claire like that. They're depending on me to pay my share of the rent. I can't just leave them hanging."

Actually I didn't know if that was true. Chase would be able to manage, even if Claire didn't find a job right away. She would be upset if I didn't come back when I hadn't said a proper goodbye, and I didn't want to leave things like that after all they'd done for me.

"I need to get back," Cole said. "Bill shouldn't have to deal with Kyle on his own. And I need to help him put the shop back in order."

Bill could handle Kyle. However, Cole was right that he shouldn't have to do it alone. Kyle was a pain in the ass and not Bill's responsibility. But that didn't involve me. I'd only seen Kyle once, and he hadn't seemed to like me very much anyway. He'd never listen to the nonexistent wisdom I had to impart. I might be able to help with the shop and I really wanted to see Bill, but my primary goal was to protect Cole. That meant we were back to where we started—me leaving.

Of course, there were two small differences this time. One—Cole knew why I was leaving and where I'd be. Two—Xavier was no longer in the picture.

Hopefully.

I shook my head a little to clear out that thought.

"That's fine," I said. "I don't want to hold you up. You can go on home, and I'll call Chase to come get me."

I had no idea what Chase's work hours were or exactly how far down the road we'd gotten, but he'd be able to pick me up eventually, right? Either way, it didn't matter. I'd figure something out.

"Why are you still hell-bent on making this difficult?" Cole's frustration manifested in him pacing the small hotel room. I watched him, feeling like we'd done this before. For a couple of teenagers—well, Cole was twenty now, so he wasn't a teenager anymore—we spent a lot of time in hotel rooms. And none of the stays had been particularly happy. Though the trip to Cole's mother had started out well enough, it had ended in disaster.

Perhaps it was better if Cole and I put some distance between us and not for the sake of keeping Cole's identity a secret. It seemed like the two of us together were a bad mix. Maybe we'd be able to find happiness separately.

Ordinarily that thought might make me choke up, but I was still numb. My emotions were on lockdown. Somehow I'd managed to push the last few days—especially the last few hours—into a dark corner of my mind. Cole didn't bring it up either, and I was more than okay with that.

"I'm not making this difficult," I protested. "I made a commitment. I'm not just going to abandon them."

"But it's okay to abandon Bill?"

Bill? Or *Cole*?

I peered at him, trying to determine if I should take his words at face value. Just like back at the farmhouse, I got the vibe this was about more than only Bill.

Damn it. Why couldn't he just be up front with me? Or was this wishful thinking on my part?

"It wasn't like that and you know it," I snapped.

He threw his hands up in the air. "I never asked you to protect me." His voice was raised, almost to the point of yelling.

"Why is it okay for you to take care of me, but I can't take care of you?" If our situation had been reversed, Cole would have done whatever it took to protect me, without asking permission. So why wasn't I allowed to do the same?

Of course he probably wouldn't have messed it up as badly as I had. But we'd never know that for sure.

"You need to come home." His tone left no room for discussion.

"I'll make plans to visit Bill later, but I'm not coming home now. Not yet. You heard what Xena said. All the handlers are looking for you. It'll be easier for you to fly under the radar if I'm not there."

"I don't care about flying under the radar."

He was starting to piss me off. He acted like I didn't know what I was talking about, like I hadn't spent the last two years living the life of a seeker. Both my mother and grandmother had died as a result of this life, and it would probably be the death of me too, eventually.

"I can't hide from this," Cole said. "There's no point in trying. They're going to find me eventually."

"Later would be better than now. You've got Kyle to worry about. Wouldn't you like to get him through high school without a handler breathing down your neck?"

There was my trump card and Cole's only weakness. He shot me a dangerous look, and I could tell he wasn't happy about what I'd said. But it was the truth. I may not have gone about everything the best way in the past few weeks, but my reasons were solid. He couldn't deny that.

"I'm not going to hide," he said again. "They're going to find me, and it's up to you whether it's sooner or later."

"Exactly!" Why was he being so hardheaded? "That's why I need to go back to Chase and Claire, so it will be later."

"No. You're going to Bill's."

I crossed my arms. "Like hell I am."

Who did he think he was? I had no keeper. I wasn't taking orders from him or anyone else.

He stepped closer, so our faces were inches apart. The smell of his peppermint gum made me want to close my eyes and bask in the memories brought on by that scent, but I stood my ground, keeping my gaze even. This was no time to get sentimental.

"If you don't," he said slowly, "I'll hunt Linda down and introduce myself."

My eyes widened and my jaw dropped. *He wouldn't...* Oh yes, he would. He was completely serious. Didn't he realize how nuts that was?

"You can't," I blustered. "You don't know how to find her. You've got to stay home to look out for Kyle. You just...*can't.*"

He laughed—actually *laughed* at me. *Damn him.*

"Oh, yes I can. I'm not the hiding sort."

He was right, but it would be a lot easier if he were. Hiding wasn't a weakness when it was a strategic move. I was about to launch into a lecture on that, but I clamped my mouth shut, saving my breath. Nothing I could say would change his mind. That was one thing we had in common—we were both stubborn as hell when we wanted to be.

"Are you prepared to tell Kyle you're a seeker?" I asked in desperation. "Are you prepared to tell him about this life?"

He regarded me silently. "If it comes down to it."

Damn it.

Anger rolled through my veins in waves. I could barely see straight. Everything I'd tried to do in the last few weeks had been a failure.

Not everything.

But I could never claim killing Xavier as a win.

"Where'd you put your clothes?" Cole asked as he stuffed his things in his bag.

"In the trash."

There was no way I would ever wear them again.

Cole pulled a plastic grocery bag out of his duffel bag and handed it to me. "We shouldn't leave them here. They're evidence."

And right now I hated Cole for pointing out something I should have realized.

Evidence... Right, because I'd committed a crime. A very, very bad crime.

Cole was all business, checking around the room to make sure we had everything, even though we'd been here less than an hour. Now that he'd blackmailed me into going home, he'd gone back to not meeting my eyes.

Damn.

Aside from asking about my clothes, he hadn't asked about what had gone down in the barn. Should I bring it up? Offer some kind of explanation for my crazy actions?

An explanation would be nice...I could use one myself. The truth was I didn't know what had come over me.

Temporary insanity? I hoped so. It would be a shame if that craziness were permanent.

CHAPTER 10

ONCE WE WERE BACK IN the car I texted Claire to let her know not to expect me home. She texted back immediately, wanting to know how things had gone.

My fingers hovered over the screen, trying to come up with a suitable reply.

Mission accomplished.

That about summed it up. I knew she'd have a lot of questions, so I quickly texted I'd call her later. I didn't want to have that conversation at all, much less over text messages.

Next I fired off a text to Xena, letting her know where we were going. I also added the same *mission accomplished* line. I wondered if she would want to know all of the details. If anyone had a right to know, it was her. I kind of hoped she wouldn't ask though. I wasn't proud of what I'd done. And I was still trying to convince myself it was necessary.

It struck me how much I actually cared what Xena thought of me. For all our differences in the past, I respected her.

I leaned my head back against the seat and closed my eyes, but I didn't sleep. I was basically hiding behind my closed eyelids. Cole still hadn't asked any questions, which was surprising. They were inevitable, though.

We stopped for lunch after a little while and I ordered a burger and fries, even though I doubted I'd be able to eat. Cole didn't seem to have any worries about that and ordered an ungodly amount of food, as usual.

As we sat across from one another at the table, heavy silence hung between us. Cole kept his head down, focusing on his food, still not looking at me despite my attempts at staring him down.

Eventually I gave up and tried to choke down my food. My stomach was not happy about it, and ninety-seven percent of it ended up in the trash.

As we got closer to home, a feeling of anticipation came over me. I really had missed Bill. Shenice too, for that matter. I hoped she wasn't too pissed at me, but I wouldn't blame her if she was. Tidewater was definitely more home to me than anywhere else I'd lived. I'd learned at a young age not to get too attached to anywhere or anyone since we moved so much. Obviously that didn't work in this location, but these were definitely extenuating circumstances.

What would it be like to settle down permanently and allow roots to flourish? Since I'd gotten a GED instead of a diploma, I didn't think my college applications would be competitive, but there was a local community college I could start at. If Shenice would still have me, I could continue working for her and eventually find an apartment, maybe with a few roommates.

Something foreign swelled in my chest and I realized it was hope. Immediately, I shook it off. *Foolish thoughts.*

About an hour from home, Cole called Bill to let him know we were almost there. When we pulled into the driveway, Bill was waiting on the porch. He stood as soon as he caught sight of the car and a shy smile emerged. To anyone else, it might seem like his feelings about seeing us were slight, but for Bill, those two small things were a huge show of emotion. For my part, I didn't bother acting coy. I flung open the door and ran into Bill's waiting arms. The scent of motor oil that always clung to his skin and clothing was comforting, and I nearly wept.

"I missed you," he said gruffly.

"Me too," I said. God, I really had.

Bill disentangled himself from the embrace and shuffled backward, shoving his hands into his pockets. "I didn't know y'all were coming, or I would've gone grocery shopping. We'll have to order pizza or something."

That made me wonder what Bill and Kyle had been living on. Bill wasn't much of a cook. I wasn't a master chef or anything, but because of my mom's erratic work schedule, I'd learned at a young age to fend for myself.

"If you make a list," I said, "I can go shopping tomorrow." I didn't know how long I'd be staying, but it was the least I could do.

"I'd appreciate that. The shop's been keeping me busy."

"I'm sorry to hear about the break-in," I said. Bill had worked hard to build the business, and it had a solid reputation. I hoped this incident wouldn't scare customers away.

Cole came up behind me. "I'll go in early tomorrow and help."

I hadn't thought about it, but the robbery wasn't the only challenge Bill had been facing. With Cole being gone, he was shorthanded at the shop since it was just the two of them working there. Under normal circumstances, they both stayed pretty busy. Although Kyle had been pitching in, I doubted he was much help. Bill had been doing the work of two mechanics.

"I can manage if you need to rest from your trip," Bill said.

Cole shook his head. "It'll be nice to get back in there." His words were sincere. Cole had never cared for school, but he both loved and excelled at his job.

We went inside to find Kyle lounging on the couch, a glazed look on his face as he flipped through the channels.

He didn't even glance at us. "Hey," he said. I was surprised we'd gotten that much of a greeting. Had he even noticed his brother had been out of town?

Cole stared at him for a moment before stomping up the stairs with my bag, which I hadn't realized he'd taken out of the trunk. When he came back downstairs, he paused just long enough to say, "I'll be in the shop by seven. See you tomorrow." And then he left without even talking to his brother. Or me, for that matter.

Kyle, for his part, didn't seem to notice Cole had left.

It hadn't dawned on me Cole wouldn't be staying for dinner. But he was probably eager to check out the shop and survey the damage as well as double check to make sure his apartment was okay.

I was disappointed. As awful as the past few days had been, I'd enjoyed being around Cole. We'd have to figure out a new normal, hopefully one that involved him actually looking me in the eye. *Ugh.* Things were totally awkward.

"I'll go order that pizza," Bill said, disappearing into the kitchen.

I stared at Kyle for a moment before joining him. He was still flipping through the channels at breakneck speed.

I was surprised when he spoke to me. "So Cole retrieved you too, huh?"

"What do you mean?" It was a knee-jerk reaction, but I knew exactly what he meant. His description was pretty accurate. Cole's intention in coming to Penn State had probably been to "retrieve me" as Kyle referred to it. I hadn't wanted to come home, but here I was.

"Cole thinks he knows what's best for everyone." Kyle still hadn't taken his eyes off the TV.

That was another accurate statement. In Kyle's case, it was true—Cole did know what was best for his brother. But did he know what was best for me?

Considering how glad I was to see Bill, maybe so, at least in this instance. I didn't run away because it was good for me, though. I left because I thought it was the right thing to do for Cole. The jury was still out if it actually had been the right thing. I hoped so because I'd hate to think I put myself and Shenice through all that for no good reason. If nothing else, I was glad I'd met Chase and Claire. One of my goals had been to find other seekers and I'd succeeded, so there was that.

Bill came back into the room. "The pizza will be here in about thirty minutes."

I stood. "I'm going to go unpack."

Bill nodded. "Your room is just as you left it."

He wasn't lying. The room was exactly as I remembered, unmade bed and all. The sight of it filled me with guilt, which was ridiculous. After everything I'd done in the last few days, an unmade bed made me feel remorse?

I needed to re-examine my priorities.

I chucked most of my clothes into the hamper, which was halfway full from when I'd left. Since Bill had been spending so much time at the shop, I bet he hadn't had time to do any of his own laundry, so I'd do his tomorrow when I did mine. I wanted to help out as much as I could for as long as I'd be here.

But I drew the line at doing Kyle's laundry. That brat could figure it out on his own.

Unpacking had only taken a few minutes, so I sat on the bed, looking around the room. When I'd first arrived those many months ago, the room had still been Jill's, Bill's dead daughter. Pictures of her had graced the edges of the mirror and some of her belongings were still in the closet. But now it was mine. There were no traces of Jill anywhere. I didn't quite know how to feel about that. I could never take the place of his daughter and I wasn't trying to, though I knew he did think of me as a daughter. I hoped I wouldn't have to break his heart again.

I wandered down the hall to my mom's room, pausing to take a breath before pushing open the door. A faint odor greeted me, and I wrinkled my nose in distaste as I looked at the dirty clothes streamed throughout the room. Those were Kyle's clothes because this was not my mom's room anymore. In my sleep deprived haze I'd forgotten Bill told me Kyle was using the room now and that he'd packed up all of her stuff. It angered me to see how careless Kyle was with the space she had painstakingly taken care of.

Assuming Bill had put her stuff in the garage, I wandered out there. Sure enough, there was a stack of boxes clearly labeled in Bill's chicken scratch handwriting. This tiny tower of five boxes made up the entirety of her life. We hadn't been minimalists by design—rather it had been out of necessity. Now, though, it made me sad to think that was all she had left behind, especially considering most of it was probably clothing and other things I would donate to charity.

Since the pizza would be arriving soon, I didn't have much time, but I figured that might be a good thing. Though there wasn't much to sort through, it was going to be tough so a little at a time might be the best approach.

I pulled the box at the top of the stack. Kneeling next to it, I carefully opened it as if it contained fine china rather than my mother's castoffs. Neatly folded clothing lined the inside. It only took me a moment to rifle through and determine there was nothing in this box I wanted to keep. I pushed it aside and pulled down the next box.

This one had more of the same, but I did pull out her favorite cardigan. Even though it was nearly worn through at the elbows and missing a button, she had worn it at home nearly every winter for as long as I could remember. Feeling somewhat silly, I brought it to my face, hoping it would smell like her. But it had been washed since she last wore it, so it only smelled faintly of laundry detergent.

The third box was a little more interesting as it contained books and papers. I found a bedraggled copy of *Good Night Moon*, which she had read to me every night when I was a little girl. I didn't realize she had saved it, which surprised me considering how frequently I had helped to pack and unpack boxes. However, there were usually one or two we didn't bother with. This must have been kept in one of those.

She'd also kept a few of my elementary school art projects and several report cards from the last few years. I'd known about those but had never really thought about them. It was interesting to see which ones she'd valued above the others. When I was in the third grade I'd made a picture book titled *Furry Puppy Gets a Home*. I hadn't been a good artist even by eight year old standards but when I'd given it to her, frustrated by my perceived mistakes, she'd made such a big deal about how great it was I'd forgotten all about them and actually become proud of the project.

She might not have done everything right, but she was a good mom.

COLE AND I WALKED INTO the mall Saturday afternoon as people streamed by. All seemed to be in a hurry—mothers tugging toddlers along with one hand and pushing strollers with the other, tweens giggling while staring at their phones, and pairs of old ladies power walking as far as the eye could see.

Cole shoved his hands in his pockets, looking uncomfortable and incredibly out of place. The mall had never been my favorite place either, but I at least enjoyed shopping every once in a while. It was just that I never had much money, so it was usually frustrating looking at all the pretty things I couldn't afford.

I sent Cole to find us a table in the food court while I stood in line at Chick-fil-A. The food was a peace offering and the best I could do. Even still, as I set the food in front of him, he shot me a skeptical and displeased look that had nothing to do with the chicken sandwich.

I sighed. He wasn't happy about being here, but he would have to get over it.

"You know we need to do this." I sank into the seat across from him.

"Yeah, so you tell me."

I drummed my fingers on the table, biting back a sharp retort. *Be nice.* Even if he was being a jerk today, I didn't have to sink to his level. But it was oh-so-tempting.

All we knew was he was the seeker with no limits. But what exactly that meant we had no clue. True to handler form, none of them had explained the term any further. So here we were, seeking the information ourselves—trial by fire.

Cole said he wasn't going to hide from Linda and the other handlers who might be after him, but he seemed perfectly willing to hide from himself. He'd never had a reason to test his abilities, but besides that he was happier ignoring them. But ignorance could be dangerous. I just didn't understand his position. If I were him, I'd want to know everything I could about my abilities. It had taken a lot of coaxing to get him to come today, and he might have agreed just to shut me up.

"Let's get this over with," I said.

"Can I finish eating first?"

I stared at him for a moment but ultimately decided to ignore his sullen tone. "Suit yourself."

Things had been even more off between us. While we had fallen into a steady and comfortable rhythm at the farmhouse, every time I'd seen him since then had been tense—either that or he avoided me all together. The first time it happened, I let it go. The second time, I grew suspicious. But the third time, I could no longer fool myself—he was definitely going out of his way to avoid me. And now the air between us was so tight you could bounce a quarter off it.

You would think torturing someone with the intent to kill would be more stressful than a trip to the mall, but you'd be wrong.

I hated this—the way my palms were slick because of nerves, the way he wouldn't look at me, and the way my stomach rolled.

Maybe we needed to talk about what happened. He seemed to want to pretend it had never happened, and while I was fine with that, I wasn't fine with whatever *this* was between us.

It hurt. Every time I looked at him, I was struck with a pang—I still loved him. And I didn't see that changing anytime soon.

We were connected by the fact we were both seekers and in our shared history—how he'd become one and the awful situation with Xavier, not to mention our romantic history.

He was the first—and only—person I'd ever slept with. I hadn't forgotten about the one and only time I'd been with him. For the most part, I tried to block it out because what had been a beautiful experience had turned into a painful memory. Did he ever think about it? How did he feel about being my first? Given our current circumstances, did he even care?

As I looked across the table at him, my heart felt like a noose was tightening around it. I never in a million years thought I'd ask those questions because I thought I'd mattered to him and I always would, no matter what happened. But now I wasn't so sure.

I needed to figure out a way to live with it. We had Linda to deal with and despite what Cole might think of me, I wasn't going to leave him to deal with her on his own. I also wasn't willing to cut Bill out of my life for the sake of saving myself the heartache of seeing Cole, so our paths were bound to cross.

Yawning, I covered my mouth, fighting the urge to pull my compact out of my bag to check my face. I'd never been one to wear a lot of make-up, but lately I'd been piling on the concealer in an attempt to cover the dark circles under my eyes. I hadn't left the house in the last few days, living in yoga pants like a zombie, trying to catch up on sleep. When that of course didn't work, I distracted myself by cleaning and doing laundry. The trouble with those two activities was they were mindless, giving me too much time to think.

The highlight of my days was when Bill came home and sat at the kitchen table while I finished making dinner. We chatted about everything and nothing, and it was lovely. Even Kyle, with his surly attitude, couldn't ruin it.

I looked at Cole, who was taking his sweet time eating, and saw a sudden resemblance between him and his brother. Both of them were pains in the butt.

While waiting for Cole to finish his meal, I picked out people I suspected had white auras. I did it without thinking—old habits died hard. When I lowered my guards to check, my guesses were right on, as usual.

I hadn't lowered my guards in so long the sight of the auras was dizzying, giving me a slight headache. I wished there was a way to strip this ability out of my body. It was a tumor in my life, and I'd kill to get rid of it.

Poor word choice.

My point was I'd be happy if I never had to look at auras again.

No, not *if...when.* One way or another, this mess would be over soon. I didn't care if they threatened me—I was never turning in another soul. And if they threatened my loved ones...

I wasn't okay with that, but somehow I'd have to deal with it *without* giving in.

I'd already killed one handler...

Horrified, I stripped the dark thought from my mind, shooting a conscience-stricken look at Cole, as if he could read my mind. He didn't seem to notice, so I looked away guiltily.

Cole scrunched up his food wrapper, a signal it was go time.

I pointed to a woman who looked to be in her early twenties, easily within Cole's age range. She had an infant strapped to her chest. "What color is her aura?"

A look of unease crossed his face as he peered at her, concentrating in a way I knew meant he was lowering his guard.

He turned back to face me. "Pink."

I looked around to find a slightly older subject and settled on a young family with two thirty-something parents and three young kids. I jerked my head in their direction. "What about them?"

"He's tan and brown. She's tan with a touch of purple. And the kids? Creamy white, pink, and light blue."

"How did you..."

He just shook his head as if the answer were obvious, which of course it was. He was the seeker with no limits. His ability wasn't restricted by age range like mine was.

I hadn't expected him to tell me the colors of the children. Since I started turning in names when I was sixteen, I'd never been concerned much with the auras of those younger than me. Sixteen seemed to be the minimum age for both seekers and the souls seekers turned in. Then again, supposedly there was a rule that seekers couldn't be made until they were adults, but considering Chase and Claire, I guessed those rules were loose guidelines rather than laws. Either that or someone had royally screwed up.

I twisted in my seat, trying to find another subject for Cole. But before I could, he spoke.

"Let me save you the trouble. I can see the auras of everyone in this room."

In theory, I already knew that, but even still, it was shocking. I wished I could determine if he saw them any differently than I did, but there was no way to figure that out.

"Okay," I said. "But what else can you do? Like..." As I tried to figure out what might be expected of him, I remembered that while I could see seekers' auras, I couldn't determine they were seekers, not like Chase and Claire could.

"What about me?" I asked. "What does my aura look like?"

His features twisted into an *are you crazy?* expression. "Do you really want to know?"

I recoiled. We had an old agreement we wouldn't check out each other's auras, and I hoped he hadn't looked at mine along with everyone else's. His reaction made me wonder though—either he had already seen it or like me, he suspected my recent actions turned it black beyond repair. His question echoed in my ears—*did I really want to know?*

No, I didn't. There was nothing I could do about my past actions and the truth of it was I would do the same thing again. Xavier needed to be ended and I was the one who did it—end of story. But we still needed to know if Cole could determine I was a seeker based on my aura.

"Just tell me if it looks different from everyone else's," I said.

He paused for a moment, dragging his gaze away from me before replying. "It's more shimmery."

Shimmery, how? Dark shimmery? I was dying to ask. Despite my earlier claim of not wanting to know, it was difficult not asking the question. Maybe it would be better to put myself out of my misery and find out.

But when I opened my mouth to ask, the words wouldn't come. I was too scared.

"Did you happen to look at Chase's or Claire's auras?" I asked.

"No," he said. "I don't look at auras. Not if I can help it."

That last comment was a jab at me for making him come here, but I didn't care. He was being obstinate for the sake of being obstinate. It reminded me of when we'd first been forced to spend time together for a class project.

But damn. I assumed the shimmer he mentioned was an indicator I was a seeker, but unless we had any other seekers to test that theory on, I couldn't be sure.

Except...a seeker was sitting right in front of me. If he had no limits, he should be able to look at his own aura.

"What about yours? Does it have a shimmer like mine?"

Cole held out his hands in front of him and turned them over before tucking them back under the table. "Yeah."

Looking at his own aura obviously made him uncomfortable. I understood. I could project mine, which mostly happened unintentionally in my sleep, but if I really concentrated I could do it at will. I didn't like to. Having your shortcomings manifest in tangible evidence wasn't pleasant.

"I think the shimmer is unique to seekers," I said.

He nodded, seemingly uninterested.

My fingers curled into fists. He was finally starting to piss me off. I got it. I truly did. He just wanted to be normal. But he couldn't have it both ways. He couldn't claim to take ownership of being a seeker, saying he couldn't run from it and also choose to ignore it.

"Look," I said, tempering my voice to keep it neutral even though I wanted to scream at him. "I know you don't want to, but we need to know what you're capable of. It might help us figure out what the handlers want with you."

"I'm sure they want the same thing they want with all seekers," he said. "For me to find pure souls. But it doesn't matter because I'm not doing it."

His logic was unarguable, but I still worried. Nothing was ever as straightforward as that. Hadn't he learned anything in the past few months?

"I wish there were handlers nearby so we could see what they look like to you."

"There is one."

My body went on full alert. "What?"

Oh, shit. They were on the hunt for Cole and here we were—sitting ducks in the middle of the mall.

Cole inclined his head. "Over there at McDonald's, getting coffee."

Though my instincts were screaming at me to grab his hand and run out of there, I lowered my guards and peered at the woman Cole had picked out. But it was pointless. She was probably twenty years older than me so even if she was a normal person, I still wouldn't be able to see her aura.

I was about to suggest we get the heck out of dodge, but the lady disappeared into the crowd. It seemed she hadn't noticed us and I was being overly paranoid.

I whirled back around toward Cole. "How can you tell?"

"I don't know if she's a handler," he admitted, "but her aura is the same as Xena's. So she's a fallen angel at least."

My eyebrows shot up before I could stop them, but I quickly schooled my expression. When had he checked out Xena's aura? Hadn't he just made a huge deal about *not* looking at auras? *Hypocrite.*

I dismissed the unkind—but true—thought.

"How so?" I asked.

"It's metallic."

"White metallic?"

"Yeah, white. But metallic, almost like it's fixed."

"What do you mean—fixed?"

"You know how normal auras waver between colors? Like how they shift?"

I nodded. It was an accurate description.

"Their auras are solid," he explained. "The colors don't change at all."

"And Xena's is white." I wanted confirmation. "It doesn't change."

Cole nodded.

Huh...very interesting. Not only had he checked out Xena's aura, but he'd obviously done it more than once.

And it was white.

I had mixed feelings about that. Xena always did what she thought was best, but sometimes—hell, *most* times—that didn't align with what she was supposed to do. So what did that mean? Was rebelling against her superiors actually the right thing to do? Did that make her superiors in the wrong? It brought up the question of morality and who had the right to play God. Who had the right to pass judgment? What determined the color of our auras? Was there a fixed code? Or did it vary depending on circumstances?

Every new bit of information I learned only brought more questions. It was so frustrating.

I wished I had understood Cole's ability a week ago. "Did you happen to look at Xavier's aura?"

"No."

Xavier was evil—of that I had no doubt. If he'd been human his soul would be black. But because he was a fallen angel, did that mean he had a fixed white aura? Did all angels, whether or not they were deserving, get a free pass? Somehow that didn't seem right. They could inflict as much hurt and harm as regular humans. Actually, no—scratch that. With Xavier's freaky ability, he'd been able to do much worse damage.

I quizzed Cole on a few more auras, but it was overkill. He could see every one—from the newborn strapped to the mother's chest to the elderly man in the wheelchair.

We left. I had a moment of confusion in the parking lot since I wasn't driving my own car—no, that was still with Chase and Claire. At some point I'd have to figure out a way to retrieve it. In the meantime, I was driving my mom's car, which she'd transferred into my name shortly before she died.

While I drove Cole back to his apartment, he stared out the window, not talking. An uncomfortable silence ensued, compounded by the fact I was acutely aware of it.

"You want to talk about it?" I didn't have to tell him what "it" was.

"No," he said, firmly leaving me no doubt of his conviction. "I want to forget it ever happened."

I wanted to sink into the seat, for it to swallow me whole. I'd brought him into this mess, and he was finally starting to blame me for it. I deserved it, but it still hurt.

I wished I could leave the past behind—not all of it, but so much of it. That wasn't a possibility. Every time I closed my eyes I saw Xavier's clothes as they caught fire, the flames as they moved to his flesh, his eyes widen as he realized he was being burned alive.

And the smell...though it didn't haunt me like the image did, I would never forget it. And that was what I thought about as I lay awake at night.

My lack of sleep concerned me for obvious reasons—humans needed sleep to be healthy—but also because since I hadn't been sleeping, I hadn't gotten any visits from my mother. She didn't visit me every time I slept, but if I didn't sleep at all there was no chance.

I wanted to tell her about what I'd done, to ask forgiveness. I hadn't made a mistake, not exactly, but I needed to make a confession to someone who understood. After my mom died—and heck, even before she died—that person had been Cole. Now I was left with no one.

When I pulled into the lot, Cole quickly hopped out with a muttered, "See ya." I watched him enter the building and continued watching for a few moments before I drove away.

CHAPTER 11

I PARKED IN FRONT OF Nice Beauty, surprised to see the lot fuller than usual. Then I sat there for a moment, staring at the neon sign while it blinked to alert potential customers the shop was open.

I felt bad about how I'd left things with Shenice. I should've contacted her before now to apologize, but I supposed late was better than never. Hopefully she'd feel the same way. But I wouldn't blame her if she wanted nothing else to do with me. I'd been an inconsiderate jerk, not to mention ungrateful. She'd done so much for me.

I pushed open the car door and shoved my hands in my pockets as I walked to the door. Even more surprising than the full lot was the full waiting area—every chair was occupied. We'd never had more than one customer at a time and more times than not, we had no customers at all.

The shocking sight of the waiting area distracted me so much I didn't notice Xena sitting behind the receptionist desk.

I did a double-take. "What are you doing here?"

She was wearing her usual black and her dark hair had a dramatic streak of purple running through it. She also wore a deep purple lipstick, which would have looked ridiculous on most people, but she pulled it off. She definitely looked like she belonged working in a beauty parlor.

Xena arched one brow. "She was shorthanded, so I offered to help."

I ducked my head, feeling properly admonished. I'd been home nearly a week, and I hadn't even thought to find out if Shenice needed help. I was too busy hiding. Yes, I was definitely an inconsiderate jerk.

I glanced up to see Shenice look over at me, her smile faltering for a moment before she returned her attention back to her client.

Damn.

"Does she hate me?" I asked softly. Perhaps I should just leave. Perhaps surprising Shenice in the middle of the workday had been a horrible idea. I honestly hadn't thought she'd be busy, but I was glad she was.

"No," Xena said. I knew her response wasn't just blowing smoke because Xena wasn't the type to sugarcoat things. "She's a better person than that."

She was a better person than me, then. But that wasn't news.

I rested my hip on the edge of the desk. "What gives with all these customers?"

"She got featured on Groupon. It was last-minute and now she's scrambling to hire another stylist."

"I guess that's a good problem to have."

Shenice got her client settled under a hairdryer and walked over. She looked me up and down, making me squirm and stand up straight and wish I'd brushed my hair before coming to see her.

"You want to work?"

I blinked. *Sooo* not what I expected to come out of her mouth. "Yes, ma'am."

"Good," she said. "And cut it out with the ma'am crap."

I couldn't hide my blush. I had no idea where that had come from, other than my need to suck up. I guessed it wasn't subtle.

Shenice put me to work washing hair and sweeping up the floors. I easily handled the sweeping, but I was nervous at first to be working with actual clients. I'd only ever assisted with washing hair, and that was just once. It didn't take long to get the hang of it though, and anyway I would've done anything, even a song and dance to entertain the waiting customers, to get back in Shenice's good graces.

When things died down, I took a break in the back room. As I sat there picking at my ragged cuticles and chewed nails, hoping Shenice didn't notice them, Xena joined me.

"You look like hell," she said. "I hope your sorry state didn't drive customers away."

"Thanks," I said dryly.

She shrugged. "The truth is the truth."

"Yeah, but that doesn't mean you have to say it all the time."

Xena cocked her head, looking at me like what I said was a new revelation. It had probably never occurred to her it might be more polite to keep her opinions to herself. I wondered what Xena had been like when she was human. I had no idea what time period she had lived in, but it wasn't that long ago women were expected to be seen and not heard. Xena would have been way ahead of her time because she answered to no one.

"Sorry," she said, and I nearly fell out of my chair. Xena was apologizing? "I didn't mean to make you feel bad. How have you been?"

I stared at her for a moment, trying to discern her motive. But it appeared she had none.

Okay, that wasn't fair. Xena cared in her own way. It was just that she was bad about showing it, and her actions weren't always easy to interpret.

"I haven't been sleeping much," I said.

"Do you want to talk about it?" Her question echoed my words to Cole. And just like his answer, mine was a definitive *no*.

I shook my head.

"You could get some sleeping pills or something," she suggested. "I hear there are pretty good ones these days."

I'd already considered that, but I didn't want to take medication if I could help it. I was running out of options, though. I couldn't go on like this—I needed sleep. For starters, I simply felt awful most of the time. It also probably wasn't safe for me to drive. But the most important reason I yearned for sleep was because I wanted to see my mother again.

"I'll think about it." I hesitated for a moment then decided what the heck? "Have you seen my mother?"

Xena started and squinted at me. No doubt she was trying to determine if I had a few screws loose in addition to being sleep deprived.

"In heaven, I mean," I clarified. "Or anywhere else."

"I haven't been to heaven since I became a handler."

"Oh." I wondered if that bothered her, if she missed it. But that definitely broached the territory of too personal where Xena was concerned so I didn't bother to ask.

"Why do you want to know?"

From the way she was looking at me, I could tell she knew something was up. That was fine. I wouldn't have asked if I wasn't ready to share.

"She visits me in my sleep." Even though we dealt with much stranger things, I still looked at her, searching for a sign she thought I was crazy. But her expression was curious rather than dubious.

"While you're sleeping?"

"Yeah, like in my dreams."

I half expected Xena to tell me I was just dreaming it rather than it actually happening. A skeptical person who didn't believe in the supernatural would explain it away by saying my dreams were simply a product of how much I missed my mother. But Xena herself was proof of the supernatural, so I knew she wouldn't dismiss it.

Even still, I hurried to provide an explanation to prove I wasn't imagining it. "These aren't like other dreams. I can feel her presence."

What a lame explanation. The truth was I didn't know how or why it worked, only that it did. I knew in my heart it wasn't all in my head.

"I've never heard of that happening."

My heart plummeted down toward my knees. Xena usually knew about these kinds of things.

Shenice came into the room, weariness evident in her motions.

I jumped up. "Do you need help?"

She shook her head. "The chemicals have to set up for about ten minutes." She crossed to the mini fridge and pulled out a soda.

"Have you ever seen angels in your dreams?" Xena asked.

"Nope." Shenice took a long swig from her soda. "Thank God. They're enough trouble while I'm awake. Just the other day one snuck up on me while I was grocery shopping. I dropped an entire carton of eggs." She shook her head at the travesty of it. "The only dead family member I've ever seen was my great uncle Leo, and all he wanted was to gripe about my granddaddy stealing a job from him back when they were in their twenties."

"He sounds like a peach," Xena commented. "How did he manage to get into heaven?"

"He was senile at the end, but they must not have held that against him. I saw him shortly after he died so I guess some of the senility was still there."

"Makes sense."

Shenice turned to me. "Have you been seeing angels in your dreams?"

"Only one."

Shenice nodded knowingly. I didn't have to tell her which one. "I wish I could help you, Ava. I could ask the other sensitives in my family, but nothing like that has ever come up, so I doubt they've experienced it."

Just my luck I was surrounded by two "angel experts," and they didn't know a thing about this.

"It's been a while since I've seen her. Not since before... You know..." And there it was—my fear I'd never see her again because of my recent actions.

Though I hadn't told Shenice about what had happened with Xavier, Xena would have told her—well, as much as she knew, anyway. Xena didn't know the specifics, either.

Shenice and Xena exchanged a look. As usual I had no idea what it meant. For someone who was so good at predicting the color of people's auras, I was horrible when it came to reading these two.

"I need to go back out there," Shenice said.

"Wait," I said before she could leave the room. This was the first we'd spoken other than her giving me directions for work. "I need to tell you I'm sorry." Simple and not nearly enough, but what else could I say?

She regarded me thoughtfully. "I know you are. And I'll forgive you...eventually." She left the room.

A small weight lifted. Things still weren't right with Shenice, but I was now confident they would be. I'd take it.

"Who is your father?"

"What?" I stared at Xena, perplexed by the abrupt change of topic.

"Your father. Who is he?"

"Nobody," I said. "I never met him. He was gone before I was born."

Xena pursed her lips, an exasperated look on her face. "Just because you never met him doesn't mean you don't carry his DNA."

"He was basically a sperm donor. He and my mom had a fling that only lasted a few weeks. So why does it matter?"

Xena stared at me like I was dense. "I'm just wondering if he passed some sort of trait to you that allows your mom to visit."

I *was* dense. Lack of sleep meant my brain wasn't firing on all cylinders. What Xena was asking about made sense. Unfortunately I didn't have much information to go on.

"His name was Michael. That's all I know."

"Isn't he on your birth certificate?"

I shook my head.

"That's going to make finding him a lot harder."

My eyes widened. "Do you really think I got this from him?"

Xena shrugged. "It's the best I can figure. You also have that weird ability to project your aura. Maybe it's all connected."

I'd never considered my father might have some abilities. I had assumed everything came from my mother and my aura projections were a fluke.

Who my father was had never played a factor in my life. Sure, there were times I'd wished he were around, but my mom and I made a pretty good team. I'd never needed him.

Yet, hope surged in my chest. What I hoped for I didn't know. I had Bill now, so I definitely didn't need another parental figure, especially since I was a legal adult.

But did I want one? It would be cool to meet the man who fathered me. I was ninety-nine percent sure he didn't know I existed. I didn't know if that would make this whole situation better or worse.

The thought occurred to me that just because Xena was going to track him down, it didn't mean I actually had to meet him. Probably knowing his identity would be enough to determine if I had inherited any abilities from him.

"You think you'll be able to find him?"

Xena gave me a look that told me how stupid she thought my question was. Yeah, I definitely wished I had known Xena before she became an angel. She was a bad ass.

"Thank you," I said quietly. "I don't always give you enough credit, but I appreciate all you've done for me."

Xena's face softened for a moment, so quick I almost missed it before her expression returned to its normal detached state.

"Yeah, well... Don't try to hug me or anything."

I grinned. "I wouldn't think of it."

But truthfully? I totally had.

WHEN I DROVE HOME THAT night I was exhausted. I hadn't planned on working all day, but my sore muscles and tired feet were welcome. Maybe for once I'd be able to fall asleep and stay asleep.

I pulled into the driveway next to the Rustinator and took a few moments to compose myself before going inside.

Bill, Kyle, and Cole sat in the living room. The sight of the three of them shooting the breeze with scattered soda cans and chip bags on the coffee table and the TV blaring in the background made me smile.

When Cole's eyes turned toward me, the grin slipped from his face and he looked away, standing. "I need to go."

It was like an icicle had pierced my heart and shattered, the tiny slivers like razors cutting me a million times.

"No, you can stay," I said quickly. "I'll just go..." I pointed to the stairs.

"I was leaving anyway."

As I wordlessly watched him walk to the door, my hurt shifted to irritation and settled at rage. What was his problem? We didn't have to be best friends or anything, but he should be able to handle being under the same roof as me. It pissed me off he was being so immature. It wasn't fair to anyone—me, Bill, or Kyle.

Forget this. I was done tiptoeing around him.

I marched out the door after him. "What is your problem?" I called from the porch.

He pulled his hand away from the driver side door handle and slowly turned. "There's no problem."

"Bullshit."

"I said it's nothing." Even though he looked at me this time when he spoke, I still didn't believe him. He was treating me like I was some kind of contagion or something. What was he worried about catching? Because I had news for him—thanks to Areli, he already caught it.

I walked down the first few porch steps. "No, it's not. If you're going to treat me like that, the least you can do is let me know why."

"It's not you, okay? It's me."

Oh no, he didn't. Did he seriously just use that line? But yes, I agreed with him. *He* definitely was the problem. I wasn't the one running away with my tail between my legs every time I saw him.

"Fine," I said. "So tell me what's wrong with you."

"Nothing."

I blew out a breath. "If this is going to continue to be a problem for you, I'll find another place to live."

"Bill wouldn't want—"

"I'm not going to cut him out of my life, but you worked hard to get Kyle down here. It's important you keep coming around for his sake."

Cole snorted. "Kyle doesn't care what I do. He doesn't notice if I come around or not."

"That's not true," I said quietly. Kyle and Cole were alike in this way—neither one was good at sharing his emotions. Though Kyle continued to be a royal pain in the ass, I could tell Bill and Cole's attention meant something to him. He'd never had a consistent positive adult influence or anyone who cared about him like Bill and Cole did.

"Yeah, well..." Cole dragged his gaze away, then turned toward his car again.

For a moment I was prepared to let him go. Maybe he would work through this on his own. Or maybe things would continue to get weirder. Even though I threatened to move out, I couldn't afford it. I would figure it out if I had to, but I hoped it wouldn't come to that. Self-preservation had me speaking again.

"I want us to be civil, maybe even cordial. Why is that so hard?"

Cole had opened his door, and now he wrapped his fingers around the top of it. "I'm doing my best."

"I guess I just don't understand," I said. "What changed between the farmhouse and now? We had been getting along just fine." More than fine, actually.

He whirled. "You changed. Okay? That's what."

I took a step back, looking him up and down and considering what he'd said. Had I really changed that much? Change was inevitable, but I was still the same person.

"No, I haven't," I protested. "Maybe a little, but not enough to warrant treating me like a pariah."

"Maybe you haven't then," Cole said. "Maybe I just didn't see you like this before. But after what happened at the farmhouse..." Sighing, he shoved his hands in his pockets.

"What?" I whispered, the word catching in my throat.

"I can't look at you the same way."

I wasn't proud of my actions, but my hand had been forced. And if I recalled, Cole had been bloodthirsty himself. I'd just beat him to the punch.

"That's not fair," I said.

"Maybe, but I can't help it. After seeing what you did to him…"

Technically, he *hadn't* seen. He didn't even know exactly what had happened. All he knew was I'd taken care of Xavier and set the place on fire.

"What would you have had me do?" My voice matched my stony expression.

"I don't know."

"I did what I had to. Do you think I liked it?"

"No…" But he hesitated. How could he even begin to think I enjoyed torturing Xavier? I was the first to admit I was glad he was gone, but seriously? That hurt.

"That's not fair," I quietly repeated my words from earlier.

Cole had the grace to look chagrined, but that wasn't what I wanted from him. I wanted him to take back his words, to tell me I was the same girl he fell in love with.

Except they would be lies. The core of who I was hadn't changed, but I'd definitely come a long way in the last year. I'd like to think after everything I'd been through I'd come out better. Or if not better, at least even.

But Cole didn't see it that way.

"It's not like I wanted this to happen," he said.

"And I did?" *That's right, Ava, get angry.* Anger was preferable to feeling sorry for myself. "You think I wanted you to turn into a seeker? You think I wanted my mom to die? You think I wanted to commit murder?"

"None of this is my fault."

I seethed, not responding right away. I looked at him, the boy I loved more than anyone else on earth and I just felt…disappointed.

I thought back to when he'd first come to find me in Pennsylvania and how everything had gotten so screwed up. Mostly I remembered what he said to me—he didn't know why he still cared. At the time, it had been encouraging because he'd admitted he still cared. His words had given me hope. They took on an entirely different meaning now.

"I guess this'll just make it easy for you to finally stop caring." I turned my back on him and went inside.

I FINALLY GOT AROUND TO calling Claire the next morning. We'd been texting since I'd gotten to Bill's but only about stupid, little things, like her new job as a hostess and her manager's horrible comb-over. I had thought those were an urban legend from the seventies, but apparently they were alive and well.

"Are you happy to be home?" Claire asked.

"Yeah," I said truthfully. "I missed Bill. A lot. I didn't realize how much until now."

"I understand." She was silent for a moment, probably thinking of her father. I knew she felt endless guilt about leaving him alone.

"Have you been able to check on him?" I asked gently.

She sighed. "No. There's no way to do that without giving away our location. But maybe this will be good for him, right? Maybe now that he has to rely on himself, he's straightened up."

Not wanting to burst her bubble, I murmured, not saying what I really thought—he was probably worse off without her. I wasn't a pessimist, but I was definitely a realist.

"Enough about me," Claire said. "Everything is boring here. We both just go to work and come home. Tell me more about you."

I thought about what I should tell her, whether I should try to make everything sound more exciting than it was because I didn't have a whole lot going on either.

"I'm working at the beauty shop again," I said. "And trying to catch up on my sleep, but that's about it."

What I didn't tell her was that even though I was trying to catch up on sleep, I wasn't very successful. I knew she would worry and there was no point stressing her out.

"You're not telling me the good stuff. I know you must have made up with Cole by now. I want to hear about that."

I laughed bitterly before I could stop myself. "Not exactly. More like the opposite."

"Aww... What happened?"

Sighing, I told her all about our recent conversation, about how he didn't "see" me the same way anymore. When I was finished, she was quiet for a moment.

"How about you?" she asked. "Do you still see him the same way?"

I hadn't thought about it, to be honest. To me, he was just Cole. He would always just be Cole, except there was no "just" about it. I realized I put him on a sort of pedestal, but at the end of the day he was just a person with flaws and shortcomings, like me. But my feelings about him hadn't changed. Despite everything, I still loved him.

"Ava?"

I had been silent too long.

"I don't think I'm good for him. I brought so much heartache and so many terrible experiences into his life. I wouldn't blame him if he doesn't want to look past that."

"No relationship is perfect."

"Agreed," I said. "But not all relationships involve sadistic fallen angels and dying. This isn't exactly the normal relationship drama."

"It's coming to an end though, right? Xavier is gone."

It was true we shouldn't have any more trouble from Xavier, but I said "shouldn't" instead of "wouldn't" because I didn't want to jinx it. Part of me still expected him to rear his ugly head and cause trouble. But even if that didn't happen, there was still Linda and whatever other seeker mess awaited me in the future. The only thing I could guarantee was I wasn't turning in any more souls, and I wasn't naive enough to think that would go over well with the handlers. I hadn't figured that part out yet.

"I think I should let him go," I said. "It's time for me to step away."

And perhaps that would be better for me as well. I'd always have love for him, but he wasn't the only one who was negatively affected by the horrible things we went through together. They were memories I'd never be able to escape, and I wondered if his presence in my life made it harder for me to move past those things. Maybe staying with Chase and Claire was the right idea after all. I could still visit Bill from time to time.

"Is that what you really think?" Claire asked quietly.

"I...I don't know." I was so tired. My brain was fuzzy and I couldn't think straight. My emotions were a tangled web of highs and lows.

"I don't know what happened between you two since you left, but I saw the way you looked at each other. If someone looked at me that way, I wouldn't give up so easily."

I didn't know how Cole had looked at me when Claire had been around, but he sure as heck wasn't looking at me like that anymore. He'd said it himself—he saw me differently.

"I wish you were here," I said. "I miss you." I hadn't realized how much I did until we'd started talking.

"Me, too," Claire said, then she laughed. "I mean, I miss you, too. And I wish you were here, not that I was there. Chase misses you, too."

I snorted. "Yeah, I don't think that's true."

"Sure it is. With you around, I chattered in your ear. Now he's stuck with listening to me."

I laughed. "I don't think he minds."

"Eh...he's used to it, anyway. Take care of yourself, okay? The door here is always open if you want to come."

"Thanks. I might take you up on that. But for once I'm going to think about things for a while before I make any decisions."

"What? Thinking before you act?" She laughed. "The horror of it all."

I smiled. "Bye, Claire."

CHAPTER 12

WHEN MY PHONE RANG AND I didn't recognize the number, I was tempted to decline the call. But in the end I decided if it was a telemarketer, I could just hang up. So I answered it.

I was glad I did.

"Ava." Kyle's voice was missing the usual attitude, which set me on high alert. I immediately thought of Bill. He wasn't old, but things happened. Panic began to set in.

"What is it? Is Bill okay?"

"Bill's fine, I guess. I haven't seen him. Some lady showed up at the shop, and Cole kicked me out, telling me to call Xena. Who the hell is Xena?"

Dread trickled through my veins. "What did the lady look like?"

"Like she had a stick up her ass."

That wasn't the description I was expecting, but even still I knew exactly who it was. *Linda.*

"Shit, shit, shit," I muttered.

"What's going on?

"Just don't go back there. I'll take care of it." I tried my best to sound authoritative and like I knew what I was doing so perhaps he'd listen to me. That boy usually did the opposite of what he was told to do.

"No. If my brother is in trouble, then—"

"Kyle, you have to trust me on this." On one hand, it was actually refreshing to see Kyle show concern for Cole, but this was the worst possible time for him to embrace the brotherly love. Kyle getting mixed up in seeker business would only make things a million times more complicated.

"Screw that."

"Listen to me," I snapped. "You're just going to make things worse. Now I need to go and call Xena."

I yanked open my nightstand drawer and fished around for my gun. I checked the chamber to make sure it was loaded, wasting unnecessary seconds. Of course it was. I'd kept it loaded since Cole had brought it to me in Pennsylvania.

"I shouldn't have left. I should've—"

"Kyle!" I shrieked, not able to control the shrill tone of my voice. So much for sounding cool, calm, and in control. "I'm going to hang up now and I need you to do what Cole told you to do, what I'm telling you to do now. *Stay away from the shop.*"

Angry at having wasted precious moments arguing with Kyle, I disconnected and called Xena while grabbing my keys and running out the door.

She answered on the first ring and I sighed gratefully.

"Linda found Cole." My hands shook so badly I had a hard time getting the key into the ignition.

"Where are they?"

"The shop."

I threw my phone down on the passenger seat so I could put two hands on the wheel. If I didn't hit many red lights, I could be there in less than ten minutes. But I of all people knew ten minutes with a vicious handler could be an eternity.

The drive only took eight minutes, but in those four hundred and eighty seconds I pictured all sorts of horrifying things happening to Cole—his blood being frozen or boiled, his airway being closed, or him being poisoned like my mom. And that had just been what Xavier was capable of. Who knew what tricks Linda had been hiding?

I paused before bursting in the shop, my rational side kicking in. I needed to think about this first. It wouldn't do Cole any good if Linda incapacitated me as soon as I walked in. But she probably already knew I was here. Handlers had a way of knowing these things, so sneaking up on her was unlikely.

Taking a deep breath, I slowly pushed open the door with my left hand. In my right, I held my gun at the ready. It was a small comfort since I knew it couldn't kill her. But hopefully if it came down to it, it would slow her down.

There was a car up on the lift in Cole's work bay. I could see under it to where Linda was standing on Bill's side of the shop. She didn't even turn to acknowledge my presence.

Where the hell was Cole?

There—on the ground on his hands and knees, his head hanging low. His eyes were closed, but he didn't look to be in pain. Instead, he had a crazed look on his face. What had she done to him?

Behind me, I felt a presence, so I whirled, squeezing the gun. It was Xena, who had her finger up to her lips. *Shit!* She shouldn't sneak up on people with guns like that.

I nodded acknowledgment, then turned back to look at the scene between Cole and Linda.

She slowly circled him, like a shark in bloody water. It made my blood rage. How dare she look at him like he was her prey? I double-checked to make sure the safety was off my gun, aiming it at her. God, it would feel so good to unload a few rounds in her back. Except, no—not her back. I wanted her to see who was hurting her—I wanted her facing me.

I blinked rapidly, clearing my hazy vision. Holy crap, where had those thoughts come from? I didn't like how quickly my mind turned to violence. Then again, I'd do anything to protect the ones I loved.

Even if he didn't love me back.

Even if he had been a complete asshole lately.

Even if it took a moment like this to make me realize I wasn't ready to let him go.

"This is just the beginning," Linda said haughtily. "You will do what I ask."

Cole didn't move. His lack of reaction scared me. What had she done to him?

Linda cackled. "What's that? I can't hear you." Then she laughed again at her little joke.

Bitch.

Beside me, Xena inched to the right, sidestepping around the car.

Linda glanced over her shoulder. "You can just stop right there. And the girl can stay where she is as well."

The girl? She knew my name. That was just insulting. I hated to admit it got to me.

"By the way," Linda continued, "you owe me a name. Don't think I've forgotten."

I totally had, mostly because I hadn't planned on giving her one.

"Go to hell," I said.

"Tsk, tsk." She shook her head. "Did you forget what happens to seekers who don't earn their keep?"

She might as well have reached into my body and punched all my vital organs—her words had the same effect. I hadn't forgotten what Areli had told me—I'd simply pushed it aside. Now I was reminded my life belonged to them. Reapers had saved me from death before, but once I was no longer useful, they'd take me out.

The gun shook in my hands and I exhaled, trying to keep control.

"What are you doing, Linda?" Xena asked, her tone conversational, almost bored. I worked to keep the shock off my face. The last time Xena had seen Linda she hadn't been nearly so cordial.

"This doesn't concern you." Linda tapped her chin thoughtfully. "Or perhaps it does. I'm sure everyone would be interested in the fact he was hiding right under your nose. Or—" Linda let out a theatrical gasp. "Maybe you were even helping to hide him."

Xena leveled her gaze at her. "I'm going to ask you again. What are you doing?" Her voice was tighter this time. Her body was tense, like a panther preparing to strike.

God please let her be prepared to strike. Xena had never shown any violent powers—just her superhero speed thing—but now would be a great time for her to reveal a secret ability.

I wanted to run to Cole to look him over and make sure he was okay, but I was smart enough to know I needed to stay back. That didn't stop me from keeping my gun trained on Linda though. She hadn't even looked at me. Obviously she didn't consider me a threat.

If she only knew I was the only person to ever kill a handler, maybe she wouldn't dismiss me so easily.

Linda smiled tightly. "Convincing Mr. Fowler that helping us is in his best interests."

I nearly snorted. She was delusional. Cole hadn't moved from his position on the floor—whatever she was doing to him wasn't in his best interests.

"It's in your best interests to walk out of here." Behind her back, Xena motioned with her fingers for me to move closer. "If you leave now, we can forget this ever happened."

I slowly stepped over to Xena, coming to a stop just behind her.

Linda laughed. "You're stupider than you look." When Xena didn't take her bait, Linda continued. "No matter how much you wish you were human, no matter how much you like these imbeciles, you're one of us. It's time you acted like it."

There was a blur and suddenly Linda's left shoulder jerked backward, followed by her right. It took me a moment to realize Xena was no longer standing beside me, and I no longer had possession of my gun. Xena held it outstretched in her arms, pointing it at Linda, whose mouth formed a shocked "o."

"You really are an asshole," Xena said simply.

Truth.

I rushed to Cole, kneeling beside him. When I touched my hand to his shoulder, he thrashed wildly, knocking me off balance. My knee slammed hard into the pavement, throbbing painfully as my vision clouded. *Damn, that hurt.*

"Cole, it's me," I whispered into his ear.

No reaction.

"*Cole,*" I said louder. Still nothing. I whirled toward Linda. "*What...did...you...do?*"

Despite the two bleeding holes in her chest, she laughed. I bared my teeth, barely holding back a growl.

Xena shot her again, this time in the thigh.

"She asked you a question," Xena said.

Starting to sweat, Linda clasped her hands over her leg, trying to stem the flow of blood. "I took his senses away. He can't hear or see anything."

I touched him again, prepared this time when he lashed out. His mouth moved, but no sound came out.

"Oh, and he can't speak, either," Linda added with a sadistic smile.

Xena shot her in the shoulder again.

"Damn it, Xena!" Linda shrieked. It was odd hearing the curse come from the evil schoolmarm's mouth.

"Get out," Xena said calmly.

Linda snarled. "You're never—"

Bang!

This time the bullet hit Linda in the middle of her chest. She collapsed on the ground, coughing up blood.

"I have an endless supply of bullets, and I'm prepared to use them all. The choice is yours."

"Real nice," Linda ground out through clenched teeth. "You're turning on your own kind."

Xena cocked her head. "We are all part of humanity. You yourself were once human. Or did you forget?" She glanced at me. "How is he?"

"I can't tell." I watched as Cole sank to the ground and rolled onto his side, his body shaking. His eyes were open but he saw nothing.

"Is your car outside?" Xena looked at me pointedly and I understood her meaning. Though she told Linda to get out, she'd been shot so many times she might not be able to move on her own. And anyway, we needed to hide Cole so she couldn't find him again.

I put my hands under his arms and tried to drag him. It was a miserable failure. Even if he wasn't fighting me, which he was—I caught a fist in the eye—he was too heavy for me to move on my own. Xena had to keep Linda under guard, and anyway I doubted she was much stronger than I was.

I needed help. It was either Shenice, Bill, or Kyle. All three were bad options, not because they wouldn't help me, but because I didn't want to involve them.

I wished Xena had been a little more conservative with shooting Linda. I'd admit seeing Linda bleed was immensely satisfying, but if not for that last shot she might be able to leave.

I pulled out my phone and called Kyle. I hadn't wanted to bring him in, but Linda had already seen him and he'd been so eager to help earlier. Might as well let him.

"How far away are you?" I asked when he answered on the first ring.

"Around the block."

Good. I figured he hadn't gone far, even though I told him to. For once I was glad he didn't do what he was told.

"Ava," Xena said as soon as I hung up. "What's that?" She nodded at the ceiling in the corner of the room. A camera's red light blinked ominously.

"Shit," I said. "That wasn't there before. Bill must have gotten a security camera after the break-in."

"Can you do something about it?"

"Umm…"

I went closer to inspect it. That sucker was screwed tight into the wall, so I couldn't take it down. I didn't want to break it, either, because it looked expensive. Besides that, it had been filming this whole time. I didn't know a lot about security systems, but the footage had to be saved somewhere.

Bill's office was locked, but I felt above the top of the doorframe for the extra key, easily finding it. *Sigh.* His new security wouldn't be much good if he left keys in easy-to-find hiding spots.

A shiny new hard drive was hooked up to his computer, which was powered on. He *never* turned that thing on.

I heard the shop door open, so I quickly disconnected the hard drive and stuck it in my back pocket and exited the office.

Kyle stood there, his eyes bouncing back and forth between Xena and Linda like he was watching a ping-pong tournament. "What the hell?"

"Hi, you must be Kyle. I'm Xena." Her smile was incongruous with the gun in her hand and Linda bleeding all over the floor.

"Yeah," he said slowly, obviously trying to wrap his brain around what he was witnessing.

"Kyle." I clapped my hands to get his attention. "Don't worry about them. Pay attention to me. We need to move Cole into my car."

His gaze shifted to his brother, who was unaware of his presence. Or anyone else's for that matter. "What's wrong with him?"

"I'll explain later. Just—"

"Yeah, I got it." Kyle walked over and leaned down to heft up his brother.

"Watch out," I warned. Too late. Cole jerked his leg, kicking Kyle in the groin.

"Shit!" Kyle glowered at his brother while clutching his crotch.

"He doesn't know what he's doing," I said. "He can't see or hear."

"What the...I know, I know...you'll tell me later." He reached for Cole again and narrowly avoided a punch to the nose.

"We'll have to subdue him," I muttered. "Either that or knock him out."

Kyle looked at me, and I could tell by his expression he wouldn't mind making his brother unconscious.

"Tape," I said. "We need duct tape."

I hopped up and rummaged through one of the cabinets. I remembered seeing tape *somewhere*, but I couldn't recall exactly where.

"Guys, if you could move this along," Xena said through clenched teeth. "That'd be great."

I found the tape in the third cabinet. For a moment, I considered binding Linda, but we wanted her to leave as soon as she was able. Tape wouldn't help with that objective.

Using my teeth, I ripped off a length of tape as I hurried back over to Cole.

"Hold his hands together," I told Kyle.

Kyle grabbed one wrist, but even in his weakened state, Cole was still stronger than his brother. Before Kyle could get hold of Cole's other arm, Cole struck him, sending him flying back.

"Ow!" Kyle clutched his nose. When he brought his hands away, they were covered in blood. My stomach twisted, but luckily for me, I'd developed a small tolerance for blood during the ordeal with Xavier.

And come to think of it, Linda's blood hadn't bothered me one bit. *Progress.* Then again, I was so damn pissed about what she'd done to Cole I could barely see straight.

Cole rose to his knees and put one foot out as he tried to stand. With a yell, Kyle rushed him, knocking him to the ground and using his weight to keep his brother pinned. I seized the opportunity and wrapped the tape around one wrist, holding the remaining length out and trying not to get it tangled while Cole flailed.

"Help me get his other wrist." There was no way I could get it on my own. I was barely able to hang on to the first one.

Blood dripped from Kyle's nose onto Cole's t-shirt as he wrestled to get control of his arm. It took three tries to secure the remaining tape. I quickly ripped off another piece and wrapped it around his wrists.

I dragged my forearm across my forehead, wiping away the sweat. Damn, Cole was strong. Part of it was probably adrenaline.

"Let's go, kids." Xena's voice was laced with irritation.

Kids? What the hell? I got that she was stressed out, but she didn't have to be condescending. I'd like to see her do this faster.

"Come on," I said to Kyle. "Grab his other arm."

As soon as we got him upright, he kicked his feet out backward, kind of like a donkey, and made contact with Kyle's knee with a loud *crack.*

Kyle stumbled back, stunned. Then with a growl, he rushed his brother again, wrapping his arms around his midsection and pushing him back into a metal shelving unit. Boxes of what I hoped contained oil filters and not heavy metal parts fell on them.

"Stop!" I screamed just as Kyle clocked his brother in the mouth. "We'll have to tape his legs together and carry him out of here."

Any trace of brotherly love Kyle had from earlier had vanished from his expression. He didn't speak as he forced Cole to the ground, pressing his face into the pavement and using his weight on his torso.

Poor Cole. None of this was his fault, and he had no idea he was hurting us instead of his enemy.

I looked over at Linda, who was watching us with a hint of amusement. Well, on second thought, maybe some of this was Cole's fault. If he had cooperated with me, maybe Linda wouldn't have found him. He'd been so eager to face her down, not even knowing what she was capable of. *Foolish.* It irritated me because he hadn't listened to any of my warnings and when it came to menacing handlers, I knew what I was talking about. All things considered, though, this could've been much, much worse.

But we weren't out of the woods yet.

I made quick work of wrapping Cole's ankles and tossed the tape aside. "I'll get his feet."

Cole twisted and bucked as we carried him toward the car. He was lucky we only dropped him once. He was probably even luckier Kyle didn't hit him again. Even I had been tempted to toss him in the trunk instead of the back seat.

Kyle sat in the front passenger seat, slamming the door behind him and muttering curses. It was kind of laughable how the tables had turned between the brothers, except I wasn't in a laughing mood. I sincerely hoped one day they'd be able to look back at this and chuckle—one day in the distant, *very* distant future.

Xena ran out of the shop and hopped in the driver's seat while I was still arranging Cole in the back, trying to make him as secure as possible. If we took a tight turn at a fast speed, he wouldn't be able to brace himself. I didn't anticipate a high speed chase, but I also hadn't anticipated Linda turning Cole into a big sense-deprived lump.

"Keys," Xena demanded, holding her hand out over the seat.

Guess she's driving. I dug into my pocket for the keys and passed them over.

I was still buckling my seatbelt when she peeled out of the parking lot. As I looked at Cole, guilt hit me. With his arms strapped behind him and the seatbelt pressing him to the seat, he couldn't be comfortable. As I reached over to loosen it, his body jerked, straining to be free. I yanked my hands back.

"Who the hell was that?" Kyle asked.

Xena looked at me in the rearview mirror, her question evident. *Should you tell him or should I?*

I decided to go with the bare minimum for the present time. Once we got Cole back to normal he could decide how much he wanted to tell Kyle.

"That was Linda and she has certain...powers."

"What, like Batman or some shit?" Even though he'd seen it with his own eyes, he was disbelieving. And I didn't have the heart to tell him Batman didn't actually have superpowers—he just had really fancy toys.

"She can block people's senses," Xena explained. At Kyle's blank stare, she sighed. "You do know what senses are, right?"

I jumped in before Kyle could make a smartass retort. "So she blocked his sight and hearing and his ability to talk. Can she block the other senses as well?"

"Probably," Xena said. "It just depends on how skilled she is. But blocking taste and smell doesn't really serve a purpose."

"Is it permanent?" Kyle's question hit me like a million needles piercing my stomach. When Xavier had used his abilities to hurt me, it hadn't been permanent, so I just assumed what Linda did to Cole wasn't either. But what Xavier had done to my mother had been very permanent. So this could potentially be, too.

"I don't think so," Xena said slowly. "I don't think she's powerful enough. Besides that, he wouldn't be much good to her like this." The needles in my stomach receded as relief filled me.

"When will it wear off?" I asked.

"I have no idea," Xena said. We were all quiet for a few moments.

"Where are we going?" Kyle asked, breaking the silence.

It was a good question. I looked out the window and realized we were headed south, approaching the toll plaza on the bypass that would lead us to Nags Head.

"*You're* going nowhere," Xena told him. "Ava, call Bill and ask him to pick up Kyle at Southland."

"Bullshit," Kyle said. "You're not ditching me."

Xena jerked the steering wheel, pulling us off the road so fast I slid across the seat and Cole's head banged into the window.

Once the car was stopped, she turned to Kyle and poked a single finger into his chest. "Listen to me, you little shit. You're nothing but a lazy screw-up and I have no tolerance for that. You'll just be in our way."

Kyle's mouth dropped open and he swallowed. *Huh.* I guessed in today's warm and fuzzy school environment, no one had bothered to tell it to him straight. I leaned back and crossed my arms, trying hard to keep the amused smile that threatened to break through at bay.

"But—"

"Just shut it," Xena snapped. "You've done nothing but cause trouble for Cole. So under normal circumstances, you'd be nothing but a pain in his ass. With this, you're in way over your head."

"Yeah, but—"

Xena poked him again, cutting him off. "*No.* Not another word. Come talk to me once you've grown up a little. No, make that *a lot.*"

Xena stared him down and something in her eyes must have told him she meant business because he crossed his arms, clamped his mouth shut, and stared at the window.

I wanted to break into a slow clap. Not bad for a pint-sized fallen angel. If the whole handler gig fell through, she could work in a juvenile detention center.

"Call Bill," Xena snapped at me as she eased back onto the road. I did as she asked, giving him the short version of what had happened. Thank God he'd been out of the shop today. But poor Bill—he'd just gotten the shop put back together.

A few minutes later, Xena shoved some cash at Kyle as she pushed him out of the car in Southland's parking lot. "Get yourself some food. Bill will be here soon."

I'd planned to move to the front seat, but the car was moving again before I could get my door open, so I climbed over the seat. Before I buckled up, I took the hard drive out of my back pocket and tossed it in the center console.

This whole time, Cole sat perfectly still, his body tense, probably ready to defend himself again if necessary. He'd closed his eyes, much to my relief. His vacant stare was disconcerting.

I wished there was a way we could let him know we were there to help him, but that was part of the horribleness of his predicament—he had no clue what was going on around him.

"Do you have a destination in mind?" I asked. We were still headed south.

"The beach," Xena said.

I nodded, secretly pleased. Since I'd scattered my mother's ashes in the ocean, I always felt closer to her if I was near it. Maybe it would encourage her to visit my dreams again. Probably not, but I didn't have many other positives right now, so I was going with it.

"Get the number for a local rental office," she commanded, and for once I was happy to follow her lead. After being in charge on my last adventure, I was ready not to make any hard decisions.

I easily found dozens of listings on my phone. "Now what?"

"Call and see if you can get a beach rental. They're probably all booked, but we might get lucky with a cancellation."

"They'll want a credit card," I said. "We should find a sketchy hotel that will take cash."

Xena shook her head. "You barely got Cole into the car. How do you expect to get him into a hotel? We need something more private."

She had a point, but my concern was also valid.

"What if Linda can track us by a credit card?"

Xena's nostrils flared as she looked over at me, but she stopped short of rolling her eyes. "I have one with a fake name."

The *obviously* was implied in her statement. This was another Xena-ism. She probably assumed everyone had credit cards with fake names on them. I didn't bother explaining to her that wasn't normal.

She lifted her butt off the scat a little so she could reach into her back pocket then tossed me a Visa card.

Harriet McIntyre.

Now it was my turn to snort. "Really?" I asked, pointing to the name. There was no way Xena could pass for a Harriet McIntyre. It was way too...un-Xena.

"Hurry up," she snapped. Whoa... I guessed she was grumpy after her run in with Linda. "It may take you a while."

She was right. I had to call five offices before I found one with a vacancy. I quickly reserved it and entered the office address in my GPS so we could pick up the keys.

"Did you hear what Linda said?" I asked cautiously. "About if I refuse to turn in names?"

"Yes." Xena didn't look at me. *Uh-oh.* That wasn't a good sign.

"Is it true?" Both Areli and Xavier had said as much, but I didn't consider those two the most reliable of sources. I wanted it confirmed by someone who didn't have ulterior motives.

"Yes."

"Shit," I whispered, wrapping my arms around my stomach and putting my head between my knees.

"I don't think you have anything to worry about right now. Linda isn't going to turn you in because then she'd have to admit she can't handle you. And even if she did, I don't think they'd do anything, at least not right away. You're the last born seeker. They want you to procreate."

So my life wasn't important enough to save, but my womb was. It was only slightly comforting, but it bought me time.

"What about Chase and Claire?" I asked. "They're not planning to seek anymore, either."

Xena scrunched her mouth to one side, considering. "I wouldn't worry about them right now. They didn't choose to become seekers, so that's a big gray area. Besides that, Niles would have to report them. Considering how he feels about Claire, I don't expect him to do that anytime soon."

"Okay," I said. One problem at a time, then.

I spun around to look at Cole. If I didn't know better, I would've thought he was sleeping. But there was no way he would let himself sleep in a situation like this. He would be on high alert. Except without his senses, how could he be?

I hated seeing him like this. I'd seen him vulnerable before, but this was different. He was helpless.

Well, not quite. I remembered Kyle's bloody nose. Not completely defenseless but definitely powerless to help himself.

"What are we going to do?"

Xena sighed, some of her fierceness seeming to leave her with that breath. "I don't know."

That made two of us.

CHAPTER 13

ALMOST TWO HOURS LATER WITH keys in hand, we pulled to a stop in front of the ugliest beach house I'd ever seen. It was made of cinder blocks and had a flat roof, making it appear squat and dumpy, especially compared to the surrounding mega-mansions. The yellow paint was the color of something you might sneeze up. A rusted basketball hoop was mounted at the front of the driveway and tall reed-like plants encroached upon the pavement. A window unit air conditioner hung out of the front window.

"Perfect." Xena grinned and got out of the car.

"Whatever you say, Harriet," I muttered. I glanced back at Cole, hesitant to leave him alone in the car. But with his hands and feet still bound, it wasn't like he could go anywhere.

Ugh. I was the worst.

I joined Xena at the front door just as she turned the key. A musty smell wafted out, but compared to the stench that greeted me at the farmhouse, this might as well have smelled like a hot Krispy Kreme doughnut.

We took a quick tour of the place. It was small and the furniture was dated, but it was clean and most importantly, it didn't share walls with any other buildings, which meant we'd be less likely to be overheard. Though come to think of it, since Cole couldn't talk, that probably wasn't an issue. Still, Xena had been right—this was much better than any hotel would've been.

"Okay," Xena said. "Let's bring him in."

We trooped outside and both of us stopped to stare at Cole sitting in the car. Some traffic passed on the road and my stomach dropped to my knees. But no one paid us any attention. We needed to keep it that way. How would we manage to move Cole without turning it into a spectacle? Kyle and I had barely gotten him in the car and that was with Kyle carrying the bulk of the weight. How in the heck were Xena and I going to do this alone?

"It would be much easier if he were unconscious," Xena muttered.

"No." I shot her a deadly look, lest she decide to take matters into her own hands. It *would* be easier, but just...*no.*

She put her hands up, palms out. "Okay, okay. It was just a suggestion."

"We need something with wheels," I said. "Like an office chair or something like that. He's too heavy for us to carry."

We went back inside to look, but since there was no office there was no desk with a wheeled chair. All of the other furniture had solid wood legs, as furniture usually does. I had just about given up when Xena called to me from the second bedroom.

"How about this?" She pulled a portable crib out of the closet.

"Will it fit through the doorway?"

"Only one way to find out."

It took us nearly twenty minutes to figure out how to set the stupid thing up. It was maybe two feet by four feet and the wheels were wobbly and unstable. It was also about three feet deep, so we'd have to dump him in there. It wasn't ideal by any means, but it was the best we had. So we'd have to make it work.

It barely fit through the doorway, so my estimate about its width must have been way off. It was probably closer to three feet. Luckily there was a sidewalk that led from the driveway to the front door, which made it easier to push, but one of the wheels spun wildly and tilted to the side, like it was about to fall off. It would be a miracle if this worked.

"We need to be fast," Xena said. "Even I can't come up with an explanation for this if someone sees us."

I could just imagine that conversation. *You see, Officer, we tied up my ex-boyfriend for his own good. And even though he's fighting us, if he could see, talk, or hear, he'd tell you he wants us "helping" him.*

Yeah...

I wondered how long it would take them to get Xena and me in handcuffs.

Ex-boyfriend... This was the first time I'd referred to Cole like that, but technically that was what he was. He'd made it perfectly clear we weren't together. God, this sucked. It would be nice if I knew he'd be happy to see my face when he could actually see again. But I didn't have time to dwell on it.

Xena opened the car door, and I pushed the crib right up next to Cole. His eyes were open now but by the way he stared blankly in our direction, I could tell his vision was still gone. He seemed to sense we were there though, and for a moment I was hopeful maybe he was getting his hearing back. But then I realized it was probably the change in temperature or air pressure caused by us opening the door that alerted him to our presence.

We tried pulling him out by his shoulders, but it was hard to reach him around the crib. He also jerked away every time we touched him, making it more difficult.

Xena went around to the other side of the car and got in the back seat next to him. As soon as she touched him, he tried to headbutt her, hitting her shoulder. She put one hand on his head and the other on his body, shoving him while I tried to guide him into the crib. The only trouble was Xena and I weren't in sync with our efforts and he tumbled down into it on his back, smacking his head against the corner support bar. *Ouch.* His torso took up the entire bottom of the crib, leaving his legs sticking up at a ninety-degree angle.

This was going so much worse that I thought it would.

Another flaw in our plan became evident as soon as we began pushing him toward the door. He was so heavy the bottom sagged down to the ground. So instead of having one of us on either side, we both went to the side where his head was and lifted, pulling it toward us. Luckily he remained still during this process. I wondered what he must be thinking of this cruel and unusual treatment. Could he even figure out what was going on? Suddenly, I was glad he couldn't see—I didn't want him to witness this circus act. Of course, if he could see, we wouldn't be in this situation.

We paused at the front door and I wiped the sweat off my forehead. The car was only four or five yards away, but it felt like we'd gone an entire football field.

I nodded at Xena and we lifted the crib again, preparing to shimmy it over the threshold, but the wheels in the back gave out, sending that end crashing to the ground. Thank goodness we had his head near us, otherwise he would've cracked it on the cement.

We were the worst kidnappers ever.

"Screw this." Xena went around to the other side near his feet. Taking a deep breath, she lifted it with a grunt. "Pull him out," she said through clenched teeth.

I knelt into a squat and put my hands under his arms, pulling as I took a step backward. Xena wedged the crib out from under him and then came around to help me pull.

"Oomph!" I fell on my butt and he landed on top of me, his head smacking my chin and making my teeth rattle. Hurriedly, I crawled away like a crab before he could start lashing out. Xena yanked his legs the rest of the way inside and then slammed the door.

Looking down at him, she put her hands on her hips. "This is good."

I narrowed my eyes at her. "Xena—"

"I know, I know," she said in exasperation.

He stayed relatively still as we moved him to the couch. His eyes had a wild look in them, and I found that interesting considering they were useless right now. God, I wished there were some way for us to let him know he was safe. Not only would it give him peace of mind, but he'd be a lot easier to manage.

I sank down to the floor to rest.

Xena snatched up the keys from the table. "I'll be back."

"Where are you going?"

"We may be here a while, so I'm going to get supplies. It's best I go while he's good and tired."

In other words, while he couldn't cause much trouble.

I turned to look at him. He did look tired. His adrenaline had probably been at an all-time high for the last few hours. His face was starting to swell and bruises sprinkled his body from his fight with Kyle. I wished we didn't have to keep him bound, but until he regained his senses or we figured out how to communicate with him, I didn't have a better solution. Maybe handcuffs would be preferable to tape, which might be rubbing his skin raw. But would handcuffs be any better? Every time he struggled, they would cut into his wrists. And that still left us with his feet. Shackles, perhaps? *Yeah, right.* Tape it was.

Except we didn't bring the tape with us. Now in addition to being the worst kidnappers ever, we were also the most ill-prepared.

"Get duct tape," I said. "And handcuffs if you can find them."

"On it." She left.

The thought of handcuffing Cole like Xavier had been turned my stomach, but the two situations were nothing alike.

Yeah, keep telling yourself that.

We were holding Cole against his will, but he didn't know better. If he knew what was going on, he'd want to be here.

God, I hoped I was right.

I brushed a piece of hair off his forehead and he flinched, baring his teeth. I was close enough to smell the peppermint on his breath and my stomach went into a full-on gymnastic routine, flip-flopping and somersaulting all over the place.

The pain that filled my heart was bittersweet because if I had it to do all over again, I would. The time I had with Cole was worth the pain of losing him. I just wished I hadn't wrecked his life so badly.

He'd wrecked one thing for me forever—peppermint. The faintest whiff of it reminded me of him, specifically of kissing him. At one point, that had been my favorite pastime. I loved the way his tongue—

Nope. Not thinking about that.

I sighed and blew out a breath.

Though I had messed up a lot of things in his life, at least I didn't destroy a common taste for him because I didn't have a penchant for munching on one thing like he did. I didn't have a particular taste or scent.

Except...I had to taste like *something*.

As I stared at Cole, an idea formed in my head. It was crazy but no crazier than taping him up and driving him across state lines. Damn...did that make our little act a federal crime?

I shook that thought free. *Stupid.* Even if Cole didn't thank us for what we'd done, he wouldn't press charges or anything.

Maybe my plan would work, making it easier for all of us. If it didn't, I would feel like an idiot, making me glad

Xena wasn't here for this. But if it might make things more pleasant for Cole, then I had to try.

I needed to stabilize him. Though his hands and feet were bound, he still had a fair range of movement. His arms were strapped behind him, so given his position on the couch, they shouldn't cause too much trouble. But he could easily hurt me using his knees and feet if I got too close.

Think, Ava, think.

I needed something to strap him to, like a gurney. Obviously, I wouldn't find one at a beach house, but what could I find? A surfboard? No, too big and probably too heavy. A boogie board? Too small and weren't they made of Styrofoam? Cole would easily be able to break that. I paced the living room, looking for something that would work. Coming up empty, I wandered around the rest of the house, opening cabinets and closets.

I hit pay dirt in the utility closet. Tucked beside the washing machine was an ironing board. *Perfect.*

I pulled it out, scraping my knuckles on the wall in my haste. Damn, I'd have to text Xena and tell her to get some peroxide and Band-Aids. But later. I needed to do this before I lost my nerve.

Holding the ironing board in the living room, I tried to figure out the best way to do this. It was then I realized I didn't have everything I needed. I had the board, but I didn't have anything to strap him to it.

I set the board on the ground and went in search of rope. But of course I didn't find any because this was a beach house—why would they have rope here? What I did find was several extension cords. I pulled them taut, trying to determine how much stress they could withstand. They didn't seem like they would rip easily, but it didn't matter—they were the best I had, so I'd have to make them work.

I lined up my supplies next to the couch so I'd have everything within arm's reach. Still, this was going to be tricky. Even tied up, Cole was much stronger than me. So I'd have to be fast and get it done before he figured out what was going on.

I reached under him to set up the extension cords. As I did his body stiffened. He probably figured out by now fighting wasn't doing him much good, so he was conserving energy. As soon as he realized what I was doing to him, that would go out the window. Let's hope it didn't take my pride with it.

Once everything was in place, I quickly flipped him onto his belly and put the board on his back. Except crap! I'd forgotten to take into account the fact his hands were tied behind him so his back wasn't a flat surface. He was struggling against me and I wouldn't be able to hold him much longer, so I didn't have time to fix that problem. I knotted the extension cord at his arms three times before moving to the one near his feet.

With a grunt, I flipped him back over and realized I'd had his face smashed into a throw pillow. *Shit!* No wonder he struggled. He probably thought I was trying to suffocate him. Instinctively, I put my hand on his arm to give comfort, but he jerked his body away from my touch. *Ouch.* I knew he didn't know what he was doing, but the truth was these days he would probably jerk away from me under normal circumstances as well. I needed to develop a thicker skin where he was concerned.

Or maybe I needed to suck it up and admit to myself he was lost to me forever.

Stepping back, I surveyed the situation, both to make sure everything was in place and to mentally prepare myself. Because if my feelings had gotten hurt a moment ago when he'd jerked away from my touch, this could end up being a real bitch.

But it wasn't about that. It was about making sure Cole understood he was safe and that we were there to help him. My feelings weren't relevant.

I blew out a breath. I couldn't put it off any longer. It was *go time.*

My hands shook as I stepped toward him and a lump formed in my throat. Then I stopped myself and laughed out loud. I was being totally ridiculous. I had slept with him for crying out loud. This was just a kiss and it meant nothing. It was a means to an end.

I pounced on him, using my body weight to make sure he remained still. Cupping my hands on his cheeks, I held his face steady even as he began to thrash.

Then I lowered my mouth to his. My lips brushed over his, but I quickly realized that wouldn't be enough—I had to kiss him deep enough for him to taste me.

I licked his lips and his mouth opened slightly—the effect I was going for. Hoping to God I was right about this and he didn't bite my tongue off, I plunged it into his mouth, tasting peppermint.

He stilled, not kissing me back, but not resisting anymore either. A second later, his tongue swished against mine, his lips hungrily lapping at my mouth.

Tingles formed deep in my belly despite my best efforts to tell myself this was a clinical kiss—there was nothing sensual or romantic about it.

Yet we devoured one another.

I let the kiss go on for way longer than I should have and when I pulled back, I saw his lips form my name.

CHAPTER 14

I STARED AT COLE, AMAZED my little plan had worked. I was even more amazed he had kissed me back. My fingers traced the ridges of my lips, still warm from his.

He craned his neck, stretching like he was reaching for me. I put my finger to his mouth, and he gently suckled my fingertip.

He knows it's me.

I took my finger away and leaned down to kiss him again. This time the kiss was slow, not as urgent, but even sweeter.

I realized I was still lying on top of him so I quickly moved off. And damn, I had gotten so lost in the feeling of his mouth on mine I'd totally forgotten he was all tied up. I tugged at the knots in the extension cords and they easily came undone. I wasn't so lucky with the duct tape. When I pulled at it, all I did was scrunch the tape tighter together, making it impossible to tear.

I trotted to the kitchen in search of scissors but came up empty. I hesitated before grabbing a knife because if he squirmed while I was trying to cut the tape one of us could get really hurt. But now that I was confident he wouldn't fight me, I couldn't leave him bound. I'd just have to be careful not to slice open one of our wrists.

"It's going to be okay," I said, placing my hand on his cheek. I said that more for my benefit than his because it seemed like he still couldn't hear. When he leaned his face on my hand, my heart threatened to burst.

Carefully I slipped the knife under the tape and sawed away. The knife was dull and I was extra careful, so it seemed to take forever to free his hands. As soon as the tape broke away he pushed himself to a sitting position and blindly reached out, grabbing hold of my shoulders. His hands followed the path of my neck up to my face, and he traced my features with his fingertips.

His expression was a mix of relief and joy, though his eyes were still vacant and unseeing. I raised my hands to put them on top of his and he brought them to his mouth, kissing my knuckles.

I could've stayed like that forever, but I wanted to free his legs. Once I did, he swung his legs to the ground. Pulling me into his lap, he wrapped his arms around me and held me.

And I was happy to let him.

"WHAT THE..." XENA STARED AT us in disbelief. "I obviously missed something."

Cole and I sat next to each other on the couch, our hands clasped. We hadn't been this way the whole time she was gone, though. We'd spent some time dealing with practical matters like me guiding Cole to the bathroom, getting him some water to drink, and preparing a towel full of ice for his face. Some color had come back into his cheeks, and he was a lot less panicked than before, a calmness having settled over him once he had figured out I was with him. He was definitely still agitated, but who could blame him?

"He knows it's me."

"Yeah, I figured out that much."

I grinned. Without meaning to, I'd pulled a classic Xena move—stating the obvious. Her annoyed reaction was pure gold.

My expression sombered as I started to explain what I had done. By the end of my story, Xena was the one grinning.

"I guess making out with you left an impression on him."

I blushed stupidly. But whatever. Xena could be amused at my expense. My plan had worked and that was all that mattered.

"What did you get at the store?" I asked.

"Food, clothing, the usual," she said. "I had to guess at your sizes."

She tossed a bag in my lap. Looking through it, I found some basic clothing as well as first aid supplies. Thank goodness—I'd forgotten to text and ask for those. The blood on my scraped knuckles had dried a while ago, but it still stung. I detached myself from Cole. He seemed very reluctant to let me go and once again I couldn't blame him.

"Come here," I said to Xena. "We need to let him know you're here too."

She arched her eyebrow. "I'm not kissing him."

I rolled my eyes, not bothering to point out that unless they had a secret to tell me, kissing him wouldn't do any good. "Just let him put his hands on your face. That should be enough for him to figure it out."

"Not too long ago he was doing his best to headbutt me in the face. I'm not really eager to give him a clean shot." But she did as I asked and came closer, kneeling in front of him. I guided his hands to her face and he ran his fingers over it, also feeling her hair. When he pulled his hands away he held his pointer finger in the air and spelled out her name.

"See?" I beamed at her.

"Yeah, yeah. You're a genius."

"Thanks." I ignored her sarcasm, feeling proud of myself on multiple levels. "Do you need me to help carry things in?"

"Take care of your hand first."

I went to the bathroom to do that, and by the time I was done the living room floor was filled with bags.

"Holy cow," I said. "How much stuff did you get?"

She shrugged. "Let's just say I made sure we'd have everything we need."

I glanced over at Cole sitting on the couch. He tapped his fingers nervously on his knee, making me want to go sit next to him again. But I needed to help Xena put the groceries away at least.

As I emptied the bags, I thought of something. "Hey, did you happen to get paper and something to write with?"

Xena pursed her lips. "No. That's one thing I didn't get."

"I was just thinking we could give pen and paper to Cole, and he could use it to communicate with us. It wouldn't be perfect but it's better than nothing. Maybe there's something here we can use."

We found a notepad in one of the kitchen drawers and we had a pen from the rental office, but it turned out Cole didn't have much to say anyway. I was sure he had a million questions, but he probably realized there was no point asking them while he wouldn't be able to hear the answers.

The one thing he did say—or write rather—was that he was hungry. No surprise there. Even though Xena had just bought tons of food, neither one of us wanted to cook, so she went out again in search of pizza.

When she returned, we sat around the kitchen table. Cole sat next to me and I guided his hands to his food. It was so weird. I couldn't wait to get him back to normal.

"We need a plan," Xena said.

I frowned. "Right now there's not much we can do, right? We need to wait for Cole to get better."

"It won't take Linda long to regroup. I'd rather be on the offensive."

Xena made a good point.

With Xavier I felt like we were always on the defensive, trying to counter whatever move he had made. It would be nice to be the one calling the shots for once.

That thought almost made me laugh out loud. When had I ever called the shots? I was barely a legal adult, so up until recently I'd had my mom and teachers at school to answer to. And then of course I'd also had Xavier telling me what to do. It wasn't until recently that I started making decisions for myself, a lot of which I'd screwed up royally.

I looked over at Cole, suddenly realizing something. I didn't know at what point his mother completely abandoned the guise of parenting, but Cole had to have been a young teenager at the oldest. Since he was twenty now, that meant he'd been making his own decisions for nearly a decade. He wasn't like me—he wasn't used to having other people tell him what to do. Bill was his boss, but their work arrangement was more like a partnership. Cole may have made some questionable choices in his life, especially when he was younger, but at least they'd been his decisions. He'd had control. So yeah, I could totally understand why he'd gotten bent out of shape when I'd left without consulting him in the decision when it had been him I was trying to hide. My heart had been in the right place, but Cole didn't see it that way and I could finally see why. I couldn't believe it had taken me this long.

I turned to Xena. "We need to wait."

She glared at me over her pizza, the thought of waiting repugnant to her. "Why? We're wasting time just sitting here."

"This involves more than just us." I gestured to Cole. It was kind of a shame he couldn't see me sticking up for him, but I wasn't doing it to prove a point to him. I was doing it because it was the right thing to do.

Xena pursed her lips. "We don't know how long he'll be this way. It could be days or weeks or..." In seeing the horror on my face, she trailed off. *Weeks?* And what had she been about to say after that? *Months?* This couldn't go on that long. It had only been a few hours and that was long enough. Cole had such a big presence, and it pained me to see him like this. It had to be horrible for him, not only not being in control, but having no idea what was going on right in front of him.

"I understand that," I said. "But I think we should at least give it a day or two. I also don't want to make any rash decisions."

Although I'd previously been planning to leave Tidewater, when I'd actually left, it had been a rash decision because I'd recently decided to try to figure out how I could stick around. But then Xena had showed up, followed by Linda a few minutes later, and everything went to hell in a handbasket....whatever the hell *that* meant. All I knew was I hadn't been thinking straight.

Cole had finished his pizza and was feeling around his paper plate for another slice, his expression serious. It was kind of funny actually. At least this whole experience hadn't wrecked his appetite. I hooked him up with more pizza, debating whether or not I should try to eat more. My appetite was still spotty, but I was working on it.

"There is one thing we can do now though," I said, sitting down with an empty plate. I doubted I'd be able to keep a second piece down.

Xena eagerly leaned forward. "What?" She never was one to sit still.

"We need to figure out why the handlers want Cole so badly. I know he's the 'seeker with no limits'—" I used air quotes for that. "—but I still don't get it. So he can see the auras of everyone regardless of age. Why is that such a big deal? There are seekers at every age level so it's not like he's reaching a population they previously couldn't get to."

She tapped her chin. "I've been wondering about that, too."

Though Xena was a handler herself, she didn't conform to the norm, so I wasn't surprised she was also curious. I'd only ever met three handlers aside from Xena, but that was enough. Two were sadistic and one was a spineless weasel.

"Part of it is he's a novelty," Xena said.

"That can't be all it is, though," I said. "I mean, let's be honest here. It's not like he's shooting flames out of his eyeballs or something exciting like that. Surely they can get their kicks some other way."

"I agree their fascination isn't for entertainment purposes. What you said is true—there's a lot of other things handlers can get into that are way more exciting."

We stared at each other for a moment, both of us sporting perplexed expressions. I'd been so worried about the fact handlers were after Cole I didn't even stop to think *why*—a huge flaw. Maybe I was finally getting smarter. Not smart in the sense I knew what the hell was going on, but smart enough to realize I didn't know what was going on and I should try to figure it out rather than simply react.

"We need to find out what they want with him before we make any moves," I said.

"Okay." Xena sighed in disappointment. "I wouldn't have minded shooting Linda again." She didn't even bother to look chagrined.

But that reminded me.

"Do you still have my gun?"

"It's in the car."

I nodded. "We should bring it inside."

"Good idea." She left to get it. I hoped Xena wouldn't get another chance to shoot Linda, but we needed to be prepared.

Cole had polished off yet another slice so I loaded him up again. Xena returned to the kitchen, placing my pink gun and a box of ammo on the table.

"Is there anyone who might be able to help us?" I asked. "Surely you know someone who knows what's going on."

"I don't know." She frowned and I could tell she was bothered. "These days it's getting harder and harder to figure out who I can trust. I can put some feelers out but I don't know if I'll learn anything. Even when I was officially assigned to him, they didn't tell me anything."

"Huh," I couldn't help saying. "That seems to be a common theme with you guys."

Xena shrugged, ignoring my jab and not bothering to deny the truth of it. "Everything's on a need-to-know."

"This is something we definitely need to know."

"Agreed."

THAT NIGHT I SLEPT CURLED around Cole, our limbs tangled and our bodies so close I could feel his heartbeat. It was—in a word—perfect. The familiarity of him was comforting, and I slept the best I had since before the farmhouse. I slept so well in fact I dreamed of my mother.

"Is everything okay?" she asked, pulling me close to her and then holding me out at arm's reach so she could look me over. Her gaze traveled over my body, her lips pursed. No doubt she was noticing how thin I'd gotten.

I hesitated. My recent conversation with Cole about how he saw me differently made me reluctant to tell her about what had gone down with Xavier. My mom was my mom and she would always love me, but even still, I didn't want her faith in me to be ruined. I couldn't stand seeing disappointment in her eyes.

Yet again, I was sick and tired of all the lies and secrecy. I wanted to live a normal life.

Of course, talking to my dead mother in my dreams wasn't exactly normal.

I decided to go with the selective truth, telling her about Linda finding Cole and everything that had happened as a result. Well, not everything. I didn't tell her about how terrible things had been between me and Cole, nor the scheme I'd used to show him I was with him. I knew I could talk to her if I wanted to, but talking to my mom about my love life would just be *ick*.

By the time I was done talking, my mom was visibly upset. She shook her head in disbelief. "I can't believe they let handlers get away with that kind of thing."

I looked at her strangely. "Do you not remember Xavier?" *You know, the man who killed you?*

"Of course. I just thought he was the exception and not the rule, especially after having met Xena."

"The other handler I met isn't evil, but I wouldn't label him as a good person, either," I said, thinking of Niles. It was worrisome that all these fallen angels were lowlifes, though. "What are the other angels like?"

She shrugged. "Just like normal people, really. I like some better than others."

Hmm...not exactly what I expected of heaven's inhabitants. Shouldn't they all be best friends with no judgment? I guessed even angeldom couldn't change human nature.

"Have you heard anything about why handlers want Cole?" I asked.

"There aren't any handlers here. Fallen angels don't come around."

Damn. For a moment I'd gotten hopeful.

"I can't figure it out." My voice was laced with frustration. "He's special and he has no limits as far as seeker abilities go, but even still that's not all that extraordinary."

My mom shook her head helplessly. "I wish I could help, but I'm even more lost than you."

I doubted that because I had no freaking clue.

"Maybe you can help with something else," I said, not meeting her eyes and letting the words out hurriedly. "I told Xena about seeing you in my dreams, and she says she's never heard of that before. So she has a theory that perhaps I got this ability from my father."

I peered up at her to gauge her reaction.

She sighed, her expression weary. "So you're trying to find him."

She didn't argue with me or try to convince me not to, but she seemed disappointed. For so long, both of us had accepted it was just two of us, so it felt wrong, almost like I was cheating on her or something.

"Yeah," I rushed on, wanting to get this part of our conversation over with. "Any information you remember about him might be helpful."

"I don't even have a picture. And this sounds awful but after nearly twenty years I barely remember what he looked like. It was a crazy time for me."

I'd already known this, but even still it was disconcerting to hear about my mother's loose ways. She had been wild for a few years, but she mostly kept that time in her life under wraps. She hadn't wanted to share and honestly, I'd never wanted to know until now.

"Anything you remember would be helpful," I said. "Xena is going to look into it, but she doesn't have anything to go on other than his first name."

"Williams," she said. "His last name is Williams. And he was two or three years older than me."

Michael Williams. The name echoed in my mind, but I felt nothing but annoyance. *Great.* He couldn't have a more common name if he'd tried. At least I could be reasonably confident he still had that name, unlike women who changed theirs when they got married.

"Do you remember anything else?"

"He had blue eyes and light brown hair. He drove a Jeep Cherokee. At the time, he was obsessed with Green Day." She smiled wryly and put her hands up.

That wasn't a heck of a lot of information to go on, but it was more than I'd had a few minutes ago.

"Do you remember the year of the Jeep? Or maybe the color?"

"I don't remember the year, but it was older, I think. Not brand new anyway. I think it was green, but I can't guarantee that." She looked away, and it occurred to me this conversation might be even more awkward for her than it was for me. It must be hard for her to admit she knew next to nothing about the man she'd conceived a child with.

"Thanks. If you think of anything else, please remember to tell me next time."

CHAPTER 15

WHEN I WOKE THE NEXT morning, Cole was lying on his side, staring at me. I smiled sleepily at him for a moment before it registered.

He's staring at me.

I sat up straight, dislodging his arm that had been around my middle. "You can see!"

He blinked but didn't respond. A few seconds passed and my hopes fell. I swore he was looking at me. It wasn't just my imagination.

I held my hand out as far as I could and waited frantically. He turned his head toward the movement.

Yes! It wasn't all in my head. It wasn't just wishful thinking. He was getting better. *Thank God.*

"Can you hear me?" I yelled.

This time he tilted his head so his ear was closer to me. Then he shrugged and mimed writing. I scrambled to find the notepad and pen, spotting it on the dresser across the room. I handed it to him and as he wrote the words, I noticed his handwriting was just as bad as it was before when he couldn't see anything at all. *Damn.*

He held out the notepad. *I can see shadows and shapes.*

There was a pounding on the door and a split-second later Xena threw it open, my gun in her hand.

Instinctively, I positioned myself in front of Cole, who couldn't see she had it pointed right at us.

When she saw it was just the two of us she lowered it.

"What's all the yelling about?"

I pulled the blanket up to my chin, irrationally feeling like we'd been caught doing something naughty. Even if we had been, this was Xena. She wouldn't care. And anyway, it wasn't any of her business.

"Cole was looking at me," I explained.

Xena gave me a blank stare.

"You know, like he's getting his sight back."

Xena peered at Cole, who was looking in her general direction, but his eyes weren't focused on anything in particular. "He still seems pretty blind to me."

"Look." I held up the paper so she could read what he wrote. "He can see a little bit."

"Great." She yawned. "But next time wait until I'm awake to make all that noise." She left the room and pulled the door closed behind her, presumably going back to bed in the other room.

I lay back down beside Cole.

I swallowed my disappointment from earlier. Sure, I would've preferred if he'd gotten the full use of his senses back, but I needed to be realistic with my expectations. When Xavier had hurt me I didn't heal instantaneously. It had taken a little while for me to get back to normal. I needed to be patient, which was excruciatingly difficult because I couldn't wait to have the full Cole back. But at least he was showing progress, so we knew he was on the road to recovery.

Closing my eyes, I snuggled in next to him, but I could already tell sleep wouldn't come. My body was probably in shock from all of last night's sleep. I glanced at the clock and did the math—eight hours. I hadn't gotten that much continuous sleep in weeks.

With a sigh, I sat up, thinking I'd go and make some breakfast for everyone. But Cole flung his arm around my waist and pulled me toward him, nuzzling my neck.

On second thought, breakfast could definitely wait.

Xena crashed around the kitchen, slamming cabinets and clanging pots and pans together. Though Cole's hearing was still limited at best, even he winced at the sound. I looked at him and raised my eyebrows. He simply shook his head, but the small gesture pleased me beyond giddiness. Since he'd reacted to my slight movement, that must have meant his vision was still getting better. It had been three days since his senses started returning and though I was grateful for his progress, it was agonizingly slow. His speech in particular seemed to be taking forever. He could make sounds, but he didn't have enough control over his voice to form most words, so he stayed silent.

It gave me a reprieve from *the talk* that awaited us. Neither of us had attempted to discuss the changes in our relationship—the fact that we kissed frequently, touched each other constantly, and slept wrapped up in one another every night. Perhaps not having *the talk* made it easier for us to be together again. It was less complicated.

I peeled myself up off the couch to go find out what all the racket was about. In the kitchen Xena was on her hands and knees, her head and half her upper body in one of the lower cabinets.

I leaned my hip against the doorway. "What are you doing?"

"Ow!" She smacked her head on the top of the cabinet as she came out. "Is it too much to ask for a mixer?"

"What are you trying to make?" I asked, my voice filled with more patience than I felt. Xena had been going stir crazy and every day it had gotten worse. The first day, she was content to binge watch TV. The second day, she'd meditated and practiced yoga for hours in the living room, forcing Cole and me into complete silence, which had been harder than you'd think, even with Cole's missing voice. The third day, she'd gone out and come home with several skeins of yarn and knitting needles. She'd worked for hours trying to teach herself using YouTube videos before declaring it lame and tossing the gnarled mess of string into the trash. And now today, she'd apparently moved on to baking.

"Brownies," she said.

I picked up the box to look at the directions, even though I already knew what they were. "You can use a spoon. You don't need a mixer."

She snatched the box out of my hands. "What? Oh, for—" A string of expletives came out of her mouth.

Xena was coming unglued.

I gently took the box out of her hands. "Why don't you go out for the day? Or even overnight?"

Her brow furrowed. "I don't think I should leave you two alone. Although, you already act like you're alone."

I narrowed my eyes at her but ignored the jab at my and Cole's canoodling. Whatever. I wasn't going to make any apologies.

"We've been here four days and nothing has happened. We'll be okay on our own for a little while." But Xena, on the other hand, would not be okay being cooped up for another day. I had serious concerns about her mental and emotional well-being.

"Maybe…"

All she needed was a little push and she'd be out the door.

"You could use the time to look into why the handlers want Cole."

"Good point."

"It's a *perfect* point. Now get out of here."

Xena nodded and picked up my keys from the counter. Three seconds later the door slammed behind her and I let out a breath. *Thank God.* She was driving me freaking nuts. I appreciated that she wanted to stick around in case we needed protection, but I had my gun. I could shoot Linda just as easily as she could.

When I returned to the living room, Cole looked at me with a question on his face.

I leaned down close to his ear. "Xena's going out for a while," I said loudly.

He nodded. A sly grin cropped up on his face and he pulled me into his lap. His mouth claimed mine while his hands slipped under my shirt to feel my skin. Goose bumps formed in the wake of his touch.

There were certain forms of communication that didn't require words and lucky for me, Cole happened to be a master.

JUST BEFORE FOUR A.M., THE front door opened and I might have missed it except for the wind chimes I'd taken from the porch and hung behind the door. Cole stirred as I wrapped my hand around my gun I'd kept ready on the nightstand. When I slipped out of bed, he grabbed my wrist and pointed to himself.

I'll go.

I shook my head. The intruder wouldn't have to be very stealthy to sneak up on him.

He ran his hands over his head in frustration and I took a moment to give him a quick kiss, reassuring him I'd be okay. Chances were it was Xena, but I wanted to be prepared.

I listened at the bedroom door for a moment before opening it. After I'd moved the wind chimes last night, I'd used cooking spray to grease the door hinges to make sure this one didn't squeak.

Barefoot and wearing nothing but a t-shirt, I silently made my way toward the front of the house.

"Are you freaking kidding me?" a voice muttered, and I exhaled as I put the safety on the gun. Xena was back.

She stood in the kitchen holding the box of brownie mix from earlier.

"What's wrong?" I asked.

She whirled, shooting me an accusatory look and gesturing to the box. "Why didn't you make these?"

I placed the gun on the counter and crossed my arms over my chest. "I was busy."

"You mean you couldn't take time away from making out with Cole."

I couldn't stop the blush that spread to my cheeks. We'd been doing more than just making out, but I definitely wasn't going to get into that.

"Why are you so grumpy?"

"I'm hungry," she whined, "and I want chocolate."

I pulled a mixing bowl out of the cabinet. "You know, this is not a good attitude for you. It messes up the *I'm so cool I only dress in black* vibe you have going on."

"You think I'm cool?"

Out of everything I'd said, that was her takeaway?

Cole appeared behind me, relieved to see it was Xena. I smiled at him and squeezed his hand. Xena made a little fake gagging sound. She was in rare form tonight—no, it was four a.m., so this morning. Perhaps she was sleep deprived. I knew a thing or two about that.

But once again, whatever.

"How is he?" she asked. I was glad to see that despite her surly attitude, she did care.

"Still not talking." I eyed the measuring cup as I poured in vegetable oil. Brownies were ridiculously easy. Xena could be doing this herself.

Also, I didn't like talking about Cole right in front of him, like he wasn't here. It felt wrong and degrading toward him.

"Huh," Xena said. "To be honest, Cole being seen and not heard hasn't been the worst thing ever."

Cole gave her the finger.

"You didn't ask about his hearing," I said. "That's gotten much, much better."

Xena smirked. "I thought so."

I rolled my eyes. "What did you learn?"

"Do you want the good news or the bad news?"

A hollowness formed in my belly. At least it wasn't bad and worse news like usual.

"Good news," I decided. Despite everything, the last few days had been pleasant and I was reluctant to ruin that, even if I could only hold onto it for a few minutes longer.

"I found your father."

My entire body tensed, my hand crushing the egg I'd been holding. The slimy yolk coated my fingers and dripped onto the floor. Cole wrapped his arm around my shoulders and kissed my temple.

That was the good news?

If that was my reaction, perhaps I needed to reconsider this whole find-my-father thing.

Xena grabbed the kitchen trash can, held it under my hand, and gently forced my fingers to let go of the egg shell. Cole handed me some paper towels.

My father.

I rarely thought about him because he was a non-issue in my life. But now, millions of thoughts ran through my mind.

Did he know about me? If he did, why didn't he contact me?

When I looked at his face, would I see a piece of me staring back?

Did he have his own family? Oh, shit—did I have siblings?

Butterflies flurried in my stomach at that last thought. I forced myself to put it out of my mind. Learning about my existence might not be a happy event for them. I'd cross that bridge when the time came. *If* the time came.

Breathe. Just breathe.

"And?" I prompted. "What did you learn?"

"Not much," she admitted. "If anyone in his family is a sensitive, they've kept it under wraps."

"But that's normal, right?" I said. "It's not like Shenice advertises her abilities."

"True." Xena didn't seem particularly convinced by my logic though, leading me to believe that finding my father wasn't going to answer any of my questions. Well, the supernatural ones, anyway.

"And that's it? That's all you learned?"

"I couldn't do too much digging without raising red flags. But I do have his address."

My throat and mouth went dry. "Where?" I choked out. "Where does he live?"

"Atlanta."

Irrationally, I wondered if he was into sports—if he was an Atlanta Braves or Falcons fan. Did he live in the south because he hated the cold? Maybe I got my disdain for snow from him. My mom had always wished for white Christmases.

Stupid. Dislike of snow isn't genetic.

Cole shook my shoulder to get my attention. *Are you okay?* he mouthed.

I let out a shaky breath and nodded. This news of my father was secondary to everything else we had to deal with.

"Tell me the bad news," I said.

"News of Xavier's death is getting around."

The hollowness in my stomach turned to numbness, spreading to my entire body. My heart started beating double-time and my adrenaline spiked.

His death wouldn't go unnoticed forever. I'd known this. Still, I wasn't ready to talk about it.

"What are people saying?"

"The rumor going around is that you killed him."

It's not a rumor.

I stared at her for a moment, stunned. But I guessed it wasn't too difficult to put the pieces together. Anyone who'd heard about how my mom died would realize I had strong motive.

Except, if other angels knew about how my mom died—knew Xavier killed her—then why hadn't they done anything about it? Was Xavier just supposed to be allowed to get away with it?

"What else are they saying? Anything about him killing my mom?"

She shook her head. "I hate to say it, but humans die all the time. One human's death isn't going to rank high on their list of concerns."

Rage simmered behind my eyes, coming to a full-on boil in my veins. I wanted to punch something, kick something, shoot something. I ran my hands through my hair and clenched them, the pain on my scalp bringing the world back into focus, just a little.

But not enough.

With a scream, I hurled the bowl with the brownie mix onto the floor. It cracked, sending brown batter streaking onto the white cabinets.

"I'm sorry," Xena said quietly. "I shouldn't have been so tactless."

Cole shot her a dirty look and wrapped his arms around me. I closed my eyes for a moment, losing myself in the warmth and comfort of his embrace.

Lock it away, Ava.

When I opened my eyes, my vision was clear. I pulled away from Cole and crossed my arms. It wasn't to dismiss him—if I indulged in his comfort for too long, it would break me. I needed to be strong and right now that meant shutting down all my emotions.

"It's fine." I cleared my throat and focused on taking the weakness out of my voice. "I'm fine."

"You know I loved your mother, right?" Xena said.

"Leave it alone." Cole's voice was barely audible and hoarse, like he'd spent the day chain smoking.

Xena looked at him, surprised to hear him speak. *That made two of us.*

When he tried to speak yesterday, his voice had sputtered out and he ended up in a coughing fit, so I suspected he lost his confidence. He hadn't uttered a sound since then.

"What did you hear about Xavier?"

"Police found him..." Xena winced. "Or what was left of him anyway. It wasn't much."

I looked away, not meeting either of their eyes. I'd been savage and I was having a hard enough time coming to terms with it myself. I didn't need to see the judgment on their faces. I had judgment enough for myself.

"The fire department showed up, but by the time they did there wasn't much they could do. It wasn't until the fire was completely out that they realized a person had been inside. Luckily his body was so destroyed there wasn't enough to positively ID him. Still an angel task force was sent to retrieve his body, just in case. Their response was a bit slow because nothing like this has ever happened before. There's no protocol."

Nope. No protocol for murdered fallen angels, especially ancient, powerful ones.

"How did they figure out it was me?"

"They questioned all the handlers who had been in the area and figured out you'd been nearby."

I punched my open hand with my fist. "Linda."

"No. Niles."

I gritted my teeth and blew out a breath between them, seething. He really was a good for nothing weasel. Though I couldn't blame this on him because all he did was tell the truth.

"What about Cole? Do they know he was there?" My breath caught in my chest, every second I waited for the answer agonizing.

"No. They just suspect you."

I exhaled. That was something at least. Though I was grateful to have had him there, I wouldn't let him go down for this. It was all on me.

I opened my mouth to say so, but one look at Cole's face had me clamping it shut. Here I was again, about to make a choice for him. We'd gone right back to where we started, but I couldn't help it. My urge to protect him was so strong it was a knee-jerk reaction. I did it without thinking.

It was hard to be objective, but if I were honest I would have to assign some of the blame to Cole. Definitely not most of it—the bulk of it was all me—but he had been gung ho to take Xavier out, even more so than me at times.

I also needed to remember what I told Xena just the other day—that I didn't want to make any rash decisions. It was harder than I thought, but any decision I made right now would most likely be a stupid one because I didn't have all the facts. And honestly, what was I going to do right now? It wasn't like I could take out every fallen angel who'd heard rumors about me killing Xavier, nor would I want to. One murder was enough to last a lifetime.

CHAPTER 16

THE NEXT DAY XENA VENTURED out and came home with a slew of board games. I appreciated that she was trying to entertain herself, but I wasn't a fan of this particular form of entertainment because she made Cole and me play with her. And let me tell you—Xena was a sore loser. It kind of caught me off guard when she stormed off after I won The Game of Life. Kind of ironic really because I definitely was not winning at life these days.

Then when she realized how much luck was involved in Yahtzee she didn't even want to finish out the game, which was particularly annoying because we'd almost made it to the final few rounds of a Triple Yahtzee scorecard.

"What kind of a game is that if it doesn't require any skill?" she asked, her voice dripping with disdain. I wondered if she'd feel the same way if she were winning instead of Cole.

I shrugged. "It's kind of like gambling."

"I *never* gamble."

That didn't surprise me. Xena wasn't the type to play any game unless she thought she had a good chance of winning. Everything she did was carefully calculated.

She kicked our butts in Scrabble, but by that point, I wasn't trying too hard. It was easier to let her win. If nothing else, it was educational—I learned the ornamental end of a shoelace was called an aglet. Who knew? I sure as heck didn't. I didn't bother challenging any of her words after that. It wasn't worth seeing her gloat when she inevitably proved me wrong. Because really, would I ever learn? Xena was always right.

When she pulled out Twister, I was forced to call the gaming to a halt. It was either that or watch Cole strangle her on the bright polka dot game board.

"What are we doing?" I asked.

Xena stopped reading the game instructions printed on the inside of the box. "I get to spin this little thingy here and whatever color it lands on—"

"No," I said. "I'm not talking about the stupid game. What are we going to do?"

We were just about out of days on the beach house rental, so at the very least we'd have to find somewhere else to stay. Now that Cole was almost back to normal we weren't as worried about accommodations because we could stay in a hotel, but we couldn't stay in a hotel indefinitely. I didn't see a solution though. We couldn't stay on the run forever.

I was so tired.

I was tired of the lies, tired of the death, tired of this chess game I'd been wrapped up in my whole life, even though I hadn't even known for most of it. Part of my frustration was I didn't know my place. Was I the all-powerful queen? Or was I a weak pawn, the first line of defense and the first to be taken out—expendable.

I guessed that depended on who you asked.

"If I stay away much longer," Cole said, "Bill's going to have to hire someone to help him. He can't keep up with the work, and if he gets any farther behind it's going to damage the shop's reputation."

"But there's nothing to stop Linda from coming to find you. She could do this again and again," Xena said.

Cole balled up his fists. "I know."

I reached over and uncurled his fingers, lacing them through mine. It wasn't easy for Cole to admit weakness, but short of filling Linda with bullets every time she showed up, he had no defense against her—and the bullets thing would only work if he saw her first. I didn't want Bill's business to suffer either, but I didn't see a solution. We were stuck and completely at Linda's mercy.

"There are rules, right?" I asked Xena. "How can Linda be allowed to get away with this kind of thing?"

"Oh there are definitely rules, but there's no one to enforce them. I mean we're angels so we're kind of on the honor system."

I snorted, looking at her incredulously. Oh...she was serious.

"Have the higher angels or the people in charge or whoever even met some of these handlers? Putting people like Xavier and Linda on the honor system seems really shortsighted." That was putting it mildly. Idiotic was more accurate.

"I didn't say I agreed with it, but as long as handlers meet their numbers then they don't get involved." Xena leaned forward a little bit. "Angels are actually kind of lazy. Their whole purpose is to be a static source of good in the world, right? So that doesn't require much actual activity. And the angels who have been around the longest, meaning the ones in power, are the worst of all. Besides that, handlers are fallen angels, which means they're viewed as being less than angels still in heaven. The higher angels want as little interaction with them as possible."

"Let me get this straight," Cole said. "Handlers are fallen angels, which means they got kicked out of heaven. So being a handler is kind of like a punishment. They're using, for lack of a better term, *criminals* to make sure there's enough good in the world?"

Cole had an excellent point. I'd never thought about it that way. If it was so important to make sure good and evil were balanced by inducting new angels, then why did they give this task to those they deemed the lowest of their kind?

"Some of us choose to be fallen," Xena reminded us. "When I signed up for this job, I didn't fully realize what I was getting myself into. I just used it as a loophole to spend more time in the world. In case you hadn't noticed, I was young when I died and there are a lot of things I never got to experience."

Wow...that was the most she'd ever shared about her personal life. I really wanted to ask her how she died and who she was in life. I didn't even know what time she'd lived in and Xena most likely wasn't even her name when she was alive. I knew frighteningly little about her, but I'd never asked because frankly it wasn't my business. It still wasn't, so I kept my curiosity to myself.

"What should we do?" I asked. "I'm all out of ideas and a lot of my recent ones haven't been the greatest anyway."

"I..." Xena shook her head. "I don't know. Right now the best thing we can do is fly under the radar."

Cole pushed away from the table, his chair making a scraping sound against the linoleum. He stomped into the other room as I watched after him.

I couldn't help but wonder if maybe he finally saw my side of things, if maybe he was starting to understand why I'd tried to lead Linda away from him, if maybe he finally realized what had been at stake—his chance at a normal life. This wasn't an *I told you so* moment—well, okay, it kind of was. But I got no satisfaction from it. And I sure as heck wasn't going to say it to him.

"We need to find a new place to stay. The rental ends tomorrow, right?" I asked.

Xena nodded. "We should go somewhere else. Let's not stay in the same place too long, just in case."

I drummed my fingers on the tabletop, thinking about something that had plagued me since Xena came in with her news earlier this morning. She hadn't learned much about my father. If I wanted answers, I would have to ask the questions.

Our current predicament offered a perfect opportunity for a road trip. Atlanta would be as good a place as any.

I LAY AWAKE IN BED that night, my thoughts not letting me sleep. Beside me Cole lay still, but I could tell by his breathing he wasn't sleeping either, probably lost in his own thoughts. We hadn't spoken about our discussion with Xena on what we should do. It was frustrating beyond belief that not one of the three of us could come up with an acceptable course of action. I mean, we couldn't even come up with a bad decision. All of us were stuck.

Hiding.

I hated the principle of it. Why should we be forced to hide when we didn't ask for any of this? When we weren't the ones in the wrong.

In a way I should be grateful to this twisted system because I realized now that if higher angels had anything to do with it, human authorities would never learn of Xavier's existence.

Which meant police would never learn I'd killed him.

How would the world react if they knew angels were among us? More importantly, how would people react if they knew angels were responsible for the premature deaths of innocent people? I understood the need to balance good and evil in the world, but at what expense? Wasn't killing innocent people a form of evil? These were philosophical questions I did not have the brainpower to answer.

So instead I would worry about smaller problems— like how I planned to introduce myself to my father.

Sheesh...what did it say about my life that I considered this a small problem?

Now that I knew his location, I could probably find him online. Considering I was about to drive hundreds of miles to show up unannounced on his doorstep, it might be prudent to learn more about him. But I wasn't sure I wanted to. I didn't want to have any preconceived notions before meeting him. I had no idea if he knew he'd fathered a child. Since I'd been a seeker my whole life, I was good at reading people and I wanted to trust my instincts and first impressions without having them clouded by meaningless chatter on social media. I was hedging my bets on being able to tell if he knew about me when I met him.

Cole's fingertips danced across my shoulder.

"Are you thinking about your father?" he asked.

"Yeah," I said so softly into the darkness I didn't know if he'd heard me. Of course, he didn't need to ask the question. He already knew the answer.

He didn't say anything else, and I appreciated he didn't give me any false reassurances. Ninety-nine percent of the time when people said things like "I'm sure it'll be fine," there was no truth to the statement. No one could be sure of anything. It was one of those meaningless statements meant to provide comfort even though both the speaker and the listener knew it wasn't true.

"Do you think this is a mistake?" I asked.

He was silent for a moment, and I knew he was seriously considering the question. Once again I appreciated he didn't give me any knee-jerk assurances.

"I think you'll regret it if you don't do it," he said finally. "It might end up being a mistake, but you'll never know unless you try."

What he said was true. Before I hadn't really thought about my father because there was no point. Now that I knew his identity, I would always wonder, a deep kind of wonder that ate away at my gut, festering until it overtook me.

"What's the worst that can happen?" Cole said. "Let's say he denies he's your father or doesn't want anything to do with you. You're no worse off than you are now."

I couldn't say I agreed with that. There was a difference between your father not knowing you exist and his ignoring your existence.

No matter what happened, my self-identity would never be the same.

If nothing else, I would ask him about his medical history. There was a gaping black hole from that side of my family. At least I would know if I was more susceptible to get breast cancer or something like that. Although with my seeker healing abilities, I didn't really worry too much about illness.

I kissed Cole's neck and snuggled closer. It was well after midnight, and we planned to get an early start the next day. If I was ever going to get to sleep, I needed to stop thinking about this.

Fat chance.

COLE INSISTED ON DRIVING, WHICH turned into a power struggle between him and Xena. It was ridiculous with both of them nearly throwing temper tantrums in the driveway. It was way too early for such nonsense. I convinced Xena to let Cole drive and even let her ride shotgun, which left me riding by myself in the backseat of my own car. Wasn't that just some stuff.

I knew why Cole wanted to drive—he'd spent the last few days with no control and it was his way of taking some back. So I didn't give him a hard time about it. Xena, on the other hand, was another story. I didn't know what was up with her.

About an hour down the road, something occurred to me.

"Do you think we need to worry about Linda tracking us in my car?" I asked.

"I don't think she has any contacts in the police department."

"What about Reapers?"

The last time I'd gone on the run with Cole, Reapers had been after him and it hadn't taken them long to find him. Although I knew the handlers turned over the named souls to Reapers, I didn't have any direct interaction with them. I'd only seen them once—when Xavier killed Cole, they'd starting circling in to claim his soul before Areli scared them away. But now, I couldn't help but compare this trip to that one, which made me think of them.

Of course there was one huge difference, and she was sitting in the front seat where I should be.

"It shouldn't be a problem," Xena said. "Reapers only come into play when there's a soul on the line."

On the line...like humans were fish, ready to be caught and gutted.

As we neared Rocky Mount, Cole and Xena bickered about which route we should take. Cole wanted to take 95 while Xena wanted to take 40. I couldn't care less—both ways would get us there in the same amount of time, so what did it matter? I tuned them out and dialed Claire's number, both because I hadn't spoken to her in a while and I wanted to make myself unavailable in case Cole and Xena wanted to use me as a tie-breaker. Those two were beyond ridiculous. This was a stressful situation, but they were expending energy on pointless things. I supposed it helped them let off steam. Or something.

After five rings, my call went to Claire's voicemail and I hung up. I didn't want to leave the details about what had happened in a message.

We took the exit toward 95 and Xena sulked in the front seat. What did she expect? Cole was driving, so of course he was going to go the way he wanted.

I yawned. Normally I passed out on road trips if I wasn't the one driving, but even though I was exhausted, I couldn't sleep. I balled up a sweatshirt and put in under my head, then put earbuds in my ears. I scrolled through the app store on my phone, looking for a meditation app. I could use some zen in my life.

The car slowed to a halt and Cole groaned.

"See?" Xena cried, way too gleeful about being stuck in traffic. "I *told* you 40 would have been better."

He glared at her and I rolled my eyes, turning my attention back to my phone. I gave up on the meditation idea and turned on some music instead. There was no way I could achieve inner peace with those two around.

Fifteen minutes later, we'd probably only gone about a quarter mile, if that. I was horrible at estimating distances. Though Cole and Xena weren't talking, the bad blood in the air was so thick I could almost taste it.

"Why don't we stop and eat?" I suggested. It was almost eleven, so a little early for lunch, but we might as well take a break now. Maybe traffic would ease up by the time we were ready to get moving again.

It took another fifteen minutes to creep up to the next exit, which luckily had a few restaurants and gas stations.

"Let's go there." I pointed at a Chick-fil-A on the left side of the road. I didn't have a strong preference for where we ate, but I did have a preference for keeping the peace.

"Pure aura, my ass," Cole muttered as he slammed his door. Xena had gone ahead of us into the building.

"Hey," I said, wrapping my arms around his neck. "What gives?"

He rested his forehead against mine. "She's pushing all my buttons on purpose, I swear."

"Maybe. We need to remember this situation is probably just as stressful for her as it is for us. She's risking a lot, too."

"Yeah, I know." He sighed. "It's just hard to believe she can be such a pain in the ass and still have a pure...*shit*."

"What?"

"Before Linda took away my sight, I checked out her aura. It wasn't white."

"What did it look like?"

"It was weird. It had that same metallic white sheen I've seen with other fallen angels, but it had cracks in it."

"What color were the cracks?" I could take a guess.

"Red and black."

I was right—red for anger and black for evil.

"I can't believe I didn't think of this when Xena was talking about angel's goodness being static."

I also couldn't believe he waited until now to say something. I didn't know what this meant, but my gut told me it was significant.

"You've had some other things going on," I said. "What do you think it means?"

"I don't know. Damn. I really wish I'd looked at Xavier's aura now."

I didn't say anything because I agreed with him and I'd previously expressed that, so no need to make him feel worse. It wasn't like he could go back in time and take a peek.

"Are you two lovebirds coming or what?" Xena yelled from the door, causing the people in the parking lot to look at us.

Damn it, Xena! We should be keeping a low profile, but besides that, it was just embarrassing.

She grinned at us and ducked inside, leaving me shaking my head. I supposed there were worse things than being called out in a parking lot for cuddling with Cole.

CHAPTER 17

I PICKED AT MY WAFFLE fries, which I normally loved. This time, it wasn't my lack of appetite that was the problem. I'd pretty much recovered that. No, I was too distracted. I felt like I was missing something huge concerning Linda's aura. I wanted to ask Xena about it, but I didn't want to discuss it in the crowded Chick-fil-A. Besides that, her mood had turned surprisingly good, and I didn't want to ruin it. Perhaps she'd just been hangry before.

When we returned to the car, she *graciously* let me sit up front in my own car. *Insert eye roll here.* She lay across the backseat, not bothering to buckle up. I guessed she wasn't worried about getting hurt if we were in an accident.

We eased back onto the interstate. Traffic was still backed up, but at least it was moving now. I chewed on my cuticle and stared at Xena, who had her eyes closed. Her breathing was even, so I watched her for a few more minutes to make sure she was asleep.

"Cole," I whispered. "When did you last look at Xena's aura? Can you take a look at it now?"

He gave me the side-eye. "I'm driving. Do you really want me to turn around in this traffic?"

I considered. We were already behind schedule, but I was desperate to have a point of comparison for Linda's aura. If Linda's evil activities were reflected in her aura, then perhaps Xena's benevolent ones were reflected in hers. I could wait until we needed to stop again, but it was eating away at me.

"Can you pull off for just a minute then?"

Cole looked in the rearview, preparing to do as I asked when Xena sat straight up.

"What the hell?" she asked, her good mood gone. "Why do you want him to look at my aura? I'll save you some time. It's pure." She seemed insulted.

Cole trained his eyes back on the road and turned off the blinker, seeming perfectly happy to let me handle this one. *Thanks, babe.*

"We know that," I said and Xena scowled, realizing Cole must have looked at her aura before. I was off to a great start. "Linda's isn't white."

She shook her head. "Impossible. That's the whole point of angels."

"Are you sure fallen angels have pure auras?" I asked.

"Yes," she said emphatically. "Even though the angels are fallen, they're still pure."

"But how can that be?" I pressed. "If they're being punished for something, then wouldn't that mean they'd done a bad thing?"

Xena blew out a breath. "For the millionth time, not all fallen angels are being punished."

Now it was my turn to get annoyed. "Stop getting caught up in the technicalities. You know what I'm asking."

"Fine," she said. "In some cases, yes, they've done something that required punishment, but auras don't change once a soul is converted into an angel. They just don't."

Now I knew how the early explorers felt when they were trying to convince the masses the world wasn't flat.

"Cole has no limits, remember?" I said. "He looked at Linda's aura and it wasn't pure."

"He had to have seen it wrong. She was torturing him."

"No," Cole interjected. "I saw it right. I looked before all that started."

"Impossible."

"You keep saying that," I said, "but obviously it *is* possible because Cole saw it."

"He has to be wrong."

"Why is it so hard to believe Linda is no longer the embodiment of goodness? To be honest, it's easier to believe her aura is dark rather than it being pure."

"I just can't...that goes against everything the system works for." Xena seemed at a loss. She didn't agree with everything about the system, but I could see now she believed what she'd been told about it.

"Do you know any fallen angels who might be nearby? Ones who might be like Linda?"

"I try to stay away from those sorts," Xena said. "To be honest, I try to stay away from all sorts of fallen angels. They can be kind of..." She trailed off, as if realizing she had helped prove my point. "Let me see what I can come up with."

She worked on her phone, talking quietly to herself. After a few minutes, she looked up. "Okay. There's a handler and another fallen angel in Charleston."

"South Carolina?" I asked.

She nodded. "They're the closest."

"Can you set up a meeting?" I said. "Somewhere public where Cole can hide and check them out."

She got to work on her phone again and several long minutes passed before she spoke again. "Tomorrow. God, I hope you're wrong."

The thing was I knew I wasn't.

WE MADE IT TO CHARLESTON that night. Xena splurged and got us separate hotel rooms. She might be giving Cole and me a hard time, but I could tell by the gleam in her eye she was happy we were back on good terms. She skipped off to her own room, calling behind her that she'd see us for lunch tomorrow, which was when she had set up the meeting with the other fallen angels.

"Are you okay with waiting longer to meet your father?" Cole asked as he slid the key card into the room lock. He held open the door for me.

"It's been eighteen years. What's one more day?"

"You just seem eager to get it over with."

I took a moment to reflect on his word choice. "Get it over with" was pretty accurate because I wasn't really looking forward to it. Every time I thought about it my stomach knotted itself like a pretzel.

"This is more important anyway." I sank down onto the bed and Cole leaned against the dresser, shoving his hands in his pockets. "I wish we could see some other seekers to check out their auras, too."

Other than Chase and Claire, I'd only seen three other seekers. The most recent was the man at the restaurant. The first was Reggie, a mean old man who worked at the Eagles stadium, but he was outside my age bracket, so I hadn't looked at his aura. The other was Chase's friend Lance, who was close enough to my age that I'd been able to see his aura. It had been dark—nearly black. At the time that had surprised me because for the minute I'd seen him chat with Chase, I wouldn't have pegged him to have a dark aura, and I was usually right about these things. He was probably twenty-three or twenty-four, which would be at the far end of the age range I could see auras for. That meant if the handlers had followed the rules and made him a seeker at the earliest, he had only been seeking for five or six years. It unsettled me—a lot of damage could be done to a soul in that amount of time.

But all of this was just theorizing. I didn't have enough information yet. However, I had some educated guesses. For instance, my mom and I hadn't known any other seekers. We were also the only seekers who could see other seekers' auras. Had they kept us separated on purpose? Would other seekers even care that they were damning their souls? After all, becoming a seeker was a choice they'd made.

I was so lost in thought I didn't notice Cole studying me at first, his expression contemplative.

"What?" I asked, suddenly self-conscious. I tucked a stray strand of hair behind my ear. When Xena had gone out to get stuff that first day at the beach rental, she'd bought me clothes, but she'd gotten a lot of the sizes wrong, so the shirt and shorts I wore were ill-fitting. Miraculously, the clothes she picked out for Cole fit him perfectly. Even if they hadn't, he would still look good. His toned body, capable hands, and soulful features transcended anything he might wear. I didn't have that gift, which meant I was a hot mess.

So what else is new?

"Should we talk?" He winced when he said it, bringing a smile to my face. I hated that his discomfort brought me pleasure, but what could I say? I was petty like that.

More than that, though, I was giddy beyond reason that we'd gotten to the point I could laugh about things like that again. We hadn't had "the talk" that Cole was trying to instigate, but nevertheless, things simply felt *right* between us again. That was worth more than any words we could exchange.

"About what?" I didn't know how I managed to keep a straight face except my desire to make him squirm was bigger than my need to laugh.

Exhaling slowly, he cracked his knuckles. "I'm sorry."

Any humor I'd seen in the situation got sucked away.

He looked into my eyes and I fell into his, the warm darkness of them swallowing me whole. I gulped and my belly fluttered, my insides feeling like they were flying down a steep hill on a roller coaster. *Weightless.*

"I know."

Kneeling in front of me, he took my hands in his, kissing each palm. "I said some horrible things to you, but you still came when I needed you."

"I always will. That's what you do for someone you love."

"I've never had that in my life. I don't deserve it."

"Cole—"

"No, let me finish. I thought you were it, I could finally count on someone and then you left. That was all I could see. But I get it now. I understand why you left. You left because you loved me, not because you didn't love me enough."

"That's exactly it," I said. "I didn't realize you would think my leaving meant I didn't love you. It was exactly the opposite. But I should have talked to you about it. I shouldn't have decided to try to hide you from Linda without you having some say in it."

He laughed wryly. "We see how well not hiding from Linda went."

"True," I agreed, somewhat reluctantly, not wanting him to feel even worse about not being able to hold his own against her. "But I should know better than anyone not to make life decisions for people."

"Then let's make our choice right now—that we'll always choose each other."

I closed my eyes, letting his words wash over and through me, taking hold in my heart. But I couldn't agree just yet. I had to know something first.

"After the ordeal with Xavier, you said you don't see me the same way anymore." I opened my eyes so I could watch his reaction. "Is that still true?"

Out of everything that had happened between us, that had hurt the worst. Bringing it up now stung, making me realize I hadn't moved past it.

"In a way. I see you being ruthless enough to do whatever it takes to protect people. I see you as being willing to risk yourself for the good of others. I see you as being stronger than I ever imagined."

"I killed him," I stated bluntly. "In cold blood. I staked him to the cot and lit him on fire. I burned him alive."

The words sounded robotic coming out of my mouth, but I wanted—*needed*—Cole to understand. If he didn't know the truth, then his words meant nothing.

To his credit, he hadn't even flinched at the description of my horrible deed. But he did take his time in responding, so long I thought he never would. With a sob, I turned away, trying to jerk my hands away from him, but he held them firm.

"You shouldn't feel guilty." He moved one hand to my cheek, forcing eye contact. "Yes, it was brutal, but you figured out a way to end his pain. Who knows how many more days he would have suffered if you hadn't done what you did? There was only one way that ordeal was going to end—with Xavier dead. I'm just sorry you had to be the one to do it."

A shaky breath escaped my lungs, and I fought to keep my hands from quivering. Cole's words lifted some of the heaviness I'd been carrying around. I didn't know if I'd ever forgive myself completely, but it helped that he understood.

He pressed his lips to mine in a kiss so soft and gentle I could feel every curve and outline of his lips. "Thank you for not giving up on me."

CHAPTER 18

WE HUNG OUT IN THE hotel room the next morning until eleven, which gave us an hour to scope out the restaurant before Xena had to meet the others.

She drove. Cole put up no argument and I sent up a silent prayer of thanks. Their squabbling was enough to spur a migraine. And I'd never had one in my life, so that was saying something.

"Tell us about these people," I said, wanting to be prepared. Cole sat in the back, so I turned in my seat to include him in the conversation.

"Brian is the handler. He was thirty-three, maybe thirty-four when he died. Noel is his wife. She's a few years younger, I think. They died together in a car accident—a semi ran a red-light and t-boned their car."

"That's horrible." I shuddered and grimaced as an image automatically filled my mind. It brought back the painful memory of when the Reapers used a car accident to kill a woman whose name my mom had submitted. She'd been forced to turn in the name because I'd tried to thwart Xavier and failed—she'd done it for my sake, and it was the first time I'd seen how much being a seeker weighed on her.

The woman's death was just one of many that marred my conscience.

"Death usually is," Xena mused. "Unless a person is elderly and ready to die. Or in pain. Then it's a blessing. Anyway, Brian was selected to become a handler—and before you ask, no, I don't know why—and Noel got permission to stay with him. They've been on Earth for nearly twenty years."

"Is that a long time?" It was longer than I'd been alive, but time was relative to angels, who existed forever. Or so I assumed.

"Not really."

"What makes them sketchy?" Cole asked, bringing up the reason Xena had arranged to meet these particular fallen angels.

"When they were alive, Brian was in a band and for a little while, they both got caught up in drugs that were prevalent in the music scene. Mostly heroin. Then Noel's family did an intervention and they both straightened up. The band had broken up by then, which made it easier, and they died shortly after. Now that they're back on Earth, they've fallen back into their old ways."

"Doing drugs, you mean?" I frowned. "How would that even work? I would think their angel bodies would reject anything harmful."

"It takes a *lot* of drugs to get them high and even then, the high doesn't last very long. The rumor is they have connections with big time dealers in Mexico, and they've started dealing to pay for their habit."

"What kind of drugs?" Cole asked.

"A better question would be what kind of drugs *don't* they use. I hinted I might be looking for a fix, which is why they agreed to meet me."

"Is it dangerous?" I asked, trying to keep a neutral tone, even though the thought of Xena putting herself at risk freaked me out. It would just piss her off if she thought I was doubting her ability to handle the situation.

"I'm not worried. I can get out of there super quick if I need to."

Right—Xena and her freaky warping ability.

We found parking a few blocks away from the pizza joint where they were meeting. We totally lucked out with this restaurant since there was a park with a farmer's market right across the street. Cole and I could wait there without drawing too much attention to ourselves.

Xena stood on the sidewalk in front of the restaurant a full twenty minutes early, but we wanted to make sure she met them outside where we could see them. She was going to try to keep them outside as long as she could to make sure Cole had enough time. It would have been better if there was outside seating, but this should work.

We settled in behind a cluster of trees and the smell of pizza sauce, garlic, and cheese wafted across the street. Cole's stomach growled so loudly I worried it was eating itself.

"Do we need to get you a snack?" I looked pointedly at his belly. I could actually have gone for one myself.

Though the hotel was nice, the continental breakfast had been a little lacking, especially by the time we finally got out of bed.

"No, I'll be fine." Cole's voice was filled with longing.

I sympathized as I breathed in the yummy air. "This is a little unfair," I said. "Xena gets to eat and we get to commune with nature." I slapped at a bug that landed on my arm.

Cole looked around, focusing on a passing car that left behind exhaust fumes in its wake. "This isn't exactly nature."

"No, but you know what I mean."

"Did you notice we passed a college on the way here?" Cole asked.

I had noticed—The College of Charleston. But I ignored his question, not wanting to open that old can of worms. Here we were hiding from handlers, and he wanted me to think about enrolling in school? *Umm...yeah...*

"Ava?" he prompted.

"Yeah?"

"Did you see the college?"

I sighed. "Yeah, I saw it."

He looked at me like he wanted to say a lot more, but his mouth stayed shut. Perhaps I wasn't the only one who'd gotten smarter.

I crossed my arms and leaned against a tree, peering around to look at the sidewalk where Xena was waiting.

Shit. They were early!

I grabbed Cole's arm and squeezed. "Look."

Brian and Noel looked like any normal couple, holding hands as they approached Xena. He was tall, easily several inches over six feet. She was a head shorter than him, but given his height, that still made her taller than the average woman. He was good-looking in an edgy, hipster way, making it easy to imagine him fronting a band. She was attractive in a well put together way, making me think she probably knew all the rules of social etiquette, like which forks to use for each dish in a seven course meal.

I squinted, trying to see their faces better, searching for any signs of drug use, but they both looked perfectly healthy—clear skin, bright eyes, easy smiles. They also looked trim and in shape, like they ran 5k's for fun.

I almost laughed out loud about my previous worry of sending Xena into a dangerous situation. These two were more suited for brunch with the grandparents than making deals in dark alleys.

But I knew Xena and if she said they were drug dealers, then they were, which meant their auras had to be dark, right? Except I wasn't getting that vibe from them at all. Either I was losing my touch or they hid their true nature very well. I didn't know which one was worse.

Brian pulled out a pack of cigarettes and offered one to Xena before lighting up. Okay, so he was a smoker. If Xena hadn't already told me what he was like, I would have been surprised to see even that vice. Despite his edgy rocker look, he shared his wife's wholesome vibe.

I looked back at Cole, who was deep in concentration, staring at them. Not wanting to interrupt, I stayed quiet, but I was dying to ask what he saw.

Xena chatted with them for a few minutes outside while Brian finished smoking. Then he put the butt in the ash tray on the top of a nearby trashcan like the good citizen he appeared to be. Damn, if they really were drug dealers, they must make a killing. Everything about these two screamed *trust me!*

"What did you see?" I asked Cole as soon as they'd disappeared inside.

"Cracks in their auras," Cole said grimly. "Loads of black coming through. Hers is worse than his."

I wouldn't have guessed that at all. While they were innocent looking, he stood out a little more in contrast to her soccer-mom-esque appearance—light brown hair clipped to the side in a barrette, modest khaki capri pants and a button-up blouse, and light, natural make-up. Her attire and demeanor suggested wallflower, making me assume he was the dominant one. The fact that she gave no outward sign of how much evil her aura possessed was unsettling.

"Let's get out of here," I said.

We drove to a local Wendy's and went through the drive-thru, preferring to eat in the car rather than risk being seen. Xena hadn't mentioned any other fallen angels or handlers in the area, but erring on the side of caution was our standard M.O. these days. Also, this way we could talk without being overheard while we waited for Xena to text us she was ready to be picked up.

"Were their auras worse than Linda's aura?" I asked, picking at my fries.

"Define worse," Cole said. "Linda's had a mix of colors shining through, but these mostly had darkness."

"How much white was left?"

"Not much. You know how Xena's aura looks metallic?"

I stared at him blankly because no, I didn't know. He was the only one who could see it.

"Sorry," he said, realizing his mistake. "Anyway, it almost seems like the white in their auras is being eaten away by the black. Like corrosion or something."

"I wonder if anyone knows about this," I said. "Xena seemed shocked, but she's already admitted she doesn't know everything."

"Someone has to know, right?" Cole shook his head. "I can't believe I'm the first one who can see their auras. Wouldn't they want to be able to check up on this sort of thing?"

"You would think so, but I think there's a fair amount of ego involved. Think about Xena and how self-assured she is. Now multiply that by about a million. They don't expect anything to go wrong, just like they don't expect any of their handlers to misbehave. It's not on their radar."

"Morons," Cole muttered.

I shrugged. "Supposedly, angels have left their humanity behind, which means they've shed all the associated negative qualities."

For as much as these angels claimed to be acting for the good of humanity, they seemed to have a low opinion of people. So why did they bother? In a way, I understood it. People could be jerks. But most of the atrocities in my life were caused by fallen angels rather than people. Humanity didn't have a monopoly on being sleazebuckets.

My phone buzzed. It was Xena.

Get back here!!! Seeker!!!

"Shit," I said, reaching to take Cole's food out of his hands so he could drive. He gave me a wounded look, like I'd run over his kitten. I didn't roll my eyes, but only because there wasn't time. "Drive. There's a seeker at the restaurant. We need to go back."

He didn't hesitate, getting us back to the parking lot by the restaurant in less than ten minutes. We ran to the park across the street, taking refuge behind the same tree. A bug landed on me and I slapped it away. *Damn. Guess he isn't too happy I killed his friend earlier.* Stupid bugs.

"Now what?" Cole asked.

I looked at my phone again, but there were no new texts. "We wait, I guess."

Forty minutes later, we were still waiting—and sweating in the heat—making me think we'd somehow missed them. Xena hadn't texted again, though. I was just about ready to give up when she walked out the front door, followed by Brian, Noel, and a woman who looked to be in her thirties and was dressed similarly to Noel. She must be the seeker, but damn, I wouldn't have suspected her to be one to agree to being a seeker. She looked like a pre-school teacher, but I'd been completely wrong about Brian and Noel, so what did I know? *Too much judging books by their covers.* I wondered if this seeker was also involved in the drug distribution or if they had a strictly handler-seeker relationship.

"What do you see?" I asked Cole.

"Her aura is dark. Nearly all black."

It was what I expected, but not what I'd hoped. Dread, unease, and all kinds of other unpleasant feelings crept into my consciousness, giving me goose bumps despite the heat.

"Come on," I said. "We've seen enough."

NOT WANTING TO APPEAR SUSPICIOUS by hanging out in the car, Cole and I went back to the hotel around three, having nowhere else to go. Around dinner time, I started getting worried. Now that it was past eleven, I was frantic. Xena had said she'd be okay, but what if she wasn't?

We shouldn't have left her without backup. My common sense kicked in and insisted we wouldn't be much help in a fight against drug dealing fallen angels, but my worry silenced it. We should have stayed.

Cole lounged on the bed wearing nothing but his shorts. Normally, I'd be having a drool fest over his bare chest, but the worry gnawed at my insides.

"She's fine," he said, flipping through the channels on the TV.

"Then why hasn't she texted?" I asked.

"I don't know, but she's with her own kind. They won't hurt her."

"Oh, yeah?" I shot back. "I wonder if Linda thought the same thing as Xena continued to shoot her."

Concern flitted across Cole's face for a moment, then he shook his head. "She's fine. They have no reason to suspect her."

"We don't know that!"

Sitting up, Cole tossed aside the remote and held open his arms. "Come here."

I sank into his lap, resting my head in my hands. I was a spastic head case, but I couldn't help it. I'd already lost so much. And I was just so, so tired of it all.

"Xena can take care of herself." He smoothed back my hair. "You're stressed."

"I am," I admitted. "But I'm legitimately worried about her. She's not invincible. She can die."

Cole sighed. "Nothing I can say will ease your mind, will it?"

I shook my head.

"If I thought she was in trouble, I'd do something about it. I wouldn't just lie here watching TV. You know that, right?"

A knock sounded at the door, causing me to jump and knock my head against Cole's chin.

"Ow!" He rubbed his mouth, his fingers coming away bloody. When my head collided with his chin, he must have bit his lip.

"Sorry," I said, rushing to the door. Despite his injury, he made it there the same time I did and placed his hand firmly on the door so I couldn't fling it open like I wanted to.

"Slow down. Let me check it out first."

Right—err on the side of caution.

Impatiently, I let him peer through the peep hole, but if it was a threat, there wouldn't have been a knock. He was right to be cautious, but my gut told me it was Xena. And my heart was dying to see she was in one piece.

Cole opened the door and she strolled in, looking no worse for wear.

She took one look at his bloody lip and her eyebrows shot up. "Lovers' spat? Did you beat him up?"

"No," I said angrily. "But I might beat you up. Why didn't you text me?"

I hadn't texted her in case her phone was out and Brian and Noel saw it and figured out Xena was working with me. I didn't want my anxiety over her safety to be the thing that put her in danger.

"I didn't realize how late it had gotten. I caught an Uber so you guys didn't have to come out." She sounded miffed, like she was upset we hadn't appreciated that favor.

"Unacceptable," I barked at her. "I was worried sick."

"Okay, *Mom.*"

Glaring at her, I crossed my arms.

So maybe I was overreacting just a little, but would it have killed her to text? Now that I saw she was fine, I realized I was indeed acting like an overprotective parent, but dang it, that was a hazardous situation. She had been with dangerous drug dealers, not little old church ladies, even if Noel did kind of look like one.

"You should have texted," Cole chimed in and I shot Xena a smug look. *Two against one.*

"Fine," she said. "I'm sorry. I really did lose track of time. I got caught up trying to figure out what their deal is."

"And what is it?" Cole asked.

Xena sat in the only chair in the room, leaving Cole and me to sit on the bed.

"They're definitely dealing drugs, but more than that, they're manufacturing them."

"What kind?"

"Meth."

I didn't see that one coming. I pictured Noel in a frilly apron, standing over tubes and beakers and measuring stuff. I honestly had no idea what went into making meth, other than Sudafed, which was why you had to practically sign your name in blood to get some at the pharmacy.

"They have a lab in their basement," Xena continued. "It's a fairly extensive operation. I'm surprised they took me down there. They're awfully trusting for a pair of drug dealers."

"They probably assume you're like them," I said. "All the handlers I know are shady, so why would they assume you're any different?"

She shook her head. "Brian and Noel are idiots. It's a miracle they haven't been caught by the police yet. Most handlers are more savvy than that."

"More savvy meaning they know how to cover things up?"

"Yes," she said begrudgingly and I could almost read her thoughts. Xena did a lot of things that weren't sanctioned, so she was a master of covering her tracks. The difference between her and handlers like Xavier, Linda, and Brian was she wasn't a sadistic psychopath who hurt everyone in her path. Though she gave off an air of indifference, she actually cared about people. The others only cared about themselves.

"Their auras were dark," Cole said.

Xena swore. "And the seeker?"

"Black."

Xena let out a shaky breath, and I tried to remember a time I'd seen her so rattled. She gravely looked into Cole's eyes. "I need you to do something for me."

I knew what she was going to ask, and I could tell it pained her. While Xena had been perfectly accepting of the fact Xavier and Linda were bad, she'd resisted the notion their auras reflected that. Now I could see she was terrified of learning her aura might not be pure.

"Can you look at my aura?"

"It's white," he said automatically.

"Cole," she said, her tone deadly serious. "I want you to look right now. I need to know it hasn't changed."

Cole nodded and closed his eyes for a moment. When he opened them, he focused his attention on Xena. It only took a second for him to raise his guards again.

"Pure."

She put a hand to her chest, sinking down in relief. "Thank God."

We gave her a moment to compose herself. I was glad her pure soul was intact, both for her sake and that of humanity. It gave me hope.

"What are you going to do?" Cole asked, seeming to understand this wasn't something she could just walk away from.

"Nothing right now." Her mouth twisted in distaste. "If the cops suddenly show up on their doorstep, they'll know it was me."

"How many more handlers do you think are like them? Or Linda. Or Xavier..." I trailed off. It was a sick situation when aside from Xena, Niles was actually the most upstanding of the handlers I'd had the pleasure to meet.

"I hate to say it but I don't think this ends here. There's a lot more corruption than I realized."

"How much did you think there was?" Cole asked. It was a fair question I would have liked to know the answer to as well.

Xena pursed her lips. "I don't know for sure. Anyway, I've known about Xavier for a while, but I only recently learned about Linda, Brian, and Noel. Like I said, I try to stay away from most handlers." She paused. "People, too, really."

No shock there. Xena personified the loner mentality. It was boggling she cared so much about me and Cole. Perhaps we'd grown on her. Like a fungus.

"If you knew about Xavier, why didn't you tell the higher angels?" I asked, feeling angry. If Xavier had been taken care of before, it would have saved me a lot of heartache. And maybe my mom would still be alive.

"Xavier is somewhat of a legend among handlers. He's the oldest one, and it's well known not to cross him."

"You did," Cole said.

Xena shrugged. "I've never been one to conform. But even still, it took me a while to get up the courage, especially considering my...*relation* to him."

I'd done my best to forget about Xena being related to Xavier. So had she, I suspected, so it surprised me she brought it up now.

"Okay, I get that about Xavier," I said. "But what about Brian and Noel? It wasn't hard for you to learn about them. So why hasn't anyone turned them in?"

"Even if they were reported, the higher angels don't like to get involved. And as long as Brian fulfills his handler duties, meaning his seekers give him names, then they wouldn't see a reason to check up on him."

Something about that explanation was off. I didn't doubt it was true, but we were missing something.

"You can't be the only ethical handler," I muttered.

Ethical handler...the phrase was laughable.

An inkling of an idea that had been floundering in the edges of my brain suddenly solidified. "That's it," I breathed. I couldn't believe we hadn't put it together until now.

"What?" Cole asked.

"They don't want you because you can see all human auras," I explained slowly. "They want you because you can expose them."

CHAPTER 19

COLE AND XENA STARED AT me, dumbfounded.

"It makes sense," I said. "We all agree the 'no limits' thing with regard to human auras is no big deal. So it's got to be the other part that's important. The handlers don't want to use Cole's abilities. They want to make sure he *doesn't* use them."

Fear clutched at my heart, weaving itself into my veins and flowing to every inch of my body. Memories of being on the run from Reapers and watching Cole bleed out in front of me filled my mind. That was bad. And that was just when one crooked handler was involved. Now several of them were after him. It was about to get much worse.

The fear must have shown on my face because Cole wrapped his arm around me. "Linda could have killed me if she wanted to, but she didn't."

"She might not be the one in charge," I said. And like Xena, she seemed to do whatever the hell she wanted rather than follow orders. So did that mean she was acting alone or was she in league with others?

"Or she might have wanted to have fun with him first," Xena said grimly, and Cole shot her a nasty look as I gasped.

"That's not helping," Cole said angrily.

"It does us no good to sugar coat things. Xavier killed Ava's mom. She knows what handlers are capable of."

"Xena's right," I said, feeling sick. Cole might be the seeker with no limits, but there were no limits to the pain and destruction handlers would cause to get what they wanted.

"There's just one problem with your theory. I got the order from higher up to look for Cole," Xena said. "If they want him so he can keep their secret...then they're in on it...and we're all screwed."

"Nothing else makes sense," I said. I didn't like it any more than she did.

Xena stood and paced. "Do you know what it means if the higher angels are corrupt?"

"Do you?" Cole asked pointedly.

Xena paused, her breaths shaky. "No. I don't. But it scares me."

Shit. The fact that Xena admitted she was scared combined with her tormented expression terrified me. Even Cole looked alarmed.

Panic filled my chest like an inflating balloon.

We're so screwed. How can this—

No, I told myself. *Keep calm. Think rationally.*

I took one deep breath and then another, willing myself to be calm.

"Did the search for Cole ever get formally reassigned?" I asked.

Xena shook her head. Optimism crept in, popping the inflating balloon of panic.

"Then maybe the higher angels were simply curious. Maybe they aren't part of a conspiracy."

"It's not like we can ask them," Cole said.

"Maybe we can," I said then turned to Xena. "Can you request a meeting with them to tell them about everything we've learned?"

She looked doubtful. "I can try, but they don't generally take meetings with fallen angels. Or anyone else."

"It's worth a shot," I said. "Because like you said, if they're in on it, then we're all screwed anyway. So we might as well try."

"I don't know if I agree with that logic," Cole said. He was never one to trust authority, anyway. "I want to know if they know what Xavier and Linda have been up to. Even if they aren't part of a cover-up, if they know and don't do anything, then they're still part of the problem."

"Yeah, but that's a much different problem," I said. "Incompetence is different than evil."

Xena's gaze shifted to me. "Is it?"

In Xena's eyes, the two were probably indistinguishable. She had ridiculously high standards and expectations, which was why I didn't understand how she could tolerate the system she was entrenched in. Then again, she was like me—stuck.

"What are we going to do?" Cole asked.

"Right now?" Xena asked, the authoritative tone back in her voice, which was strangely welcome. I guessed she'd recovered from her shock. "Stay the course and go see Ava's father."

"Are you sure—"

Xena cut me off. "Yes. We need to stay hidden while we figure this out. We can do that in Atlanta just as easily as in Charleston."

It was really happening—I was going to meet my father. No more delays, no more detours.

No excuses.

Great.

As I walked up to the house with the bright red sign touting *Homes from the low 300s*, I forced myself to concentrate on placing one foot in front of the other. It was harder than you would think, considering my entire body was shaking.

My father worked for the real estate company in charge of this development, manning the model home. Basically, his job was to sit on his butt and wait for potential buyers to come in. It had been ridiculously easy to find him, but of course he hadn't been hiding.

Sweat covered my palms and I anxiously rubbed them on my shorts. I hated to say it, but this was more nerve-racking than when I'd gone to the farmhouse to deal with Xavier. Though I hadn't had all the details about what was going to happen in that situation, I had been ready to do whatever it took to protect the world from his evil. And let's face it—I'd wanted him out of my life as well.

Now, though, I had no idea what to expect. Would he welcome me? Or would I ruin his day? Which would I prefer? I couldn't shake the feeling I was betraying my mom, but that was ridiculous. I'd told her I was doing this and besides that, I had every right to meet my father.

I looked back at where Cole was waiting in the parked car. He gave me an encouraging smile and I tried to return the gesture, but I feared it came out more like a grimace.

I hesitated on the porch, not sure if I should knock or just walk right in. Since a sign in the front yard said *Model Open*, I decided against knocking. This was kind of like going into a store, right? I wouldn't knock before walking into Target, so I guessed I shouldn't now. But what did I know? My mom and I had never shopped for a house.

Upon entering, I was greeted with the scent of baking apple pie, except I could tell it was a candle or scented plug-in and not the real thing. The trouble was this apple pie had cinnamon in it, the scent of which set my already fried nerves even more on edge.

The first floor had an open floor plan, with the kitchen, dining room, and living room sharing a space. The dining area was furnished and on the table were all kinds of brochures about the development and the various housing options. The living room was empty except for a large wooden desk with two empty chairs sitting in front of it.

Behind that desk sat my father.

The first word that came to mind when I saw him was salesman, and I was talking the kind of salesman that went door-to-door and gave that profession a dirty name. He was attractive enough, with light brown hair like my mother had said, but having spent a fair amount of time in Shenice's shop, I could spot a bad dye job when I saw one. His blue eyes were squinty as he smiled at me, like he was in need of glasses but too vain to wear them.

He stood, revealing his attire of khaki pants and a real estate company branded polo shirt. "Welcome!" he said a little too brightly. "How can I help you?"

His tone indicated he didn't think he could help me at all. I totally got that. After all, I wasn't nearly old enough to be in the market for buying a house. Still, I stalled.

"These houses look really nice," I said. "How big is the neighborhood?"

He put his hands on his hips, which drew my attention to the fact he wasn't overweight or anything, but he wasn't necessarily in shape either. His body looked soft, squishy, kind of like the Pillsbury dough boy. His skin was also a little blotchy, and as he took a few steps closer, I noticed his eyes were bloodshot. I also caught a whiff of way too much cologne, like he'd bathed in the stuff, but I was grateful for it because it overpowered the cinnamon.

"There's about forty houses so far, but the development has room for seventy-five." He looked behind me at the front door, as if he expected someone to follow me inside. "Are your parents coming?"

He has no idea.

Unless I turned out to be a potential customer, I was nothing more than a mild annoyance who'd interrupted his game of Candy Crush. There was no spark of recognition in his eyes or even so much as a hint of curiosity. I realized then I'd hoped for something, like his DNA would recognize mine in some primal way.

"This was a mistake," I muttered as I spun on my heel, retreating toward the door. Then Cole's words echoed in my mind – *you'll regret it if you don't try.*

He was right.

I blew out a breath and when I turned around, my father was already seated again behind the desk. This time as I walked toward him he didn't bother to stand.

"Actually, I'm looking for Michael Williams."

He smiled, putting the nicotine stains on his teeth on display. "You found him."

Even though he hadn't invited me to, I took a seat in one of the cushy chairs across from the desk.

"Do you remember Mary Parks?"

Wrinkles formed on his brow. "I don't think so. Should I?"

My knee-jerk reaction was to bare my teeth at his casual dismissal of my mother. *Asshole.* He'd gotten her pregnant and didn't even remember her?

Taking a deep breath, I focused on staying calm. My reaction wasn't fair. She'd never told him about the pregnancy, but even still it was a slap in the face of her memory that her name seemed to mean nothing to him. More than that, though, I looked enough like my mom that the sight of me should be a blast from the past.

"It would've been about nineteen years ago that you knew her. You dated her."

He laughed, leaning forward on his elbows. "Honey, you're going to have to be a lot more specific than that. I've dated a lot of women."

I wanted to punch him in his doughy face. Maybe my mother had been right in not telling him about me. I couldn't believe she'd dated such a jackass. She'd called that time in her life "crazy and wild." Looking at the man sitting in front of me, I decided "stupid" should be added to that list.

But I'd come this far, so I was going to see this through.

I pulled out my phone and brought up the oldest picture I had of her. "Here."

He took the phone from me, and I could tell the moment he recognized her.

Chuckling, he returned my phone. "Ah, Mary. She was a lot of fun. How's she doing?"

"She's dead."

He recoiled, making me want to slam his head on the desk. He hadn't even freaking remembered her, and now he was acting like the news was painful?

Screw him.

Dial it back, Ava. I'd spoken bluntly with the intention of getting a reaction, so I shouldn't be mad I'd gotten one. I couldn't stop myself from kicking a hornet's nest.

"I'm sorry to hear that, but what's this about?"

"I'm her daughter."

He paused for a moment, not seeming to know what to say.

"Well, then, I'm especially sorry for your loss. I don't know what I can tell you about her, though. I didn't know her very well. We only dated a few weeks."

The man was an idiot. I couldn't believe he hadn't put it together yet. And I couldn't believe I had this human pile of garbage to thank for half of my DNA. My only solace was I looked nothing like him—I was my mother's daughter through and through.

"You're my father."

His eyebrows shot up so high they met his bad dye job, and his body jerked backward like I'd shot him. His horrified expression was so exaggerated, it was almost comical. The thing was he wasn't hamming it up—he really was horrified.

That made two of us.

"No." He shook his head. "*No*," he repeated as if saying that one word aloud would make it so.

I shrugged. "You can deny it, but that doesn't make it not true."

"I just...you can't..." he sputtered. Visibly shaking, he stood. "You need to leave."

I blinked. "Are you serious?" Yeah, he was a total asswipe, but I hadn't expected him to kick me out.

"Yes," he said self-righteously. "You have no proof."

"What? You mean like a DNA test?" I laughed bitterly. I didn't want my relation to this man proven any more than he did. If I had known what a weasel he was, I wouldn't have bothered, no matter how much I wanted information. "We can do that if you want."

There I went kicking the hornet's nest again.

His face paled and he wiped at a line of sweat on his brow. *He knows it's true.* Goddamn him.

"What do you want from me? I have no money to give you."

"I don't want your money," I said, thoroughly disgusted by this situation.

"Then what do you want?"

"I want to ask you some questions. Like about the family history."

He swallowed, and I could almost see the hamsters running on the wheel in his head. "No," he said finally. "My lawyer wouldn't want me to talk to you."

"Are you serious?" I asked again, but it was the only possible response.

A smug smirk appeared on his face as if he was congratulating himself on the genius of coming up with that line. There was no way this clown had a lawyer.

Or perhaps he did. He was so stupid there was no telling what legal troubles he might have had. He could have done hard time for all I knew.

"I'm going to ask you nicely one last time to leave," he said. The thing was that he'd never *asked nicely* a first time. "I'll call the police. I can't have you harassing me at work."

I gripped the armrests on the chair, trying to control my anger. When the red haze had cleared from my vision, I stood. "You didn't say 'please.'"

"*Please* leave before I call the police."

"Gladly."

I stormed out of the house, slamming the door behind me. It wasn't until I was nearly to the waiting car that I realized he hadn't even asked my name.

Chapter 20

I FLUNG OPEN THE CAR door so hard it banged against my arm, painfully hyper-extending my elbow. Tears blurred my vision as I jammed the seatbelt clasp home.

Cole remained silent as he pulled away from the curb.

Wiping the tears off my face, I laughed bitterly. "Well, apparently I'm half asshole."

Cole sighed. "Ava—"

"Do you know what he said to me? He threatened to call the police if I continued to *harass* him."

"Ava—"

"He thought I wanted money from him. And this was after he didn't even remember my mom." On my short walk to the car, I'd given myself a pep talk, telling myself it didn't matter. He was nothing to me—no more than a sperm donor. But now that I was on a roll, I couldn't stop.

I was lying to myself. As much as I wanted Michael Williams to mean nothing more than a piece of trash I might step on and not think twice about, I cared. That excuse for a man was my father. *What a letdown. How had my mother ever sunk so low?*

"Ava, you're overreacting."

"What?" I semi-shrieked. "You weren't in there. How can you say that to me?"

Even as I said the words, I heard them objectively. They were exactly what someone who was overreacting would say.

"So your father is an asshole. Join the club."

Cole never talked about his father, who hadn't ever been in his life. Chase and Claire's father also carried the asshole label. So my tragedy wasn't really a tragedy—it was just a sorry common fact of life that a lot of kids dealt with. My situation wasn't special. However, knowing that didn't make me feel any better at this moment.

"Nothing has changed," Cole continued. "You didn't have a father an hour ago and you don't have one now. End of story."

That sounded simple, which was all well and good, but it wasn't that easy. It didn't take the pain away.

"I would've been better off not knowing he existed," I said, sorely thinking he probably thought the same thing.

"Yeah, but you can't go back."

In hindsight, I wished I hadn't given Xena the green light to search for my father. I knew that once she found him, I wouldn't be able to leave it alone. The possibility of locating him had never been presented to me before.

Now I understood why my mother had never bothered to tell him about me. The only thing he might have been good for was child support payments, and given my ten-minute interaction with him, I guessed he couldn't be counted on for even that.

What a total prick.

It bothered me that I came from him. When I looked at Cole though, guilt sprang upon me so fast I didn't see it coming. I'd had one good parent—Cole couldn't say the same. If our situations were reversed, I'd tell him it didn't matter where he got his DNA from. What mattered was the person he'd become.

I'd do well enough to listen to my own sentiment.

Some people were lucky enough to be born into great families. Others were forced to find their own. I thought of

Bill, who'd only recently come into my life. If life were fair, I would've had someone like him for the last eighteen years. Still, I wasn't going to squander the good fortune that had finally brought him to me.

"Bill is my father," I said quietly. Cole reached over and squeezed my hand and I knew he understood.

I thought of Xena and Shenice, and even my mother, who although dead was still part of my life. I ran my finger along the skin on Cole's hand, focusing on every little hair and indentation. Despite all the crap we'd been through, our relationship was stronger than ever. Or perhaps it was *because* of everything.

Yeah, I could do much worse in the family department.

LATER THAT NIGHT, WE CHILLED in Xena's hotel room with an ungodly amount of Chinese food. I think Xena ordered half the menu. When I used a fork instead of chopsticks, she sent me a look of such scathing disgust I looked behind me to see if Linda had secretly snuck in. Color me surprised when Cole actually knew how to use them, too. Geez...so I couldn't use chopsticks. I wasn't sophisticated. *Sue me.*

"I'm sorry Michael turned out to be such a skeezy windbucket," Xena said. When she'd learned the meeting had been less than joyful, she started referring to him not as my father but as Michael. Stuff like this was why I loved Xena, despite all her quirks.

However, I preferred to think of him as the sperm donor.

"The worst part is I didn't even get to ask him any questions," I grumbled. "So I still have no idea why I'm such a freak."

Cole slurped up a noodle off his chopsticks. "If you're a freak, then what am I?"

"True," Xena said.

Cole chucked a fortune cookie at her, nailing her in the nose.

"Hey!" she protested. "You shouldn't say things if you don't want people to agree with you."

"It was a rhetorical question."

Xena cocked her head. "Was it?"

Since I didn't want to get pelted with a fortune cookie, I kept my mouth shut, but I agreed with Xena. Cole was off the charts on the freak-o-meter seeker scale.

Which was why we were in our current predicament.

Time to shift gears. While my father being a jackass was a personal tragedy, the situation with the handlers had the potential to be a tragedy of epic proportions.

"Did you learn if the higher angels knew about Xavier?" I asked. While Cole and I had gone to see Michael, Xena had been trying to gather information.

"No." Frustration shone through in her tone.

"Any luck on getting an audience with them?"

She laughed. "That's a big *hell* no."

"Maybe..." I hesitated to suggest this, but we were running low on options. "Maybe we should try to get in touch with Areli."

"Oh, trust me," Xena said. "I tried. He's MIA."

Figures.

"My contact list has shrunk," Xena explained. "Especially now that you're wanted for Xavier's murder—"

I winced as she said that and she grimaced, perhaps realizing she'd been too blunt. But the problem wasn't that. I could call it a mercy killing or assisted suicide all I wanted, but I'd murdered him. I thought of the fire and the scent of burning flesh. *Murdered him with gusto.* One of these days I needed to come to terms with what I'd done.

But that day wasn't today. I had other worries.

"Sorry," Xena said. "Like I said before, there's no protocol so I'm not sure what the consequences will be, but it's doubtful they'll let this go. Considering that combined with me shooting Linda and helping Cole escape, there are very few I can turn to."

It just hit me that the danger with Xena meeting Brian and Noel hadn't been that they were dangerous drug dealers. No, it was that like me, Xena was wanted. She hadn't directly said so, but how could she not be?

"Do you think Brian and Noel might have been stalling you by showing you the lab? Maybe to turn you in?"

"No. The only thing they care about is their next fix. They have no idea what's going on and even if they did, they still wouldn't care as long as I paid them."

"Wait," Cole said. "Did you actually buy from them?"

Xena nodded. "I had to. I needed to be convincing."

"How much money did you give them?" I hated to think she had fueled their lurid business.

"You don't want to know."

Well, okay then.

"One thing that's bothering me that we haven't really talked about is all the seekers with dark auras."

"Your aura isn't dark," Xena said. "Neither is Cole's."

Cole and I exchanged a look. I hadn't looked at his aura since we'd dealt with Xavier and other than that time at the mall, he hadn't looked at mine as far as I knew. My head was totally in the sand with that—I still wasn't ready to know if I'd damned my soul beyond redemption.

Because yeah, even though angels had a messed up system going on, I still cared about the state of my soul. I'd still like to get into heaven and find eternal peace or whatever.

"I haven't met enough seekers to know if my theory is correct," I said. "But the handful I have met have dark auras, and I wouldn't have guessed that."

"What about Chase and Claire?" Xena asked.

"Theirs are okay. But they're also a unique circumstance. They didn't choose to become seekers, which is why I think their auras aren't affected. Just like mine and Cole's aren't affected by our seeking activity."

"What kind of person would choose that life?" Cole asked. "I know I'm not the best person around, but I would never be okay with deciding who dies. So maybe the type of person who would choose that life is more likely to have a dark aura."

"Maybe," I agreed. "I actually thought the same thing. But I wonder about that. If handlers and other fallen angels are corrupt, then what's to stop them from lying about seeking? The people who agree to become seekers might not understand what they're getting themselves into."

I wanted to believe that. I desperately wanted to believe that no one would choose this life. Deep down I knew I was wrong. Some people would always put themselves before others. Wouldn't it be ironic if by doing that, they were actually damning their own souls?

"Yeah," Cole said. "But they continue doing it. With every name they turn in, they make the choice again. They could always stop."

"If they stop, they die," Xena reminded him. "They were marked for death once and they only get to live if they seek."

I was reminded of the saying that you should never judge another person unless you'd walked in their shoes, so I tried to refrain from judging those who had chosen that path. I was certainly in no place to judge—I'd chosen that life for Cole. And damn it, I couldn't say what I would do if I had to do it all over again. Would I be strong enough to just let him die?

Cole had said he saw me as strong, but I was weak in so many ways.

"Made seekers can't see the other seekers' auras," I said. "There has to be a reason for that. And it's probably the same reason I've been kept away from other seekers my whole life—because I can see them."

"If some seekers realized what was happening to their auras, they might stop seeking," Xena said. "They might not care about other people, but when it comes to their own soul, who knows?"

"I understand why those who decide to become seekers to save themselves might be judged for that choice, hence the dark aura," I said. "But I'm concerned with the fact that it's being hidden. People should understand what they're getting themselves into."

"We don't even know if your theory is correct," Xena said. "And the only way to figure that out is to find more seekers, but like I said before I don't have many more people I can reach out to and I'd prefer to stay off the radar. I don't know how else we'd find other seekers."

"The whole point of seeking and turning in the souls so they can be angels is to create more good in the world," I said. "But if people are made into seekers, their auras are almost guaranteed to become dark. It seems counterproductive."

"They'd probably end up with dark auras anyway," Cole said, repeating his point from earlier.

"You don't know that for sure. They should at least have a chance."

I was not one to believe in the innate goodness of people, not after seeing so many auras over the years. Pure goodness in the world was hard to find. But I also wanted to believe everyone had the potential to be good. No one was born evil.

"It's a messed up system," Xena said. "We knew this already."

"Then we should try to stop it," I said.

I'd been so consumed with figuring out how I could get away with not seeking and live a normal life, but I needed to think outside my own situation. The system was definitely screwed up, and I didn't know if it had ever actually worked. Thanks to Cole, we were the only ones who could prove it might be doing more harm than good.

"Don't you think I would have done that already if it were possible?" Xena asked.

"Nothing is impossible," I retorted. I didn't know where my optimism was coming from. I wouldn't call myself a pessimist, but I was definitely a realist. Or maybe my stubbornness was masking itself as optimism.

But dang it, I saw Cole brought back from the dead— I'd seen the impossible. Then again, that only required one angel. Stopping the entire seeker system required a whole lot more of them.

Xena stared at me for a moment. "Okay, I'm done for tonight. I'm kicking you out. Feel free to take the food with you."

Her rudeness didn't even faze me. I hopped off the bed and grabbed the container of sesame chicken while Cole stacked several cartons.

Cole's phone rang before we got to our room. I quickly opened the door so he could free his hands to answer it.

"It's Kyle," he said. It only took a few seconds for his expression to shift from mildly annoyed to angry. His brother had that effect on people. That boy was a troublesome pain in the butt. Maybe being an only child wasn't so bad after all.

Although, I still didn't know for sure that I was. The sperm donor may have donated sperm elsewhere as well. I guessed I'd never know because there was no way I was subjecting myself to being in his company again. *Ugh.*

Today totally sucked. I was physically and emotionally exhausted.

After stowing the food in the mini-fridge, I flopped down on the bed. Still on the phone, Cole stretched out beside me. I laced my fingers through his and still in my clothes, mercifully fell asleep.

I JOLTED AWAKE TO FIND Xena's face inches from mine. Hurriedly, I sat up, banging my head against the headboard.

I opened my mouth to demand to know what the hell she was doing all up in my face in the middle of the night, but she clamped her hand over my mouth and shook her head.

Putting her finger to her lips, she gestured toward Cole. I shook him awake and he stared at her in alarm. Unlike me, he was smart enough to realize he shouldn't talk, so she didn't slap her hand over his mouth.

But I was alert now.

She pointed to the window. Cole crept over to it and peeked outside. Immediately his body stiffened. Xena motioned for him to return to us.

"What is it?" I hissed.

"Two fallen angels are out there looking at the car," Cole said, not bothering to whisper. When Xena shot him a nasty look, he shrugged. "We're on the third floor. They can't hear us."

I was with Xena on this one—better to err on the side of caution. Xena had her super-freaky teleporting thing. Who was to say these two didn't have super hearing or something?

"Stay away from the window and don't turn on any lights," Xena said. "Pack your stuff. We need to get out of here."

She didn't have to tell me twice. I shoved my few belongings into my bag and slipped on my shoes. Cole and I were both ready to go in under thirty seconds.

But where were we going to go? They were stalking my car. It wasn't like we could call an Uber to pick us up.

How did they find us? And who the heck were they, anyway?

I hoped Xena had some answers. More importantly, I hoped she had a plan to get us out of here.

We headed toward the stairs, making me think we all had the same idea—they couldn't sneak up on us in a stairwell. We'd hear them come in. If we took the elevator, they could be *right there* when the doors opened.

"At the bottom of the stairs, there's a door that leads out to the parking lot," Xena said. "I'll go out the front and lead them away."

"How?" Cole asked.

"I didn't exactly have time to formulate a plan, so I'll wing it."

Cole didn't look convinced, but we didn't have a better option. They were less likely to try to hurt Xena. Besides that, she could get away quickly, as she'd told us when she had the meeting with Brian and Noel. We didn't know what we were up against with these two, and depending on their powers, Cole and I could be completely defenseless.

Well, not completely. Cole was armed and my gun was tucked into my bag. I reached in and wrapped my hand around the hilt, keeping it in the bag. I wanted to be ready, but I didn't want to run around the hotel with a gun drawn, either. Totally *not* inconspicuous.

"Be safe," I said to her.

She nodded and trotted down the stairs in front of us, exiting toward the lobby. Cole and I continued to the other door. My car was parked about twenty yards away from it.

Cole put his ear up to the metal door, motioning for me to be quiet. I hoped that would work because standing just three feet away from it, I couldn't hear anything. It must be soundproof.

He shook his head. "I can't hear a damn thing."

"Shit. What should we do?"

"I'm going to open the door a crack," he said. "Be ready to run. Do you have your keys out?"

I fished around in my bag, trying to lay a hand on them and coming up with everything from dirty socks to toothpaste. Finally, I felt the smooth metal of the key fob in my hand. Dang. It was a good thing he'd said something. We wouldn't have gotten very far if we had to make a mad dash to the car.

"Ready," I said, juggling the key fob, my gun, and my bag. If it came down to me having to shoot someone, we'd be in trouble. Perhaps it would be better if I put the dang thing away.

Cole slowly opened the door just a hair, and I cringed as the hinges whined. The crack was just wide enough for us to be able to hear Xena's voice. Actually, no, not her voice. She was *laughing*.

I strained to hear what was going on. It seemed like she was *flirting* with them. *Sooo* weird. When she said she was going to improvise, that was not what I was expecting.

Cole inched the door open a little more, and I caught sight of one of the guys. He was slight, not much bigger than Xena. In a fair and normal fight, Cole would easily be able to take him, but it was never a fair fight between handlers and seekers. Although, we hadn't verified they were handlers. They could just be fallen angels. But why would they be lurking near my car if they didn't mean us harm? That was way too much of a coincidence to be believable.

I couldn't hear what Xena was saying to him, but judging by his unimpressed expression, he wasn't going for it. *Abort!* I wanted to scream at her.

Hearing a deep laugh, I let out a sigh of relief. Xena must be having better luck with the other guy.

Cole looked over his shoulder at me. He was getting antsy. Hiding while someone else took the risk was not his style.

I blinked and the little guy was gone. What the hell? Where had he gone?

A second later, I heard Xena grunt, followed by some harsh words. It sounded like she might be threatening him.

I pushed past Cole to open the door a little wider. *Shit!* The little guy was standing behind Xena with one arm around her neck and a knife poised to slice open her throat.

How had he gotten over there so fast? He must share Xena's ability.

That left the other guy. Now that the door was open wider, I could see him and he was a beast. This pair would have made a comical duo under other circumstances—Tiny and Huge.

Huge turned, but Cole and I didn't duck out of the way in time.

"Hey!" he yelled.

I froze.

A blur of movement caught my eye. Tiny was doubled over, but that wasn't where I focused my attention. No, my attention was focused on the blood dripping off the knife.

I wildly searched the parking lot for Xena. I was so distracted I didn't notice Huge charging until he was nearly on top of us. Cole pushed me out of the way just before Huge would have flattened me. Unfortunately, that meant Cole took the brunt of the hit.

Before I could try to help him, I spotted Xena, leaning on a pole, her hand at her neck. When she pulled it away, her skin sagged, the dingy light from the streetlight illuminating the gaping slash in her throat. She was pale to begin with, but now her face was ghostly.

"Xena," I whispered. *Oh, God.* A million thoughts ran through my head in a millisecond. *She better be okay. She'll be okay. She's a fallen angel. She can heal. She better be okay.*

"Get in the car!" Cole yelled.

I dropped my bag, not caring if it got left behind as I fumbled with the key fob. My eyes ping-ponged between Cole and Xena, not sure who I should help.

Xena must have realized my dilemma because she narrowed her eyes at me and took off at a run in the opposite direction. She was fast, but not as fast as she could be. Even still, there was no way I could catch up to her.

Cole was pinned to the ground under Huge, but he had both hands on his neck, squeezing the pressure points. It didn't seem to make much difference to Huge, though.

With a scream, I jumped on his back, digging my nails into his skin where his neck met his shoulders. I might as well have been giving him a massage, though. Huge arched his back, bucking me off. I rolled until I hit the wall, smacking my head on the brick. For a moment my vision clouded.

What the heck was I thinking? This was a fallen angel, for goodness sake. My stupid fingernails weren't going to hurt him. I retrieved my gun and checked to make sure the safety was on. Then I held it by the barrel and bashed it into the back of Huge's head, breaking the skin with the third blow.

I barely noticed the blood as I continued to whale on him. Cole released his neck and slammed the heel of his hand into the guy's nose at an upward angle. Between that and me hitting him, Cole was able to get free. Maybe we lucked out, and the only thing that was special about Huge was he was, well, *huge*.

Before Huge could scramble to his feet, Cole took my gun and hit him with it several times with much more force that I'd managed. He stumbled to his knees.

"Go," Cole said, scooping up his own gun and our bags from the ground.

I wretched open the driver's side door and jammed the key in the ignition. As soon as Cole was in, I backed up. I looked down at the shifter as I switched into drive and when I looked up, Huge had recovered and was looming in front of the car.

Gritting my teeth, I gripped the steering wheel. He picked the wrong girl to mess with.

I stomped on the gas, not even cringing at the thump of his body as it landed on the hood of the car. When I slammed on the brakes and his body rolled off, I steeled my arms so my unbuckled body wouldn't slam into the steering wheel. And when I drove off, leaving him in the middle of the road, I didn't even look back.

CHAPTER 21

COLE HADN'T FARED SO WELL with my defensive driving, having hit his forehead on the dash. *Whoops.* But I hadn't had enough time to warn him. It had been a reflex. It turned out hitting thugs with a car was my signature move when it came to defending Cole.

"Did you see which way Xena went?" I asked as we sped down the road.

"No," Cole said, pulling out his phone. A moment later, he shook his head. "She's not answering."

"That guy was fast," I said. "And she was hurt. He might catch her."

"I know," Cole said grimly.

"Think, Ava, think," I muttered. "Where would she go?"

"We should stop and wait somewhere," Cole said. "She was on foot, so she couldn't go but so far."

"I don't know..." I said. Even though she was hurt, Xena's ability to get from point A to point B no matter how far apart they were was amazing. I just wished I knew where B was.

"We could be going in the complete wrong direction."

That made me pause.

"You're right. But where should we go? I don't want to drive in circles."

"Somewhere populated," Cole replied. "Let me see if there's an IHOP or Walmart nearby. They're open 24 hours."

He found a Walmart six miles away and set the GPS. Now that he pointed out we might be going farther away from Xena, I got more nervous with every passing mile. Cole hadn't seen her slit throat. Though she'd been far away from me, I'd gotten a clear look at it.

When we'd sliced Xavier's throat, he'd completely healed within a few hours. But I didn't how long it would take Xena. Angels got more powerful with age, and I assumed the same concept applied to their healing abilities. Since she wasn't a terribly old angel, it might take her a while.

Though this Walmart was open twenty-four hours, the parking lot was nearly deserted. I parked near a cluster of cars, hoping to blend in.

"She'll call," Cole said with a confidence I didn't share. "We just need to wait her out."

She couldn't call if she was passed out from blood loss. *Damn it.* That thought was not helping and Cole was right. We had no way to track her so we had to depend on her contacting us.

"Are you okay?" I asked, turning to inspect him. His lip was split and one eye looked like it was swelling.

"Yeah, for the most part. He banged the back of my head into the pavement before I got hold of his neck."

"Shit, Cole." I reached over and sure enough his hair was matted with blood. I ran my hand down the back of his head to his neck and my hands came away sticky. I closed my eyes for a moment, reliving the other time I'd had his blood on my hands. But this time it was different— he was still breathing. I could handle this. "Come on," I said. "We need to get you cleaned up."

He sighed but opened the car door.

My head was pounding from where I'd hit the brick wall, but out of the three of us, I'd faired the best. None of my blood was spilled.

The thought of spilled blood made me think of Xena again. How much blood had she lost?

I pushed the worry out of my mind. I could do nothing to help her right now, but I could help Cole.

"That guy was inhumanly strong," Cole said as we scanned the first aid supplies in the store.

"He's not human," I reminded him.

"Yeah, I know, but you know what I mean."

We took our supplies through the self check-out so we wouldn't risk a cashier noticing Cole's bloody head. Honestly, I was just glad we hadn't had to shoot anyone. I mean, I did hit someone with my car, but somehow that didn't seem as bad as using a firearm.

We locked ourselves in the family restroom, and Cole pulled his bloody shirt over his head. It was a total loss. *Damn.* We should have bought him a fresh shirt, too. He'd have to wait here while I got him one when we were done tending to his injuries.

He stuck his head under the faucet to rinse the blood away so I could see what we were working with. Unfortunately, that made the wound start bleeding again, turning the water in the sink a deep pink.

"There's a lot of blood," I said.

Cole put his hand over the wound to try to stop the flow. "Are you okay? I can manage this myself."

I paused for a moment. "You know, I am." And I was. This was Cole's blood and no part of him disgusted me.

"Are you sure? You can wait outside and—"

"Cole." I leaned down and kissed his cheek. "I'm fine. Really. I'm not going to leave you when you're hurt."

The only trouble was I had no medical training. I could handle a cut on the arm or something, but a head wound was something totally different.

"It's really bleeding," I said. "You might need stitches."

"That's not happening."

I sighed. He was right. Unless it was life threatening, we couldn't seek medical help. It would call too much attention to us.

"Hang on," I said. "Keep pressure on it."

I did a quick search on my phone for how to properly care for a head wound. How did people ever survive before the Internet?

"We need ice," I said. "Wait here."

I left him to buy ice, some baggies to put it in, a towel, and a shirt. When I returned, the bleeding seemed to have slowed a lot. Thank God. His seeker healing powers must have kicked in.

I set him up with some ice and he changed his shirt. As we walked out to the car, I clutched my phone in my hands, staring at it and willing it to ring, which of course didn't happen. A watched pot and all that.

I locked the doors as soon as we got back into the car. It probably wouldn't matter if they found us, but it was good for my peace of mind. I opened the center console to stow the extra medical supplies, but they wouldn't fit on account of the hard drive I'd taken from Bill's that was in there. So instead I tied the top of the bag closed and tossed it on the floor.

"How do you think they found us?"

"Who knows?" Cole asked. "They could have spies all over the place."

"I'm worried about Xena." It went without saying, but I needed to say it out loud. The worry was festering, eating at my insides.

"I know. Me, too. But I also think she can handle herself."

I pressed the button on my phone to check the time. It hadn't even been an hour since we'd left her. Too soon to panic, right? I had at least another hour for that.

So we'd wait.

Two hours later we were still waiting in the parking lot as the sun came up. The natural light illuminated Cole's injuries, making them look much worse than they had the night before in the florescent store lighting. They were healing, but the dried and matted blood made him a gruesome sight.

As soon as the McDonald's in front of the Walmart opened, we hit up the drive-thru. Cole didn't say as much, but he was uneasy. He'd started fidgeting about an hour ago—not a good sign. I didn't know how I was keeping the panic at bay. Perhaps because he was worried, I was able to keep it together. One of us had to.

I was halfway through my egg sandwich when my phone rang. My greasy fingers fumbled with the phone, dropping it on the floorboard. In my haste to retrieve it, I banged my head on the steering wheel, but I didn't care.

"Xena," I said. "Thank God."

"Come get me." Her voice was barely audible and it sounded like she was having trouble breathing.

I started the car. "Where are you?"

"Happy."

"What? *Happy?* What is that?"

"*B...P...*"

"B.P., like the gas station? Which one? There are a million of those."

No response.

"Xena? *Xena?*"

Nothing.

Shit. We were still connected, meaning she hadn't ended the call. Hadn't or couldn't? There was no sound coming from the phone, but until she hung up, I was staying on the line. I tapped the speaker phone button.

"There are at least a dozen BP stations in a twenty mile radius from the hotel." Cole scrolled through his phone.

I gritted my teeth, handed him my phone, and put the car into drive. "Then we'll have to visit them all until we find her. Start with the one closest to the hotel. And don't hang up my phone."

I steeled my mind against everything except the next turn. With the morning rush hour traffic, it took us twice as long to get back to the area near the hotel as it took to get to Walmart. As I turned into the lot, I was filled with anticipation.

But Xena was nowhere in sight.

Stupid. It was not like she could sit on the curb waiting for us. Considering how bad Cole looked, Xena must look ten times worse with her slit throat. Even if it had healed, her clothes would be covered in blood.

I parked and we both got out.

"I'll check the bathroom," I said.

Cole nodded and headed toward the rear of the building.

It only took me a second to realize she wasn't in the tiny one-stall restroom. Hopefully Cole was having more luck outside.

When I exited, Cole was walking over to the car.

"Nothing," he said. "There's nowhere she could be hiding here."

It had been too much to hope we'd find her at the first stop.

"What's the next address?" I asked once we were back in the car, forcing myself to stay calm by focusing on the task at hand.

The next stop was only two minutes away and it was the same deal—no sign of her.

"What if she was unconscious and someone found her and called an ambulance?" I asked, tapping my fingers on the steering wheel while I waited for Cole to pull up the next station on his phone. "Should we start asking if someone saw her? Or call the local hospitals or something?"

Cole considered for a moment before shaking his head. "She's smarter than that. She wouldn't let herself be seen."

I was about to say *I hope you're right*, but I wasn't so sure I was. If Xena went to a hospital, surely doctors would realize she wasn't a normal human. But wouldn't that be the safest place for her? She could still benefit from medical treatment.

After the fifth stop, Cole took over driving when I couldn't stop my hands from shaking. But now, I had nothing to distract me. I clutched my phone, which had yet to disconnect from Xena's call.

He reached over to squeeze my hand. "We're going to find her."

"How can you be so sure?" Atlanta was a big city, and it had been an hour since we'd started searching. Anything could have happened between then and now.

"Because we don't stop until we do," he replied with conviction. I wished I shared his confidence. It was just that the odds were against us—good old realist thinking.

Stop number six—nothing.

Stop number seven—nothing.

At the eighth stop, my phone lost the call.

At the ninth stop, tears blurred my vision. I wiped them hastily as I hurried into the building to check the restroom. Nothing.

Back outside, Cole wasn't anywhere in sight. I thought about waiting in the car for him, but something nagged at me to go look for him—probably fear I'd lose him, too.

I circled around toward the back of the building. This station was next to a business complex, which had meticulously maintained flowerbeds lining the brick walls. If Cole had still been wearing his bloody green shirt instead of the new blue one I'd bought him, he would have blended in with the bushes and I would have missed him kneeling beside them.

Hope surged in my chest and I ran across the drive, narrowly avoiding being creamed by a car. The driver's rude hand gesture didn't bother me—Cole had found something.

Not *something—someone*. As I skidded to a halt next to him, I saw a small form under the bushes.

Xena lay on her side, unconscious, but that wasn't the most alarming thing. Her shirt was gone, revealing bloody welts all over her torso, like she'd been whipped. In places, her skin was in strips and I couldn't tell if it was still connected to her body.

"Hold up the bushes so I can pull her out without scratching her," Cole said. I did as he requested, getting a close-up view of her injuries.

It was bad. So much worse than I could have imagined.

She didn't make a sound as Cole gently brought her out. Her shorts were partially intact, but her thighs were covered with the same wounds.

"Should I bring the car over?" I asked.

Cole lifted her, trying to be gentle, but there was no uninjured place he could touch her.

"No time." He jerked his head toward the office building. In the windows, two horrified faces gaped at us.

He walked briskly, but he couldn't go too fast or he'd jostle Xena. I trotted along beside him, using my body to shield her from view. At the car, I slid into the backseat and Cole laid Xena in my open arms, her body stretched across the seat.

Blood was everywhere. There was no way this upholstery was ever coming clean.

Cole got us out of there and as we drove away, I heard sirens in the distance. Hopefully no one was quick-thinking enough to get our license plate number. Or shit, take a picture of it. Oh, well. We'd deal with that if we had to.

I brushed Xena's hair away from her face. The purple streak was matted with blood and stuck to her forehead. She had leaves from the bushes stuck in her wounds. I hesitated because my hands weren't clean and this wasn't a sterile environment, but they needed to come out and it would hurt her less if she were unconscious. Besides that, I didn't think infection was an issue for fallen angels. At least, I hoped it wasn't.

I was not equipped to deal with this, and no amount of Internet searching would give me the experience I needed.

"We should get out of Atlanta," Cole said.

"Agreed." If those guys found us here once, they could probably do it again.

"Any preference as to where we go?"

"No." I continued to pick the debris out of Xena's wounds, but it was slow going, especially in the backseat of a moving vehicle.

After only ten minutes on the interstate, Cole exited.

"Where are we going?" I asked. We still hadn't made it out of Atlanta.

"I started north to throw off anyone from the BP who might have called the cops. We're really going south."

Good thinking on his part.

"Stop there at the Walgreens first," I said.

Cole didn't hesitate, quickly hopping out of the car to run in and get supplies. I didn't have to tell him what to get. He returned with bottled water, towels, and several bags of medical supplies.

"We're going to need to stop soon," I said once we were back on the road. "We need running water and..."

I didn't know what else we needed.

"I know," he said. "We're circling back around Atlanta now. Can you hold on about an hour?"

It wasn't me I was worried about. Though I didn't think Xena would die, I wanted her to have every chance to fully heal in a comfortable and safe location. Plus, what would happen if we didn't get all the dirt out of her wounds? Would her skin close around it, leaving scars? Or perhaps she wouldn't heal at all. I wasn't sure how it worked for her, especially since she was a relatively young angel.

I did the best I could to tend to the wounds, but her lower legs were out of reach, not to mention her back. I couldn't very well flip her over.

So instead I focused on her face. Her skin had been so clear and pretty, and I wanted it to return to that state. Using tweezers, I carefully picked every hair and speck of dirt out of the cuts. Luckily, Cole had gotten hydrogen peroxide in a spray bottle, which would make application easy. I cringed as I took the clear protective wrap off the nozzle. This was going to hurt.

I spritzed the worst of the cuts on her face and she moaned, her eyes still closed. She didn't deserve this.

"I'm sorry," I said to her, squeezing her hand. "I'm so, so sorry. But I've got you now."

CHAPTER 22

WE FINALLY STOPPED NEAR MACON at a hotel with room doors that opened directly to the outside so we wouldn't have to carry Xena through a lobby. She still hadn't regained consciousness, which was probably for the best. I couldn't begin to imagine the pain she would be in, and that was saying something considering I'd had my blood boiled. I thought her face was already starting to look better, but that might have been wishful thinking. Until we got her properly cleaned up, it would be hard to tell the true state of things.

Cole carried her into the room and laid her down on the towels I had ready on the bed. Using the small medical scissors, I snipped off her shorts so they wouldn't be in the way. When her whole body was exposed, I couldn't help but suck in a breath at the sight of her wounds in their entirely. Her flesh hung to her body in bloody strips.

Beside me, Cole cursed.

We painstakingly cleaned every inch of her body, throwing away the bloody towels and running out to buy new ones. By dinner time, she still hadn't woken up. Before we went to bed, I set an alarm to wake me every hour so I could check on her. That was a pointless task, though. I couldn't sleep anyway.

Every time I got up, I shifted her body, thinking her skin would heal more easily if it wasn't rubbing against the towel she was lying on. The only trouble was there was no way to position her without some of her injuries taking the brunt of her weight.

Around 4 a.m., approximately twenty-four hours after this ordeal began, I heard her mumble. I sprang out of bed and was at her side.

I squeezed her hand. "Xena, I'm here."

Her breath wheezed out of her body in painful sounding breaths. Behind me, I heard Cole sit up.

"Water," she croaked.

Cole quickly retrieved a bottle of water from the dresser and poured a little in her mouth.

"I know it's hard for you to talk, but try to tell us if there's something else we can do to help you," I said. "We did our best, but we'll do whatever you tell us."

Her nod was barely perceptible. A few moments later, she passed out.

LATE THE NEXT MORNING, XENA woke up again and requested more water. She stayed awake for a little longer this time, but not by much. I stuck to my hourly schedule, turning her body and checking her wounds. They seemed to be healing, but damn, it was slow going. Well, for an angel, anyway. This could have killed a human.

Would it have killed me? What if Cole and I had dealt with Tiny instead of Huge? Based on appearance and size, Huge should have been the bigger threat. We'd been so wrong. If we'd chosen our foes differently, Cole and I might be dead.

She woke up after dinner with a jolt, her body jerking. Moaning, she moved her hand to her head. Cole moved to her bedside with water. After drinking a little, she tried to push herself into a sitting position.

"Here," I said, putting a pillow behind her to prop her up.

"Thanks," she said, her voice sounding much stronger. Then she glanced down at her body and let out a little shriek.

"It's better than it was," I assured her. "You've already healed some."

Her eyes widened at she looked at me. "I'm naked!"

Cole backed away, a horrified expression on his face, like he'd also just realized that little fact. Neither of us had given much thought to Xena's state of undress. We had been in a medical crisis. Considering the extent of her injuries, I couldn't believe she was worried about her lack of clothing.

"We didn't want anything to stick to your wounds," I explained.

"Look away, Cole," Xena said forcefully.

"Trust me, I am," he muttered.

Rolling my eyes, I sat on the bed next to her. "How are you feeling?"

"Like I got whipped by Indiana Jones."

"What happened?" Cole asked, his eyes still averted.

"Like I said," she retorted. "I got whipped by Indiana Jones."

Oh, geez. Cole and I exchanged a glance. Was she delusional?

I put my hand to her forehead to check for fever. She slapped it away.

"The smaller one who cut me had a whip," she explained. "Who the hell carries a whip?"

"Cowboys," I said.

"No, those are lassos," Cole corrected.

Whatever. Geez, was that really important right now?

"Anyway, I was already weak when he caught up to me. I didn't even see the first lash coming." She sounded disturbed, not because she'd been whipped within an inch of her life, but because she hadn't anticipated the attack.

But I was with her—who the hell carried a whip in the twenty-first century?

"Does it hurt?" I asked.

She gave me her signature *you're-an-idiot* look. I grinned. That one small action told me she was going to be okay.

"Where are we?" she asked.

"Macon."

"That's not too far from Atlanta, is it?" she asked. "We should move."

I shook my head. "You haven't healed enough yet."

Looking down at her body, she sighed. "I suppose you're right. How long has it been?"

"We found you yesterday morning."

"Damn," she said. "I can't believe I was out that long. I've never been hurt this badly before. At least, not since I've been an angel."

That comment made me do a double take. What had Xena been through when she was living?

"Here's the plan," Xena said. "Go get me something to eat. I'm starving. We'll stay here one more night, but then we have to move. And for God's sake, get me some clothes, okay?"

Neither Cole nor I complained one bit about her bossiness and did as she commanded.

WE MADE IT JUST OVER the Florida border the next night with Xena wearing nothing but one of Cole's t-shirts, which made her look even more like a little kid. Her skin had woven itself back together, but it was very thin and delicate. It didn't take much for it to get ripped open again. The healing process tired her out, so she slept most of the drive.

Now that I knew she was going to be okay, the full weight of the recent events hit me. I was exhausted in every way possible—emotionally, physically, and psychologically.

It didn't help that Cole managed to re-open his head wound in the shower this morning.

None of us had much to say. Cole and I couldn't figure out who those guys were, how they found us, and what they wanted. Xena wasn't up for talking, but even still, I got the impression she had no clue, either. All three of us were wanted—Cole because he was the seeker with no limits, me because I'd killed Xavier, and Xena because she was helping us. So those were three viable reasons for them to come after us. Which one was it? Did it really matter?

While Cole left to scrounge up dinner, I took an extra long shower. When I came out of the bathroom twenty minutes later, Cole was back and two bags of fast food sat on the dresser, untouched. It only took half a second to figure out something was terribly wrong.

The dread that coursed through my body was expected and normal, but with it came a strain of annoyance. *What now?* I was just so tired. I couldn't keep going like this, waiting to see what next bad thing was going to slap me in the face. Slap *us* in the face.

"What is it?" I asked.

Wordlessly, Xena held out her phone. My knees threatened to buckle.

On the screen was a picture of Shenice. She was lying on her side and her eyes were closed, like she was sleeping. That alone wasn't alarming, but her wrists were bound together in front of her with a zip tie.

"Oh God. Oh no."

"It gets worse." Cole held out his phone. Bill and Kyle were in similar positions, only there was blood all over Kyle's face and it looked like his nose had been broken.

Shit, shit, shit.

"Who sent those pictures?" I asked.

Xena shook her head. "I don't know. I don't recognize the number."

I looked at Cole, who was strangely calm. Then I gasped and hurried to look at my phone, hoping I was the odd one out.

Nope.

I had received a picture of Chase and Claire. The only difference with this one was they were both awake. Chase's left eye was swollen shut and he looked pissed. Claire's eyes were puffy, like she'd been crying. I scrolled up, but there was no message—just the picture.

"I got one, too," I said grimly, holding out the phone. When Cole took it, I sank onto the bed and clasped my hands between my knees, squeezing so tightly it seemed I would break the bones in my hands.

"When is the last time you talked to them?" Xena asked.

I tried to remember, but my mind was fuzzy. It had been a while since I talked to anyone. The last time I called Claire, she hadn't answered. And come to think of it, I hadn't gotten any texts from her lately. There had been so much going on I hadn't noticed.

"I talked to Kyle the night we were attacked," Cole said.

"I haven't talked to Shenice since we left, but that's not unusual," Xena said.

"I haven't heard from Claire, either."

"Bill and Kyle were probably the last ones taken," Xena hypothesized, "and considering Chase and Claire are awake in the picture—"

I tuned Xena out and looked at Cole. His expression told me we were thinking the same thing—this wasn't going to end unless we turned ourselves in. How many people were going to get hurt because of us? How many people was I willing to *let* get hurt?

None.

It was hard to believe it had come to this, but they'd boxed me in. My life wasn't worth sacrificing five of my friends.

"Why are you two just sitting there?" Xena looked at us suspiciously.

Cole sighed. "We're done."

I stood and hugged him, not bothering to fight the stream of tears.

Xena made a face. "What does that mean?"

"They nearly killed you and they've taken everyone we love," I said. "It's not going to end."

I suddenly knew what my mom had been feeling when she'd refused Xavier's blood. She'd been done, not willing to let anyone else get hurt or killed for her sake.

"So what?" Xena asked. "You're just going to turn yourselves in?"

I hung my head. When she put it that way, I felt like a coward, like I was giving up. But what else could we do? We could try to rescue our friends, but considering how things went with the two fallen angels we just encountered, it was doubtful we'd be successful.

"It's the only chance we have to save them," I said.

"Even if you turn yourselves in, there's no guarantee they'll let them go," Xena said.

"I know, but there's no chance we can take them. We'll have to be smart about it—make sure everyone is released first."

"Then what?" Xena said.

"I don't know, but once they have us, they have no reason to go after our friends."

I had to trust that angels, even fallen ones, were lazy like Xena had said and wouldn't do something without a purpose.

"So all of this was for nothing." Xena was pissed. "You're going to let handlers like Linda win."

"It's not like that and you know it," Cole snapped. "You think I like this? They have my baby brother."

"I hate this," I said quietly. We were choosing to save our friends, but what about the rest of it? What about all the people who died prematurely because seekers turned in their names? What about people who chose to become seekers without understanding what they were getting themselves into? I was powerless to stop people from making that decision, but at least I could end Areli's line and make sure there were no more born seekers.

Xena stared at us, her disappointment evident. It made me feel so much worse, but we were out of options and out of time. We couldn't keep running. They'd find us eventually, and as Linda reminded me, eventually they'd get tired of us not holding up our end of the deal—we were only allowed to live as long as we turned in names. Sooner or later, the Reapers would come for us. Why not turn ourselves in while it could help our friends?

And couldn't Xena see we were doing this for her sake, as well? She'd almost died. What did she want from us? It wasn't like we could—

I stopped as my thoughts drastically changed direction. Perhaps hiding was the exact opposite of what we should have been doing this whole time.

"Let's expose them," I said. "The higher angels might not want to hear what we have to say, but if we broadcast what we know, then they'll hear about it eventually, right?"

"Broadcast?" Xena asked.

I nodded. "YouTube, Facebook, Instagram, all of it. Let's make it go viral."

"How can we do that?" Cole asked. "We're the only ones who can see handler and seeker auras. Who will believe us about all this crazy shit? We have no real proof."

"But we do," I said slowly. "I can project my aura."

For a moment, Cole looked encouraged, then he scoffed. "Yeah, but no one will believe that's not just Photoshop or something."

He made a good point, but that wasn't all we had.

"We have the footage from when Linda attacked you," I said. "Bill's hard drive is in the car."

"Seriously?" he asked.

I nodded.

"You can film me as well," Xena said uneasily. She'd managed to live on Earth for decades without exposing her abilities. It meant a lot that she was willing to do it now, especially since it would only get her in more trouble if our plan worked and the higher angels saw.

"It doesn't matter if people believe us. In fact, I don't care if anyone believes us," I said. "As long as the footage gets attention, the higher angels might finally take notice of what's been going on."

"This might work," Cole said. "But we need to be quick."

I turned to Xena. "What's the limit on your credit card, Harriet?"

CHAPTER 23

COLE AND I RAN OUT to buy three laptops and a new phone for Xena, since hers had gotten left behind in the bushes. As the cashier rang up our selections and I swiped the card, I held my breath, waiting for it to be declined or for the cashier to call me out for not being Harriet McIntyre. Neither of those things happened, so we raced back to the hotel.

The laptops seemed to take forever to get up and running—they kept asking for our personal information and wanting us to register warranties and set up virus protection. *Ugh.*

Cole's was ready first and he plugged in the hard drive. He paled slightly as the footage of him and Linda filled the screen. I squeezed his hand, feeling extra glad we'd turned the camera off before Kyle and I had carried him out of there.

"Where should we upload it?" he asked.

"Anywhere and everywhere," I replied. "Search for online groups about the supernatural. They're the most likely to spread them."

While Cole started searching, Xena and I got ready to film our parts. I'd only purposefully projected my aura once, when I was trying to convince Cole the whole seeker and angel thing was real. I tried to get myself into a calm and peaceful meditative state, but the images of everyone I loved tied up kept popping into my mind.

I broke out into a sweat, having sudden and panic-ridden doubt. What if their capturers saw the footage before we freed them?

"Stop," I said and Xena and Cole both looked at me. "We can't upload anything until after our friends are safe."

Cole paused. "You're right."

"Wait," Xena said. "You're still going to turn yourselves in?"

"It's the only way," I said miserably. "You once said time is irrelevant to the higher angels. Even if they hear about the videos right away, who knows how long it will be before they take action? It might be too late by then."

"If you're turning yourselves in, then I'm going with you," Xena said. "I care about them, too, you know."

"You can't. Someone has to make sure all the footage gets posted and you have the best chance of staying under the radar." She'd been incapacitated, but they hadn't taken her, which led me to believe they were less likely to come after her. Also, she wasn't fully healed yet, but I didn't dare say that aloud.

She sighed, not disagreeing with my logic. "Let's do this."

FILMING XENA WAS INTERESTING—AND easy. She'd had so much practice with her ability she had a firm command over it, unlike me. It took forever to get decent footage of me projecting my aura. Of course, Xena's ability was cool and useful whereas mine was pointless, so why would I have bothered to take the time to hone it?

By the time we got everything ready, it was three a.m. and I was exhausted. We hadn't tried to communicate with the capturers yet because we wanted to have everything prepared. Xena had suggested using the footage as a bargaining tool, and Cole and I considered for a moment before deciding against it. This was a dangerous game we were playing, and I didn't want to tip them off. I didn't want to do anything to jeopardize the footage being released. I trusted Xena to keep everyone safe if they tried to retaliate once they learned what we'd done. Cole and I certainly wouldn't be in a position to do anything.

He held his phone in his hand, finger poised over the send button. We'd composed a simple text: *Let's trade. Cole and Ava for the five of them.*

"Here goes," he muttered. I closed my eyes as the text that would seal our fate was sent.

Ten, fifteen, twenty minutes passed without a response.

"Should I send a text from my phone?" I asked, worried they somehow didn't receive it.

"This is still a stupid idea." Xena lay on the bed, more worn out and exhausted than me, but too proud to admit it. "You don't even have a plan."

"We don't know where they are, so how can we make a plan?" Cole asked. "Until we get more info, we're flying blind."

His phone buzzed and the three of us gulped in unison. Xena rose from the bed and we all leaned over his phone.

Columbia, South Carolina.

"What's there?" I asked.

"Nothing special I'm aware of," Xena replied. "Have I mentioned this is a stupid idea?"

"Once or twice," Cole said.

Xena blew out an exasperated breath. She might be irritated we weren't heeding her warning, but I was irritated she kept bringing it up. We knew what we were in for.

We knew we most likely weren't coming back.

Cole had already pulled up GPS on his phone. "Five hours away."

"How are we going to do this?" I asked. "We need to make sure they release everyone before we turn ourselves over."

Xena crossed her arms and plopped down on the bed, not willing to participate in the conversation.

"When do you want to leave?" Cole asked. "We should probably get some sleep, but..."

He didn't need to finish that sentence. Neither of us would be able to sleep.

I grabbed my bag and started packing. He did the same. All the while, Xena refused to look at us, anger coming off her in waves.

Cole went out to the car with both of our bags, and I stayed behind a moment to say goodbye to Xena.

"I'm sorry to leave you like this," I said. "I wish there was a better way."

Xena turned her gaze toward me. The sight of tears glistening in her eyes made me step back.

"I don't want you to go," she said stubbornly. In that moment it clicked it wasn't about us not listening to her—she didn't want to lose me anymore than I wanted to lose my friends.

"I know," I said softly. "But I can't let them hurt my loved ones anymore. And I can't run anymore."

Xena pulled me into a hug so fierce I worried she'd damage her newly healed skin. When she let me go, her eyes were clear.

"Text me when you're nearly there and I'll start the uploads."

I nodded, not able to put my million thoughts into words.

"Goodbye, Xena."

I SPENT THE FIRST TWO hours of the drive arranging the meet. Doing it via text message made it a long and drawn-out process, but I didn't want to do it over a phone call. This way we were able to discuss the situation and take our time formulating our responses.

We set up a meeting for nine a.m. in the parking lot of an abandoned mall. The capturers agreed to provide us proof our friends had been released safely, but they wouldn't specify what that proof was no matter how many times I demanded. Shortly after that, they stopped responding all together.

Cole and I didn't talk much. I kept expecting fear to set in, but I was numb. To my surprise, I even dozed a little.

When we were twenty minutes away, I texted Xena, telling her to start uploading everything.

Cole reached over and took my hand. "I love you." His voice was husky, full of emotion.

"I love you, too." I was so choked up, I could barely get the words out.

Objectively, I knew what we were doing, but now that the minutes were counting down and it was nearly upon us, the gravity of the situation set in.

Cole abruptly pulled off on the side of the road and both of us unbuckled our seat belts. He pulled my body to his. When we kissed, I tasted the salt of the tears running down my face.

"This sucks," I said, letting out a little laugh.

"Yeah, it does," he agreed. "But we're doing the right thing."

"I hope so."

He tucked a strand of hair behind my ear and I closed my eyes, concentrating on the feel on his fingertips on my cheek.

"It's almost nine," he said reluctantly.

I nodded, not wanting to end this moment with him but knowing we had to. I pressed my lips to his in one last passionate act, loving the taste of peppermint as his tongue swirled with mine.

A LARGE WHITE WINDOWLESS VAN sat in the parking lot. It was exactly the type of vehicle I'd expect a kidnapper to drive.

Cole pulled to a stop on the other side of the lot but kept the car running in case we needed to make a fast getaway. My phone buzzed immediately, and the text contained a single line that was a link to a website. I shot Cole a hesitant look and then clicked on it.

It was a feed of a camera filming what looked to be a busy downtown district. Cars streamed by and people hurried along the sidewalks. I wasn't sure what we were supposed to be seeing.

In the distance of the shot, the door of a minivan slid open and figures emerged—five of them. They were far away and out of focus, but based on the heights, builds, and skin tones, those could be our friends. It was difficult to tell on the small screen.

"I guess that's our proof," I said, hoping to God they weren't tricking us.

Cole looked at me, and I could read the thoughts going through his mind because they were the same as mine—*Screw turning ourselves in. Let's get out of here.*

Before either of us could speak, there was a knock on Cole's window.

The barrel of a gun was pointed directly at him.

Gasping, I reflexively put my hands up and pressed my back against the door, my body wanting to get as far away from the gun as possible.

Cole put his hands up as well. "Stay calm," he said under his breath.

There was another knock, this time on my window and a second gun appeared. I shifted toward the center of the car, but there was no escape.

"Get out of the car, but keep your hands where we can see them."

"We have to unbuckle our seat belts," Cole said calmly.

"One at a time."

Cole nodded at me to go and part of me wanted to laugh deliriously. *Ladies, first. Thanks, babe.*

I clicked the release button and opened my car door, stepping outside slowly. The fallen angel wielding the gun on my side was a woman—tall and blonde, with huge boobs. She looked like she'd be more at home in the Victoria's Secret fashion show than pointing a gun at a teenager in an empty parking lot.

I kept my eyes trained on her as Cole got out of the car.

"Walk to the van," the man from his side said. When I circled around the car, I saw it was Tiny. All plans of cooperating went up in smoke as I glared at the man who'd hurt Xena.

"You're a disgrace," I spat at him. "You're an angel. How can you act like this?"

He chuckled. "I'm a *fallen* angel."

Xena's explanation about fallen angels not necessarily being bad ran through my mind. Apparently he didn't share the same sentiment.

I didn't say anything, knowing it would be pointless. There was no reasoning with that monster.

Once we reached the van, the woman pulled open the door and took out two black hoods. She fixed one over my head and then zip-tied my wrists. I listened as she did the same to Cole. Then she shoved me forward, and I banged my knees on the edge of the van. I cried out in pain.

"Get in the van, sweetheart." She had a thick German accent.

I climbed in, my bound wrists making it very difficult. Cole came in next and the door slammed closed behind me.

"Are you okay?" he whispered.

"Shut up," Tiny barked from the front seat.

The van moved abruptly and we both tumbled to the floor. I scooted so my body was touching Cole's, a small comfort.

Xena had been right—this was a bad idea.

I concentrated on my breathing, trying to rid myself of fear.

Your loved ones are safe, I kept repeating over and over in my mind.

Except it wasn't completely true because Cole was here beside me. I'd had the same feeling when we were at the farmhouse with Xavier—both sorry and glad to have him with him.

I couldn't judge how long we drove—it could have been five minutes or half-an-hour. When the van stopped just as abruptly as it had taken off, I rolled, my body hitting the front seats. The door slid open and someone got inside with us. My hood was yanked off, painfully jerking my neck.

"Walk into the house," the woman said. "We'll shoot you if you make trouble."

She pulled out a switchblade and pulled it against the tie on my wrists. I sucked in a breath when the knife grazed my skin, leaving behind a thin line of blood.

"Oops." She shrugged.

Fury filled Cole's eyes and his body tensed, like he wanted to take her on.

"I'm fine," I said quickly, putting a hand on his arm.

The woman smirked as she cut Cole's ties.

"Hurry up," Tiny said impatiently.

We exited the van, and I was surprised to see we were in a posh neighborhood. Like million-dollar-house posh. The house in front of us was brick with huge rounded steps leading to a set of ornate double doors. The woman opened the door for us and we entered the foyer, which was white marble, complete with columns.

"In here." Tiny pushed me using the barrel of his gun and I stumbled. Cole grabbed my arm to keep me from falling. If I looked at his aura, it would be bright red. It was like they were trying to set him off. I definitely wouldn't put it past them.

"It's about time," said a sinister voice I recognized all too well.

Linda.

CHAPTER 24

LINDA WASN'T WEARING HER NORMAL Mary Poppins-esque garb. Instead, she was wearing what could only be described as a mu-mu or an old lady's nightgown. She probably wasn't completely healed from when Xena shot her. It was a small victory that brought a smile to my face.

Cole positioned himself in front of me as best he could without making it obvious. It was pointless, though, and he should have known that as well as I did. If Linda wanted to hurt me, she wouldn't use weapons.

Tiny closed the door behind us with a resounding thud and when he joined Linda, I saw he had traded in his gun for a whip. The brown leather was discolored with stains, and I clenched my fists, the memory of Xena's bloody body fresh in my mind.

"What do you want with us, Linda?" I asked.

Her lips stretched into a slimy grin. "Absolutely nothing."

"Then why are we here?" Cole asked.

"Perhaps that was a little fib," she said. "Before you become nothing, we want to have a little fun with you."

Beside me, Cole sucked in a breath and reached for my hand. I looked up at him. *Shit*. She'd taken away his vision, but I couldn't tell if that was all she'd done. Most likely she'd taken away his hearing as well.

I turned my attention to Tiny and the woman, expecting one of them to attack me. Instead, Linda came toward me.

"Did you kill Xavier?"

I met her gaze defiantly, not sure how I wanted to answer. She already knew I had and to be honest, I wanted her to know. I wanted all three of them to know they weren't invincible.

Yet, that knowledge gave me little comfort because she knew as well as I did that I was no match for any of them. The only reason I'd been able to kill Xavier was because he let me.

When I didn't answer, Linda sighed. "We all know you did. The only thing left is for you to confess your sin. But either way, reckoning is coming."

She reached into the pocket of her nightgown and pulled out a small silver gun.

She pointed it directly at my forehead, so close there was no way she could miss.

This was it.

I fought against the instinct to flinch and close my eyes, not wanting to show Linda weakness, even in my final moments.

Around us, the room started to darken and shadows swirled near the ceiling. A chill filled the air. *Reapers.*

Linda laughed. "They've come for you. And next they can take your boyfriend, but not before he sees your dead body. Any last words?"

I didn't know why she bothered asking that because her finger squeezed the trigger before I could respond.

I watched in fascination as the end of the gun lit up, followed by a mushroom of smoke. The bullet moved toward me so slowly I could have reached out and grabbed it out of the air.

The shadows swirled lower, surrounding me. And then they were lifting me, moving so swiftly I became dizzy. Then blackness overcame me.

When I opened my eyes, I was lying in the middle of the softest bed I'd ever lain on.

"It's about time."

Linda had said the same exact thing, but unlike her voice this one was filled with kindness.

Areli.

I sat up and all I could see was white. I looked down to see I wasn't actually lying on a bed. The white was continuous and it was like the floor had raised to cushion me.

"Is this heaven?"

Areli chuckled. "No. If it were, that would mean you're dead. But you are very much alive."

"Then where am I? The reapers came." My fingers gripped my thighs, digging half moon fingernail shapes into my skin. "Cole. Is he—"

"He is also very much alive. The Reapers saved you and brought you here at my request. But they couldn't intervene until you needed saving. I thought Linda was never going to try to kill you."

Huh. Well, that was an odd sentiment.

"This is kind of like a halfway point," Areli continued. "It's where people who are having near-death experiences go."

If I squinted, I could make out a very bright light in the distance. So this was what people meant when they said they'd seen the light.

I was about to ask why I was here when three shimmers materialized in front of me. They took on human forms but no features were distinguishable. Where their faces should have been was light too bright to look at.

Areli bowed his head reverently.

There was no sound, but still I heard a question in my mind. *Did you kill Xavier?*

"Yes."

Did he kill your mother?

"Yes."

Silence stretched on. Part of me wanted to explain more about what fallen angels and handlers had been doing, but instinctively I knew to stay quiet as if they'd silently commanded me to do so.

Is everything Areli tells us true?

I didn't know exactly what they were referring to, but I knew the answer to that question as well.

"Yes."

Tell us about the souls of your brothers and sisters.

It took me a moment to understand they were asking about my fellow seekers.

"The longer they seek, the darker they become."

And what about those who guide you?

The phrasing of that was so wrong—handlers *guiding* seekers?

"Many of them have become dark."

The shapes turned translucent and disappeared just as quickly as they had come. I felt an absence I couldn't explain, and it took me a moment to recover.

"What just happened?"

In their presence I'd been in almost a dream-like state, but now they were gone, lucid thoughts crowded my mind. Why hadn't I told them more? I'd barely said anything! There was so much they needed to know.

"Time to go back now," Areli said.

"No," I protested. "Call them back. I need to talk to them again."

Areli just shook his head. "If you stay much longer, you won't be able to return. They have everything they need. Trust me."

Shadows swirled up from below, enveloping me and transporting me again. I was powerless to stop them. And just like last time, blackness overtook me.

WHEN I CAME TO, I was lying on the hard marble floor. My brain pounded against my skull.

"Ow," I muttered, moving my hand to a huge lump on the back of my head.

"Ava, thank God."

I opened my eyes to find Cole hovered above me, worry on his face. *Damn.* I clutched at his arms and sat up quickly. *Bad idea.* My head throbbed and my vision blurred.

"It's okay," he said. "Take it easy."

By the calmness in his voice, I could tell there was no threat. When my vision cleared, I saw the room was empty. Beside me on the ground was a single bullet. I picked it up and rolled it between my fingers.

"What happened?"

He shook his head. "I don't know. Linda took my vision and hearing away and then all of a sudden it came back. Everyone was gone and you were on the floor."

I held up the bullet. "Linda shot at me, but the Reapers saved me and took me to heaven. No, not heaven. Purgatory, maybe? It was a half-way point or something. Areli was there. So were higher angels. He told them everything."

"What did they say?"

"Nothing," I said. "They only asked questions. They know I killed Xavier. And they know he killed my mom."

"Shit."

"No," I said slowly, thinking of Areli's final words. *Trust me.* As I looked at Cole, a deep calmness settled over me. "I think it's okay. It's over."

EPILOGUE

"HURRY UP!" KYLE YELLED IMPATIENTLY from the other side of the door.

I gritted my teeth and cleared my things off the counter, stowing them in a drawer. I'd been living with Kyle in Bill's house for several months now, but I still hadn't gotten used to sharing a bathroom with him. Teenage girls were supposed to be the bathroom hogs, but in our case, it was definitely reversed.

Kyle rushed past me, slamming the door behind him the second I was clear of it. Though I was tempted to stand outside and yell at him like he did to me all the time, I'd give him a pass today. He'd made the wrestling team at school, and today was his first tournament. His interest in the sport had surprised us all, but it kind of made sense given it was a solitary sport—he didn't play well with others. It was a good way for him to vent his aggression and in any event, it had kept him on the straight and narrow. His coach was a ballbuster and forced his players to maintain a 2.5 average GPA, even though a 2.0 was all that was required.

I trotted downstairs to find Bill waiting in the living room.

"That boy is going to make us late to his own event," he said.

"I know. And he'll probably blame it on us."

Bill chuckled. "True."

When Kyle finally came downstairs ten minutes later, Bill paused just long enough to turn on the outside Christmas lights before we rushed out the door. He'd put them up before Thanksgiving, excited to finally have "kids" around to enjoy them again. Kyle had given Bill a hard time about helping to put them up, but the childlike grin on his face when they plugged them in for the first time was unmistakable.

Perhaps there was hope for Kyle after all.

Cole was waiting for us outside the school's gym doors. As Kyle rushed past him to join his team in the locker room, Cole whapped him on the head.

"You're late, numbnuts."

Kyle flipped him off without breaking stride.

Cole wrapped his arms around me and kissed my forehead. Despite the cold, warmth flooded my body. That never got old.

We'd talked about moving in together in a proper apartment, but I wasn't sure I'd be able to contribute enough financially. I was starting classes at the local community college in January, which meant I'd have to cut back my hours at Shenice's shop. Cole assured me he'd pay for the whole apartment, but I didn't feel right about that. Plus, Bill would be disappointed if I moved out. So we were still figuring things out.

One thing we weren't figuring out was that we were still so much in love with one another.

In the gym we found seats and I waved at Kaley, my old friend. She'd made a lot of friends and started dating someone on the wresting team since I'd been gone. Our situations were so different now, we hadn't rekindled our friendship, but we were still friendly.

However, seeing her made me miss Claire something fierce. I'd seen her once when Cole and I made the trip to retrieve my car, but she had her hands full. She and Chase had moved back home and she'd convinced her father to enroll in AA. So far he'd only had one slip-up, which was encouraging. Like me, they were both set to start taking classes in January. Chase had even started playing baseball again, joining a club league. I wished we lived closer together, but their lives were in Pennsylvania and mine was in Virginia.

There were several matches before Kyle's, so I asked Bill and Cole if they wanted anything from the concession stand. Stupid question—Cole rattled off a long list of things. He offered to go with me, but I declined. He and Bill actually enjoyed watching the matches. I didn't care if I missed them—I was only here to support Kyle, so unless he was wrestling, I spent the time playing on my phone.

While I was standing in line at the concession stand, I thought I heard someone hiss my name from a side hallway. I peered into the darkness, seeing nothing at first. Then I saw a flash of black.

My heart pounded in my chest as I hurried over. There in the shadows stood Xena.

"Xena!" I squealed, pulling her toward me in a crushing hug. She returned the gesture for a moment before pushing me away. *Right. Too cool for hugs.*

But I didn't care. I hadn't seen her since we'd left her in the hotel room in Florida. It turned out she'd started uploading everything the moment we'd left, which was how Areli had had time to see everything. Although we hadn't been able to get in touch with him, he'd been watching us. Or so I assumed. That was the best we could figure based on the time stamps of all the footage Xena had uploaded. Just as we'd hoped, some of it had gone viral, making the rounds on social media for weeks. Of course, by that time, all the fallen angels on Earth were gone. Shenice hadn't seen any in months.

"How are you?" I asked.

She smiled. "Good. Better than good, actually."

I'd been so distressed when I didn't know what happened to her I'd searched for her, coming across a horrifying article online about a missing Japanese-American girl. The picture in the article showed Xena, looking very studious in a school picture. Her name had been Kaiyo Sato, and she'd been killed in a hate crime following the attack on Pearl Harbor. She'd been fifteen.

"What are you doing here?" I asked.

"I got permission to stay on Earth for a while," she said. "So I'm sightseeing."

"You've already seen Tidewater," I teased. "Surely there are more exciting places to visit."

"I know. I'm not supposed to see you, but I came anyway."

Xena disobeying orders? I expected nothing less.

"I'm glad you did."

"I learned more about your family," she said. "It turns out you have angel ancestors on both sides."

I did a double take. "Seriously?"

I'd actually been in touch with my father's family, but I hadn't learned that little tidbit. It was weird how it happened. Out of the blue, I got a call from Michael Williams' mother, my grandmother. He'd let it slip to her I'd come around, and she immediately hired a private investigator to find me. We hadn't met in person yet, but we'd talked several times on the phone, enough for me to conclude the asshole gene skipped generations. She'd bought me a plane ticket to visit her in January before classes started. I was cautiously optimistic.

Xena nodded. "That could explain why you're able to project your aura and visit with your mother."

My visits with my mother had become predictably regular, though more infrequent, but I was okay with that. She'd settled into her place in heaven and was at peace. And for the most part, so was I.

"What's happening with the seeker system?" I asked. From what I could tell, it was no more, but I still wanted confirmation.

"The higher angels realized that when fallen angels stayed on Earth too long, they started to take on human traits, mostly negative ones. It's like an addiction they can't stop."

Her mention of addictions reminded me of Brian and Noel. In addition to uploading our footage, Xena had made an anonymous call to the Charleston police. But by the time they'd gone to investigate the lab, all the fallen angels had been recalled to heaven, so Brian and Noel were long gone. Some poor detective was probably pulling his hair out trying to figure out what had happened to the drug dealers.

"Anyway," Xena continued. "The system has been put on hold indefinitely. They're going to leave humans to their own devices for a while to see if enough of them will become angels without interference."

I didn't like the sound of that. "So they might reinstitute the system if there aren't enough pure souls?"

"In theory, but I wouldn't worry about it. It'll be centuries before they make any kind of final decision. They're slow to act. How quickly they pulled all the angels off Earth was unprecedented." She paused. "I should get going."

I smiled sadly. "I'm glad you came to see me." I mentally added *one last time*. Somehow I knew I wouldn't see her again.

"Of course. Take care of yourself, Ava."

"You too, Harriet."

She grinned and then she was gone, leaving me in an empty hallway.

"Ava." Cole came up behind me, relief in his voice. Even though there had been no sign of troublesome handlers, his protective streak was still going strong. He'd probably come looking for me because I'd taken so long.

"Sorry," I said. "Xena was just here."

"Really?"

"Yeah, but she's gone. I don't think we'll see her again."

"That's probably a good thing," he said slowly. "What did she say?"

"She confirmed everything we suspected. No more handlers, no more seekers."

"Thank God." The little bit of worry that had taken up permanent residence in his eyes melted away.

"And apparently, I have two angel ancestors. Who knew?"

A sly grin crept across Cole's face. "I'm not surprised because I see a little bit of heaven every time I look at you."

A laugh escaped my mouth. "You've got to be kidding me." Rolling my eyes, I playfully pushed him away. He captured my hand and used it to wrap my arm around his neck. I clasped my hands together as he pulled my body in line with his.

When he lowered his lips to mine, I tasted peppermint, my own little slice of heaven.

Thank you for reading *Redemption*! I hope you enjoyed it. If you did, please help other readers find this book by telling your friends and leaving a review on Amazon, Goodreads, or your favorite book retailer. Word of mouth and reviews help authors more than you know!

About the Author

Jessica lives in Virginia with her college-sweetheart husband, two rambunctious sons, and two rowdy but lovable rescue dogs. Since her house is overflowing with testosterone, it's a good thing she has a healthy appreciation for Marvel movies, Nerf guns, and football.

To learn more about Jessica, visit her website jessicaruddick.com. Connect with her on Twitter at @JessicaMRuddick or on Facebook (facebook.com/AuthorJessicaRuddick).

Other Books by Jessica Ruddick

Birthright: The Legacy Series, Book One
Retribution: The Legacy Series, Book Two
Sacrifice: The Legacy Series, Book Three
Letting Go (Love on Campus #1)
Wanting More (Love on Campus #2)

9 781946 164070